A Sad Day in New Orleans

"Dreadful accident," the mayor said, shaking his head.

"Do you really believe Wayne's death was an accident?" I asked. "I'm not convinced that it was."

The mayor took my elbow and ushered me toward the sliding glass doors. "Let's not talk of this here," he said.

We stepped outside into the hot air and paused under a palm tree.

"I know how upset you must be, Mrs. Fletcher. Wayne was a friend to us all."

"I certainly am upset, Mayor Amadour," I said, feeling a different kind of heat rising in my blood. "I'm particularly upset that the police department made such a quick decision on the nature of Wayne's death. I really can't believe it."

"Now, now, Mrs. Fletcher." He took my hand between his and patted it. "I knew Wayne for many years, and he was a bit of an odd duck."

"I don't think—" I started to say, but he wouldn't let me speak.

"He was an obsessive man," he said, squeezing my hand hard, and catching my ring in the vise of his grip. "No telling what he would do if he took a mind to it. I believe if you think about that for a little while, you'll come to the same conclusion."

I yanked my hand away, and suppressed the urge to rub my finger where the ring had made a dent in the skin.

Other books in the *Murder, She Wrote* Series

MURDER IN A MINOR KEY

A *Murder, She Wrote* Mystery

A Novel by Jessica Fletcher
and Donald Bain
based on the
Universal television series
created by Peter S. Fischer,
Richard Levinson & William Link

A SIGNET BOOK

SIGNET
Published by New American Library, a division of
Penguin Group (USA) Inc., 375 Hudson Street,
New York, New York 10014, USA
Penguin Group (Canada), 90 Eglinton Avenue East, Suite 700, Toronto,
Ontario M4P 2Y3, Canada (a division of Pearson Penguin Canada Inc.)
Penguin Books Ltd., 80 Strand, London WC2R 0RL, England
Penguin Ireland, 25 St. Stephen's Green, Dublin 2,
Ireland (a division of Penguin Books Ltd.)
Penguin Group (Australia), 250 Camberwell Road, Camberwell, Victoria 3124,
Australia (a division of Pearson Australia Group Pty. Ltd.)
Penguin Books India Pvt. Ltd., 11 Community Centre, Panchsheel Park,
New Delhi - 110 017, India
Penguin Group (NZ), 67 Apollo Drive, Mairangi Bay,
Auckland 1311, New Zealand (a division of Pearson New Zealand Ltd.)
Penguin Books (South Africa) (Pty.) Ltd., 24 Sturdee Avenue,
Rosebank, Johannesburg 2196, South Africa

Penguin Books Ltd., Registered Offices:
80 Strand, London WC2R 0RL, England

First published by Signet, an imprint of New American Library,
a division of Penguin Group (USA) Inc.

First Printing, October 2001
10 9 8 7

PUBLISHER'S NOTE
This is a work of fiction. Names, characters, places, and incidents either are
the product of the author's imagination or are used fictitiously, and any resem-
blance to actual persons, living or dead, business establishments, events, or
locales is entirely coincidental.

The publisher does not have any control over and does not assume any
responsibility for author or third-party Web sites or their content.

If you purchased this book without a cover you should be aware that this
book is stolen property. It was reported as "unsold and destroyed" to the
publisher and neither the author nor the publisher has received any payment
for this "stripped book."

The scanning, uploading, and distribution of this book via the Internet or via
any other means without the permission of the publisher is illegal and punish-
able by law. Please purchase only authorized electronic editions, and do not
participate in or encourage electronic piracy of copyrighted materials. Your
support of the author's rights is appreciated.

For Renée

Chapter One

"Hand me the bait pail, Mrs. F. I think they nibbled off my worm again."

I put down the national section of the *Bangor Times* and passed a tin bucket of night crawlers to Cabot Cove's sheriff, Mort Metzger.

It was Sunday afternoon, and we were sitting on the end of the Town Dock dangling our fishing lines in the harbor, but not getting much interest on the part of the marine population. A recent bout of rainstorms had left every garden in Cabot Cove soggy, and Mort's wife Maureen had complained that the worms were taking over her flower beds. Mort's answer had been to dig up a load of the wriggly, grayish-pink creatures and invite me to fish with him while we brainstormed about who we could get to help finance the purchase of a new patrol car for the village police force.

"The Ladies Auxiliary likes to have a pet project for their Spring Fling," I suggested.

"Now, Mrs. F.," Mort said, hesitating as he baited his hook and dropped it in the water, "I don't want to turn politically incorrect on you, and I appreciate all the ladies have done for the village. But buying a police cruiser with the proceeds from a fashion show somehow just doesn't seem right."

"I'm disappointed in you, Mort. The whole object is to

raise the money. As long as the gathering of those funds is legal and proper, whether they come from a fashion show or a pancake breakfast is not all that important."

Mort's pained expression said he wanted to disagree, but thought better of it. He picked up the newspaper I'd abandoned, and idly turned the pages.

"Have you talked to the Men's Club or the Lions or the Rotary?" I asked.

"They've already budgeted their funds for the year. Ralph Mackin needs a new roof on the old courthouse, and he got to the Rotary first. And the high school Key Club is committed to their baby car seat program for the hospital. I can't think of anyone else, can you?"

"Then it's got to be the Ladies Auxiliary, Mort. And I think we'd better approach them pretty soon, before they commit all their money, too. It's either that or wait till next year."

"We can't. The state's matching funds program is only for this year. If we miss that, we'll never be able to replace that old heap we've got."

"Is it in that bad shape?"

"It's pretty beat up. One of the deputies had to go to Tommy Brinkley's home to give him a speeding ticket because the patrol car couldn't keep up. And Tommy's old clunker is no sports car; it's a 1987 station wagon."

"I'll talk to Tina Treyz on Monday," I said. "She's a terrific fundraiser, and she's on the organizing committee for the ladies' luncheon."

"Well, she's a driver, all right," Mort said, warming to the idea. "If anyone can get us to the goal, she's it."

We sat quietly for a while, Mort bouncing his line and reading the paper.

I breathed in the fresh, spring air. The sky was full of mares' tails, the high cirrus clouds a sure sign of impending rain, but it was perfect Maine April weather, crisp and bright, occasionally warm enough in the sun to take off your sweater, and chilly enough at night to keep two blankets on the end of the bed.

"Say, aren't you going down to New Orleans next week?" he asked.

"Yes. Why?"

"Take a look here. Got a strange murder there, it says."

I leaned over Mort's shoulder and read along with him.

AP—New Orleans police are investigating the possible connection between voodoo practices and an apparent murder that took place yesterday in the Crescent City, as the Louisiana metropolis is also known. The body of Elijah Williams was found sitting up against the tomb of nineteenth-century voodoo queen Marie Laveau in the city's oldest graveyard, St. Louis Cemetery Number One. Police said the victim appeared to have been strangled, but declined to elaborate further. An autopsy is pending.

Laveau's tomb is a popular attraction in this Mississippi River city, where swamp conditions forced citizens to "bury" their dead in above-ground vaults for over two centuries. The cemeteries, known as Cities of the Dead, are regular stops on sightseeing tours, but the two St. Louis cemeteries are located in what are now considered dangerous neighborhoods, and visitors are warned not to wander from the safety of their tour groups.

Mayor Maurice Amadour reassured the public there was no cause to be alarmed, and announced that a special security detail would be assigned to the cemetery for the next month. However, merchants in the French Quarter complained that the mayor's office was not doing enough to safeguard the tourism industry.

Police said Williams, whose age was not known, was at one time a guide in the bayous. He disappeared fifteen years ago on a fishing trip during which a prominent

politician died. The politician's badly mauled body had
been recovered from the alligator-infested waters. An
NOPD spokesman said Williams had been presumed dead
as well, and the discovery of his body on Saturday was a
surprise. An investigation is under way to uncover
Williams's whereabouts for the last decade and a half, the
spokesman said, and the NOPD was calling on local residents to come forward with any information pertinent to
the case.

"Hmmm, interesting story."

"Now, Mrs. F., you be careful down there. I hear that
New Orleans is a dangerous city."

"You have to take the same precautions you would in
any large city, Mort, and I always do. I had no problems
when I was there last year, and I'm looking forward to seeing all the things I missed on the first visit. And yes, I'll be
careful."

He harrumphed.

A slight tug on my line returned my attention to fishing.

"I think I may have caught something," I said gleefully.

Mort eyed the slight curve at the top of my pole.

"More likely you've hooked a weed," he said. "Whatever
it is isn't giving you much of a fight."

I quickly reeled in the slack in my line and pulled back
on the rod. When the end of the fishing line cleared the
water, hanging from the hook was a tiny fish, no more than
five inches long.

"Got a dab there. Definitely not a keeper," Mort said,
deftly netting my catch.

Apologizing to the little flounder, I gently extracted the
hook from its mouth and leaned over the edge of the dock
to release it back into the water. The fish hesitated a moment and then flapped away, back down to the bottom of

the bay. I wondered if the experience would change the life of that little fish. Would it shun temptation from now on? Would it approach an easy meal with suspicion? Or would it forget to be cautious, only to be caught another day?

Chapter Two

A young man with a scruffy beard tugged on the neckline of his T-shirt, rose from the audience, and leaned into the microphone. "You're an investigative reporter, Mr. Broadbent, but I hear you moonlight as a sax player on the weekends."

"You'd make a good investigative reporter yourself," Broadbent replied. "You've discovered my passion. I'm a closet saxophonist."

"Are you any good?" the young man asked.

A ripple of uncomfortable laughter ran through the audience, but Julian Broadbent grinned at the young man, who held a notebook and pencil.

"Well, I'm better than Bill Clinton, but not as good as Branford Marsalis."

This time the laughter was louder, and the audience burst into applause.

Julian Broadbent was a handsome man with blond hair and light-blue eyes, who knew how to use his Southern charm. It was part of what made him such a successful investigative reporter. That charm, coupled with tenacity and writing skill, had helped him write a popular book on a recently retired Louisiana senator, whose departure from Washington just barely preceded the publication of Broadbent's exposé of him.

"He can sweet-talk the politicians right out of their trees," our host and moderator Charlie Gable had said in his introduction of Broadbent, "or right out of their Senate seats in this case."

Broadbent was one of four authors with new books out. I was among them. We'd spent this Thursday morning discussing writing in general, and our latest works in particular, as guests of Gable and the New Orleans *Times-Picayune.*

"Seriously, folks, you'll have to be the judge." Broadbent bobbed his head toward the dapper man to his left, and his Louisiana accent deepened. "My colleague on the panel, heah, once tole me 'Keep yo' day job.' But my mama was a stubborn Cajun, and I guess I inherited that trait. I'm still practicin'. So y'all come on uptown to Tipitina's next Tuesday and see if I've improved since my review."

As the audience laughed and clapped again, Wayne Copely, the man to Broadbent's left and to my right, covered his mouth with his fist and leaned in my direction. "Stubbornness never was a substitute for talent," he muttered.

I smothered a smile. Wayne, another author on the panel, was a music critic with a nationally syndicated column, and a friend of recent acquaintance. He'd been particularly helpful to me during the writing of my latest mystery, *Murder in a Minor Key,* which I'd set in New Orleans. At the recommendation of a mutual friend, I'd gone to Wayne for information on the city's love affair with jazz.

"You cannot write about New Orleans if you don't know about her musical roots," he had told me solemnly. "I will guide you."

Keeping his promise, he had given me a quick education in the range of local musical offerings, while squiring me from one jazz venue to another. We went to concert halls, sophisticated clubs, rollicking bars, down-and-dirty dives, and it seemed to me, nearly every impromptu street performance. When we parted more than a year ago, Wayne had urged me to come back for the Jazz and Heritage Festival that takes place in New Orleans each spring, although it was hard to believe that there could be even more to hear in a city already overflowing with music.

Fate had been kind and my publisher even kinder. Now that *Murder in a Minor Key* was climbing the best-seller list, I was back in "The Big Easy" for the last days of a successful, if whirlwind, promotional tour, just in time for the festival. This morning's panel of authors, which also included a historian, Doris Burns, along with Wayne, Julian Broadbent, and me, was one of a regular series, hosted monthly by Charlie Gable, book editor of *Lagniappe,* the weekend entertainment section of the *Times-Picayune,* the city's only daily newspaper. Charlie had always been complimentary in his reviews of my work, and when he'd invited me to participate in one of his Book Club Breakfasts, I'd been flattered to accept. My publisher had arranged several interviews to coincide with my visit to New Orleans, and I was looking forward to revisiting a city that had so intrigued me before.

Turning in my direction, the bearded young man asked, "Mrs. Fletcher, are you a secret musician, too?"

"I took music lessons as a child," I answered. "Perhaps many of you did, too."

I looked around the audience; heads were nodding.

"My mother used to say, there must be a special place in heaven for music teachers; they have such an abundance of patience," I said with a chuckle. "I sometimes suspected mine wore earplugs. I grew up to love all kinds of music, but I'm afraid my best musical skills are as a listener."

"Miz Fletcher, why did you choose New Orleans for your latest mystery?"

The speaker was an elderly lady in a bright, multicolored dress with a floral pattern. She held a large straw hat, an even larger straw handbag, and a red umbrella hung from her arm.

"Many writers find inspiration in particular locations,

most often those that are initially unfamiliar," I responded. "If I'm walking in a crowded city, or on a desolate stretch of road, all of a sudden I'll find myself composing plots, and characters who seem to fit the scene. Perhaps there's something odd in the sight of a particular building, or a strange smell assails me, or the eerie sound of the wind makes me shiver. All my senses are sharpened when I encounter someplace new. Those experiences end up on the page."

"We got lots of eerie things in New Orleans," the woman said.

"Probably more here than other big cities do," I agreed. "New Orleans has many qualities to stimulate the imagination. It's friendly, dangerous, exotic, accessible, foreign, and thoroughly American. You have a wonderful mix of cultures, religions, and philosophies. You have appreciation for the past, and exuberance for the present. Your food is spicy, and so is the air, perfumed with the mingled aromas of the cooking, the rich vegetation, the swamps, and the Mississippi River. Your weather is, by turns, sultry and refreshing. And everywhere you go, and in everything you do, music accompanies you. The whole city is a mystery, and I love to unravel mysteries."

The ovation from the New Orleanians that greeted my description of their city made me blush. I hadn't intended to wax so poetic, but I wouldn't take back a word. Visiting New Orleans was an adventure, and as different from my hometown of Cabot Cove, Maine, as it could possibly be. I was eager to explore it again on this visit.

When the applause died down, Charlie spoke up.

"Mrs. Fletcher, thank you. You make us see our own city with fresh eyes."

He checked his watch.

"We're coming to the end of this session of Book Club Breakfasts, but we still have time for a few more questions."

The lady in the flowered dress waved her straw hat at Charlie. "I have a question for Doris Burns, too," she said.

"Go ahead, ma'am."

"Ms. Burns, do you have another project you're working on?"

"I'm so glad you asked me," she said, beaming.

Doris Burns was a historian, the youngest woman ever to be made full professor at Princeton. She was striking, tall and narrow with an angular face, lively brown eyes, and short brown hair that curved softly toward her delicate chin, not precisely what you'd expect a historian to look like, but just right somehow.

"Mrs. Fletcher is right about the wonderful possibilities in New Orleans. I'm currently researching a book on the history of cult religions. Since a sizable percentage of the population practices voodoo, this is a great place to start. As long as I have the floor, I'll add that I'm staying at the Royal Hotel for the next two weeks, and would appreciate hearing from any of you in the voodoo community. I'm making tape recordings of what voodoo means to those who practice it, and how their traditions may differ from their neighbor's. If you can give me a half hour or so, I'd love to get you on tape."

There was a rustle of papers around the auditorium as people noted the name of the hotel. Wayne leaned forward and pulled the table microphone to him. "Speaking of recordings," he said, "as long as we're asking for research assistance here—this okay with you, Charlie?"

Gable nodded. "We'll let you have the final word, Wayne, in this question-and-answer session."

Wayne fingered the floppy yellow paisley bow tie that rested on his royal-blue shirt. He took his time pulling a large white handkerchief from the jacket pocket of his cream-colored suit and dabbing it across his shaved head. The spotlights pointed at the stage were hot; it was nearly noon and the air conditioning in the large room was struggling to counter the heat wave outside.

Finally, he spoke.

"As my good friend Jessica Fletcher noted, we have an appreciation for our past. And like my colleague Ms. Burns, I'm also interested in recordings, but old ones, not new ones. In fact, I'm looking for original cylinder recordings made in Thomas Edison's day."

He paused.

"You can help."

He fell silent again to let his suggestion sink in.

"As many of you know," he continued, "I've been hunting details on the life of Alphonse LeCoeur, known as Little Red. He played trumpet 'round about the same time as Buddy Bolden. They may even have known each other, perhaps played together. No surviving recordings of either of these talented gentlemen have ever come to light, but rumors about Little Red's recordings have persisted, and I believe he did, indeed, put down some tracks on wax cylinders."

I listened as Wayne mesmerized the audience with tales of a moody, cerebral horn player, an introspective man who lived his life in the bayous, and rarely played in public, but one who deserved a place in the pantheon of jazz greats. He described how the celebrated musicians of the day found their way to Little Red's shack, to coax him to perform with them, or just to listen in wonder to a talent shared with so few. Wayne's voice rose and fell like a preacher exhorting his congregation.

"He drew the other musicians of his day like ants following a trail of honey," he intoned. "They were hungry for his sound, in awe of his skill, his 'chops' if you will, and jealous of his talent. Some claimed Little Red was possessed by a voodoo spirit, a *loa*. When under its spell, the notes that poured from his horn were magic—sweet, melodic, inventive music, in sharp contrast to the boisterous style of Buddy Bolden that was so popular in the frenzied days that followed the turn of the last century."

Wayne peered over the half glasses perched on his nose. His eyes roamed up and down the rows of occupied seats.

"For years, I've tracked rumors that claim the existence of those cylinders. So far, they still elude me. But if those recordings exist, I aim to uncover them. They represent an important link between Little Red and those who came after him."

"I'll bet they're worth some money, too, aren't they?" Broadbent put in.

Wayne looked momentarily taken aback before replying, "They will have tremendous worth as a historical treasure, Mr. Broadbent, linking the traditions of Ragtime, Dixieland, and more modern jazz. Every jazz musician today owes a debt to Little Red. Oh yes, his influence isn't as obvious as that of others—Bolden and King Oliver, Louis, then Roy Eldridge, who bridged the gap between the older style of trumpet playing in New Orleans and Chicago with the modern giants—Dizzy and Sweets Edison, Fats Navarro and Miles Davis. But even though today's artists never heard Little Red play—which I hope to rectify by finding those cylinders—his legend, which has been passed down by word-of-mouth, has had a profound impact on the way our current jazz stars *think* about the music they create."

Letting his gaze rest on Broadbent, he added, "And with today's sophisticated digital recording capabilities, I'm certain they can be remastered and released to the benefit of all musical aficionados, yourself included, of course."

He again addressed the audience. "As to their monetary worth, I believe were there to be any fiduciary gains, they would go to any legatees of the LeCoeur family, should they survive."

Wayne cleared his throat, and carefully wiped his forehead with his handkerchief. He let the silence in the auditorium grow. Looking up, he took a deep breath, audible throughout the room.

"Go home," he boomed, startling those whose attention had wandered. "Search your attics and your storerooms. Scour the secondhand merchants and antique dealers. Bring me any cylinders you may find, and perhaps"—his voice rose—"together, we can make musical history."

Silence greeted this pronouncement. And then a rumble of voices swelled, filling the auditorium, as people rose from their seats, gathered up their belongings, and started for the doors, intending, I was sure, to hurry home to search their attics for wax recordings of Little Red LeCoeur to bring to Wayne.

Charlie Gable saw his program breaking up without his own closing comments, and rushed to stem the exodus. "Hold on, folks," he said.

About half the room turned back to the stage.

"Before you go, let's have a hand again for this morning's authors: historian Doris Burns, jazz critic Wayne Copley, investigative reporter Julian Broadbent, and mystery writer Jessica Fletcher."

There was some spirited applause from those who hadn't yet made it out the door.

"Don't forget to visit your local bookstore to purchase the books written by these good folks, or you can order autographed copies from the Book Club Breakfasts website." He rattled off the web address for his book club. "And thank you all for coming."

As the auditorium emptied, those of us on the panel got up from our seats. I looked around for Charlie, to offer my thanks for including me in the program, but he was deep in conversation with a man dressed in a blue pinstriped suit, and holding a tan cowboy hat. The serious expression on Charlie's face discouraged me from approaching them.

Julian Broadbent swiveled his seat around and regarded Wayne with a disdainful air. "Quite the little drama queen, aren't you," he sneered.

Wayne pulled his glasses from his nose and let them dangle from the purple cord looped around his neck. Unperturbed, he gathered up his papers, inserted them in his leather case, and gently took my elbow to guide me off the stage. Looking back at Broadbent, he said, "When one has substantive material to discuss, drama comes naturally."

"Are you suggesting my work isn't substantive?"

"Nonsense. You're a fine writer." Wayne emphasized the final word.

"Oh, is this another snide 'day job' comment?"

Broadbent was getting hot. He stood quickly, sending his chair rolling to the back of the stage. His six-foot frame towered over Wayne.

Doris Burns stood watching the exchange, an amused smile playing over her mouth.

Wayne gazed down at his black-and-white "spectator" shoes. He licked his right index finger and leaned over to wipe a smudge off the toe of his left shoe. Straightening, he looked at Broadbent and said, "You must admit, your writing is far superior to your abilities, such as they are, on the saxophone."

"At least, I know how to play. You only know how to complain."

"Criticism is a noble, if occasionally underappreciated, profession," Wayne announced to me in an easily heard aside.

"Noble, is it? You're about as noble as a swamp rat."

By this time, I was tugging at Wayne's arm, attempting to draw him away before a battle-royal ensued. It was Charlie Gable who jumped between the mismatched combatants, the man in the blue suit at his side.

"Ladies and gentlemen, may I introduce Mayor

Amadour's top aide, Philippe Beaudin. Philippe, please say hello to our distinguished speakers. This is Ms. Burns and Mrs. Fletcher, and of course you know Mr. Copely and Mr. Broadbent."

Philippe Beaudin flashed a dazzling smile that was probably a powerful weapon in the political arena. Smoothly, he greeted each of us with murmured compliments, gently calming the waters and distracting Broadbent and Wayne from their rancorous exchange.

"The mayor hopes you'll be his guests at a party he's throwing during the Jazz and Heritage Festival," Beaudin said. "There'll be the usual warm Louisiana hospitality, good food, stimulating company, and wonderful music, which I *know* you'll all enjoy. Lots of politicos for you to pursue, Mr. Broadbent."

He winked at Broadbent, smiled at Wayne and me, and said, "Wayne, tell these nice folks what a wonderful host our beloved mayor is."

"You do just fine in the telling yourself, Phil," Wayne responded.

Beaudin turned to Doris Burns. A flicker of interest lit his eyes; his voice dropped, becoming husky.

"A few of our voodoo disciples will be present, *cher*," he said, using the familiar Cajun endearment. He moved closer. "Fertile ground for your research. I hope I'll see you there."

"Please tell the mayor I'll be happy to attend," she said coolly, apparently accustomed to discouraging unwanted male attention.

"I'll do just that."

Beaudin donned his cowboy hat, and pulled a sheaf of papers from his breast pocket, handing them around. "The directions and other details are here," he said brusquely, all business now that his mission was accomplished. "You can let Charlie know if you're coming and he'll have transportation arranged if you need it. I look forward to seeing you all again." He tugged on the brim of his hat and left the stage.

Broadbent jogged after Beaudin as the mayoral aide swiftly walked up an aisle in the direction of the auditorium exit. "Phil, is the mayor eyeing former Senator Lunsford's seat?" I heard him inquire loudly, reverting to his investigative reporter role and apparently having forgotten his confrontation with Wayne. I couldn't hear Beaudin's reply as the two men barreled through the double doors to the lobby.

"Well, that was a timely interruption," Doris Burns noted. She turned to me. "I understand we're staying in the same hotel. Would you like to walk back together?"

"Wayne and I planned to have lunch at one, but you're welcome to join us."

"Please do, Ms. Burns," Wayne jumped in. "New Orleans is famed for its unique cuisine and we are titillating our palates today at Antoine's."

"Please call me Doris, both of you. But may I take a raincheck on lunch? I really should prepare in case today's invitation to tape voodoo followers brings in some calls."

Wayne assisted us down the narrow stairs at the side of the stage and we followed him to the lobby outside the auditorium. The young man who had asked Julian Broadbent about his saxophone playing was perusing posters on the wall. He turned when he heard our voices.

"Excuse me, Mrs. Fletcher," he said. "I'm David Stewart. I write for the Tulane student newspaper. I was hoping you might give me a short interview."

"You go ahead," Wayne urged. "I'll walk Doris to the hotel, and meet you there when you get back. That gives me time to confer with the chef at Antoine's to see what special dishes we should order today. I promised you a gustatory delight, and so you shall have it. Doris, my dear, are you sure you won't reconsider?"

Wayne ushered Doris to the door, delighted at the possibility of another acolyte to introduce to the delights of the Crescent City. He tucked her hand under his arm and escorted her out the door, his short, sturdy physique a contrast to her tall, slim one.

"I won't keep you long, Mrs. Fletcher," Stewart said. "I already have a lot of notes from this morning's program, and I just need to fill in some details."

He flipped back the cover and the first few pages of a narrow notebook with spiral binding at the top, the classic "reporter's notebook," and pulled a pencil from behind his ear; the eraser was chewed down, and there were teeth marks denting the yellow paint. A nervous young man.

"What would you like to know, David?"

"Uh, how long will you be visiting New Orleans?"

"I'm not sure exactly. My publisher has arranged a few interviews for me with local media—I have to call about the times and locations—and there will be a signing at Bookstar."

"Are you going to the Jazz and Heritage Festival?"

"Oh yes. It's one of the reasons I came here. But whether I'll stay for both weekends is uncertain."

"Have you been to it before?"

"No. This will be my first Jazz Fest."

He scratched a note on his pad.

"You know it's a pretty big event out at the racetrack," he said. "It can get pretty confusing. There's thousands of performers, and so many people it's hard to walk."

"I'll feel overwhelmed, I'm sure, but Wayne Copely has promised to escort me."

He stared at the page he was writing on, a blush rising on his face. "You know," he said, "if he can't make it one time—if you need any help getting—you know, like around, I'd be happy to take you."

"Oh, David, that's very generous of you, but I believe Mr. Copely has a full schedule planned for me."

"Well, just in case he can't make it, you can always call me."

He reached into the front pocket of his well-worn jeans and produced a card on which he had already scribbled his name and phone number.

"I'll keep it in mind," I said, opening my shoulder bag and tucking his card into a side pocket. "I really must go now. I don't want to keep Mr. Copely waiting."

David rushed to open the door for me. A blast of hot air nearly pushed us back inside. The sun was blinding.

"You know, I do a little mystery writing myself," he said, tugging at his wispy beard as we stepped outside.

"Oh?"

"I had a story published in a magazine once. It took first prize in a student writing contest."

He was talking fast now.

"Would you, uh—could you, ah, maybe read my latest mystery story sometime, if you have the time, that is?"

"I'm going to be pretty busy while I'm down here," I said.

"Oh, yeah, of course. I shouldn't have asked. It's not important anyway. It's just a silly story." He tucked his head down and studied his sneakers.

I sighed. Would-be mystery writers often pressed their work upon me, and the task of reading so many manuscripts could become burdensome. I longed to turn them down, but as a former teacher, I also hated to discourage literary effort.

"Listen," I said, "why don't you drop off a copy at my hotel. I'm staying at the Royal. I'll read it on the plane on my way home. Just be sure to include your address so I can write to you and return your story."

"Really? Oh, cool! Thanks so much. I'll go get it right now."

"That's not really necessary . . ."

But my words went unheard. He had already sprinted halfway down the street.

The French Quarter was awash with tourists as I made my way back to the hotel, and the tide swept me toward Jackson Square. Walking slowly, I followed the crowd, my progress hindered by knots of people who'd stopped to admire the colorful artwork hanging the length of the cast-iron fence that surrounded the park, or to consider the work of caricaturists and portrait painters who'd set pictures of movie stars and other familiar faces atop makeshift easels to entice tourists to sit for them. The square was named for Andrew Jackson, and his statue took pride of place at its center. I glimpsed Jackson through the iron pickets of the fence. The victor in the Battle of New Orleans in the War of 1812 was silhouetted against the white expanse of the St. Louis Cathedral, sitting astride a rearing horse and tipping his hat to all the visitors, most of whom ignored his sculptured likeness in favor of the surprising variety of live entertainment along the pedestrian walkway. Clowns, magicians, tarot card readers, tap dancers, and musical trios, duos, and solos all vied for the attention of the flood of visitors who were happy to comply, tossing coins into hats or open instrument cases on the flagstone in front of the performers.

Conscious of Wayne waiting for me at the hotel, I made a note to myself to return when I had more time to enjoy the performances, and browse the art. But my way was blocked. A young clown on roller skates, his nut-brown face painted white with a big red mouth, and a battered top hat perched on his bright-orange curls, was at the center of a group of giggling children, their parents and others watching from behind them. Bent in half, the tall clown pulled coins and flowers from behind the youngsters' ears and from under their arms, affecting a look of amazement at each discovery. One of the children reached out to touch a little skull dangling from a chain around the clown's neck. He tucked it into his shirt, and opened his hand to release a white dove. The crowd burst into applause. When he pulled the hat from his head to take a bow, the orange wig came with it, revealing his own mop of black curls in much the same style. He set the hat down, brim side up, orange curls drooping around the crown, and thanked those who dropped in coins and the occasional bill.

"Where y'at, folks?" he called out. "That's Nawlins' speak for "How y'all doing?" Welcome to the Big Easy. Y'all're standing in the heart of the *Vieux Carré,* the French Quarter to you out-of-towners. Anyone heah a native?"

The crowd laughed.

"Where y'all from?"

Voices shouted names of home towns.

"Cleveland."

"Indianapolis."

"Nachez, Mississippi."

"Anchorage," yelled a man standing next to me. He wore plaid shorts and a white T-shirt damp with perspiration.

The clown skated toward us, leaving his hat on the ground.

"Anchorage? I could sure use some of your cool air on a day like today. Bring any with you?"

"'Fraid not," said the Alaskan. "Wish I'd thought of it."

"Me, too." The clown made an exaggerated swipe across his brow with a bandana, and delighted his onlookers when water poured onto the ground as he skated in a circle pretending to wring out the cloth.

Coming back to me, the clown said, "And you, ma'am? Where y'all hail from?"

"Cabot Cove, Maine."

"Another cool state! Whatcha doin' here?"

"Well, actually," I said, laughing, "right now I'm just trying to navigate through the crowd to St. Louis Street to get back to my hotel. I have an appointment and I don't want to be late."

"Is that all? I can help you there."

He glided back to where he'd left his hat and scooped it up, picking out the change and bills and stuffing them into his pocket. *"Laissez les bons temps rouler!* Let the good times roll," he proclaimed. "I'll be back in a little while. Y'all hang around, now, heah?"

The open circle the spectators had left for him quickly filled as the throng moved on to other entertainment. The clown skated back to me. "Ready to go?" he asked.

"Oh, you don't have to bother," I said, not expecting the special attention.

"No bother at all to help a famous visitor," he replied. "You'll never make it without me. See all those people? They're like a wave on the ocean. If you don't go with the flow, you'll get washed out to sea. It takes special skills to get through."

I looked around and had to agree. "Okay, how do we do this?" I asked.

"Single file is best. Grab on to the top of my trousers in the back, but don't pull too hard or we'll both be very embarrassed."

The clown's black-and-white checkered trousers were attached to a hoop around his waist, and held up by a pair of green suspenders. I grabbed the hoop with one hand and held tight to my shoulder bag with the other.

The clown pushed his way through the multitude, pulling me along behind. His height, extended by the roller skates, allowed him to peer over the tops of the heads in front of him and select a pathway. His loud voice also ensured co-operation.

"Step aside, folks. Coming through. Excuse us. Make way."

The sight of an almost seven-foot-tall clown in checkered

trousers, dragging a woman in his wake, must have been enough to startle the dawdlers and the curious, who stepped aside to let us pass.

We escaped Jackson Square, dodged the milling tourists on Chartres Street and soon reached the corner of St. Louis Street. My colorful escort doffed his hat and dipped into a low bow in front of me. The little skull on a chain dropped from his collar and swung out in front of him.

"Napoleon DuBois at your service, Mrs. Fletcher."

"How did you know . . . ?"

"Your picture was in the book section of the paper this morning. And it's on the back of a book I just bought."

"Well, Napoleon, that was timely service you provided, and I'm very grateful," I said, unzipping my bag. I pulled out my wallet. "Something for your assistance? You must lose a lot of doves."

"No," he said with a smile. "Goes right home, will be there when I get there."

His eyes flew up to the sky and he clasped his top hat and orange wig to his chest in a saintly gesture. "What I'm really praying for, though, is one of your books signed to me."

"I'd be delighted to give it to you," I said. "I have a few copies back at my hotel. I'll put one aside for you."

I gave him some money, thanked him again, and promised to leave an autographed copy of my new book with the concierge desk. He could pick it up when it was convenient. We shook hands and he skated back in the direction from which we'd come.

Smiling, I glanced at my watch and continued on to my hotel. New Orleans was such a colorful city, full of interesting people, fascinating places to see, and surprises, like a gallant street entertainer who'd rescued me from being late. I'd have a good story to share with Wayne over lunch.

Chapter Three

"You must have the Oysters Rockefeller, definitely the oysters. You do like oysters?"

"I'm from Maine. I love all seafood."

"Well, this is where the dish was invented years and years ago. And it was named after Rockefeller because the taste is so rich. It would probably be called Oysters Trump if it were invented today."

"Then let's start with that. What else do you recommend?"

"I think the *pompano en papillote*. The fish is topped with shrimp and crab and then cooked in parchment. You'll love it."

I smiled at Wayne. He was in his element here. He'd been greeting other diners, and waving at the restaurant staff ever since we'd entered Antoine's.

"We'll have an order of the soufléed potatoes to share," Wayne told the tuxedoed waiter who stood at his elbow, a white cloth draped over his left arm.

"Certainly, Mr. Copely."

"How's the family?"

"Very well, sir. Thank you for asking."

"Did you like that CD I left for you?"

I tuned out Wayne's conversation with the waiter and released a sigh I hadn't even realized I was holding. I was happy to be sitting down and in air-conditioned comfort.

We'd walked to Antoine's from my hotel, but even though the distance was short, it was uncomfortably hot. New Orleans was experiencing a heat wave with temperatures close to one hundred, high humidity, and no relieving rain in sight. I noticed that many of the women on the street wore large hats, or carried umbrellas or parasols to shield themselves from the sun's fiery rays. While I had brought lightweight clothes in anticipation of warm weather, the only hat I'd packed was a baseball cap I occasionally wore when jogging, not appropriate headgear for going to lunch at an elegant restaurant. Thank goodness for the lovely iron-work *galleries* on the upper floors of buildings in the French Quarter. They'd provided a shaded walk almost the entire route to the restaurant.

Antoine's, one of the city's venerable establishments, dating to 1840 when it opened in a different building, was now situated in what had been a private home that had been built in 1868. Wayne had led me past the front room with its Austrian shades, down corridors and up and down flights of stairs, and through a maze of rooms with glittering chandeliers, polished dark woods, and antique furnishings. As we went, he kept up a running commentary on the city's oldest and most famous restaurant. By the time we finally sat down in the Rex Room, where colorful Mardi Gras costumes were displayed in glass cases, I had worked up a good appetite, and was ready to sample the signature dishes for which Antoine's was noted.

The waiter went to place our order, and I unfolded a white linen napkin across my lap.

" What are you having, Wayne?"

"The chicken *bonne femme*. They make it very well here. And I took the liberty of ordering a baked Alaska for us for dessert. I hope you don't mind."

"Not at all."

"Well, Jessica," he said, rubbing his hands together, "that was a productive morning, wasn't it?"

"I think it went well."

"Yes, except for that little contretemps with Broadbent."

"Why do you dislike him so?" I asked.

"I don't care about him one way or the other, but I think he's hardly the objective investigative journalist he presents himself to be."

"What makes you say that?"

"He's an old buddy of Beaudin's, probably been on and off the political payroll for years."

"On and off?"

"Politicians in New Orleans are always changing bedfellows. No one can agree with anyone else for very long. They're known for switching sides, opinions, friends. In fact, it's a miracle to me that Phil Beaudin has been Maurice's assistant as long as he has."

"And you think he and Broadbent . . ." I hesitated.

Wayne snorted. "Julian's stories always manage to give the administration a boost. Look what he did to Senator Lunsford just when Maurice was thinking about moving up. You know, Jessica, even though our mayor is an old family friend, I have no illusions about honest politics in New Orleans."

"Do you think he's corrupt?"

"Let's just say he's part of a longtime, honored tradition of not letting the law get in the way of good policy. Plus, he's been very lucky." He pulled a piece off the roll on his plate, and buttered it. "So, what else would you like to discuss?"

"Oh, come on now, Wayne," I said. "You can't just drop a bomb like that and retreat. How has the mayor been lucky?"

Wayne chewed thoughtfully. "He's been reelected on his own merits for years," he said after a moment, "but he never would have made it into office in the first place if his opponent, Virgil Franklin, hadn't had such a timely death."

"And you think Franklin's death was suspicious?"

"I couldn't say for sure. But Virgil was way ahead in the polls."

"How did he die?"

"He fell out of his pirogue in the swamp, and supposedly drowned in three feet of water. 'Course by the time the alligators and vultures got through with him, there was really no way to tell how he died."

"How awful!"

"Yes, but it was just what Maurice needed. The other party couldn't come up with another strong candidate, and he's been voted into office in every election since."

"You don't think Broadbent had anything to do with Franklin's death."

"Who's to say? But what reporter worth his salt sits in the pocket of a politician?"

"Can you be sure his book on Senator Lunsford was written deliberately to help Amadour?"

"No, of course not. But it's just like New Orleans politics to have something happen so conveniently. I guess I just don't believe in coincidence."

The waiter interrupted our conversation by setting down our Oysters Rockefeller, six plump specimens set in a pan of rock salt.

Wayne closed his eyes, leaned over the dish, and took a deep breath, inhaling the tempting aroma of oysters, greens, and anise.

"I'm in heaven," he cooed. "Let's eat, and then I'll tell you all about Jazz Fest."

"You just want to change the subject," I chided.

"You're right." He winked at me. "But you can bring it up again another time."

The food was delicious, and Wayne was a wonderful

host, entertaining me with stories of his exploits on the road promoting his new book. I reciprocated, regaling him with the tale of my earlier trip through Jackson Square as the caboose of a top-hatted clown.

"I'm looking forward to taking you to Jazz Fest tomorrow," Wayne said as the waiter cleared our plates. "I'm tied up this evening, but after that I've cleared my calendar, and except for time spent following up any new leads on Little Red LeCoeur's recordings, I'll be at your disposal."

"I hope I won't be taking you away from important business."

"Not at all. Attending Jazz Fest comes under my job description. I checked my answering machine a little while ago. Apart from the usual death threats, I have no other pressing appointments."

"Death threats! What do you mean, death threats?"

"It's a critics' affliction, my dear. Goes with the territory, I'm afraid. Nasty letters, phone calls. They come from all over the country, probably the world. I got my first a dozen years ago when I gave a local band a poor review, and their national tour was canceled. I don't think it was my review. They were dreadful players, decidedly second-rate. They had no sense of tempo, much less musicality. However, they and their friends took offense at my appraisal, and for about a month I was plagued by a series of vicious calls, impugning my manhood, of course—but I'm used to that—and detailing the unpleasant way they were going to take revenge. It's one of the reasons I bought an answering machine, to put a little technological space between my detractors and myself."

"Someone threatening you with death is more than a detractor, Wayne. I hope you've told the police."

"I did the first few times, but the investigations never turned up anything. In those days, you had to keep the caller on the line to do a trace, and I wasn't willing to listen to that filth for more time than it took to replace the receiver. After the third or fourth instance, I became inured. Now, I simply toss the letters, erase the messages, and go about my business. As you can see, I'm perfectly hale and hardy, perky even."

He tucked his chin down and batted his eyelashes at me. I couldn't help but smile.

"You can make jokes, Wayne, but it's really not a laughing matter. Most of the time, the kinds of people who make threats like that get satisfaction just thinking they're scaring you. But you can't count on that. You could be in real danger. Why don't you ask the phone company for Caller ID, so you can see the number of the person making the call and report them?"

"I'm not sure I want to know who they are. They might be my friends." He grinned, and added, "Tell you what. If they get me, I'll leave you my antique Chinese box. You'll love it, all kinds of drawers and hidden compartments."

"Wayne, don't kid about that."

"Don't worry about me, Jessica. I'm fine, and I've learned to ignore these messages with typical New Orleans aplomb. You know, it's ingrained in our personalities from childhood not to take life too seriously. *Laissez les bons temps rouler,* and all that. We live for the day, the hour, the minute even. It's part of our charm."

Although Wayne was flippant about the threats made against his life, I could sense tension beneath his show of bravado. "I've been on the receiving end of death threats, too," I admitted. "I know what you're going through, and it's not a comfortable feeling."

"You have?" He was obviously astonished. Frowning, he sat back in his chair and crossed his arms. "You never told me," he accused.

"There's still a lot we don't know about each other," I answered. "It's not something I enjoy discussing any more than you do, but it's important to take action."

"Tell me what happened."

I took a deep breath, struggling to find simple words to describe what had been such a disturbing experience. "It was an obsessed reader," I said at last. "He sent me threatening notes at every stop on my book tour, said he was watching me and would know when his time had come."

"Did you hire a bodyguard?"

"I came close once, but changed my mind at the last minute. I didn't want to give the perpetrator such power over my life." As I talked to Wayne, I could feel the fear and the anger that had filled me during those days flowing back. I hurried to conclude the story.

"It was not a successful tour for me, although the books sold very well," I said dryly. "I notified the police in every city, but since I wasn't staying anywhere for very long, there wasn't a lot they could do."

"You see?" Wayne interrupted.

I held up my hand to stall his comments. "But when I got home," I continued, "our sheriff, Mort Metzger, conducted an investigation, set up a stakeout, and caught the fellow."

"Where is he now?"

"In a mental hospital. I hated pressing charges, but it was the only way to ensure the stalker got the treatment he needed. I fervently hope the doctors will be able to help him conquer his problems."

"You're very generous," Wayne remarked. "If my stalker is ever caught, I hope he spends the rest of his life on a chain gang, pounding boulders into gravel."

As we'd been talking, our waiter had slipped plates of baked Alaska in front of us. It was a spectacular dessert, the warm meringue, delicately browned, coating cold ice cream, the combination of textures and temperature a delight to the tongue.

Wayne sat back, wiped his lips with his napkin, patted his stomach, and blew out a satisfied sigh.

"Terrific! Never a disappointment."

"Yes, it's really wonderful."

"Let's talk music. Do you remember the jazz lessons I gave you last year, Jessica?"

"I recall going to more concerts and performances than I'd ever been to in my life. And I remember you telling me that the biggest change in jazz in your lifetime has been the emergence of the bass player. And you said that most improvisation is based upon chord changes, and that jazz is really America's only indigenous art form. Oh, and bebop is the most challenging form of jazz for musicians to play—let's see, the leading bebop musicians were Charlie Parker, a drummer named Kenny Clark, oh, and of course, Dizzy Gillespie, and . . ."

I recounted for him other things he'd told me about jazz. When I was finished, he shook his head, smiling. "Whew! I'd say you learned your lessons well." Consulting a schedule he'd pulled from his breast pocket, he added, "Tomorrow, you'll have an opportunity to sample all kinds of jazz, and there'll be a host of trumpet players to listen to this year because opening day is dedicated to the memory and spirit of Little Red LeCoeur. I had to push hard for that, but the organizers finally agreed. I'm sure they'll have T-shirts and little trinkets with his image on them, so you can even bring home a memento of his influence."

"Wayne, do you really think there's any chance of finding those recordings you spoke of this morning?"

"I'm not sure. But I may know a lot more after tonight."

"Someone has already responded to your challenge?"

"It could be a false lead, but if you don't track them all down, you never know. I won't say any more. I don't want to jinx it."

"You're not superstitious, are you?"

"Everyone in this city is superstitious. I should have gotten a special *gris-gris* to wear till I find the cylinders. Maybe I'll pick one up at Jazz Fest tomorrow."

"I've heard that term, *gris-gris,* but I don't remember what it is."

"It's a voodoo charm, a pouch containing a mixture of ingredients, which vary depending on what you need—something to bring you luck, protect you from evil, help you get a job, attract a lover, that sort of thing. You wear them on a string around your neck. I never have, but lots of people do. I wonder if Doris Burns knows about them. We should enlighten her."

The bill came and Wayne and I had a good-natured debate over who would pay for lunch.

"This one's on me," he said. "After all, I chose the restaurant. You can buy me lunch tomorrow at the racetrack. That's where the festival takes place."

"I'll be happy to buy you lunch tomorrow, so long as you let me take you to dinner at a restaurant later on. As wonderful as a Po' Boy sandwich or other festival fare may be, they can't compare to a lavish meal like the one we just had. You must let me treat you to a special place."

"We'll see."

We exited the restaurant and stood for a moment in the shade of the gallery overhead, acclimating ourselves to the heat.

"Oh, I almost forgot," I said. "I brought along the book you asked for."

I pulled from my shoulder bag a hardback copy of my latest mystery, which I had already inscribed to Wayne.

"Wonderful! I'll start it tonight." He squeezed the book into his leather case along with his papers from the morning's panel.

"I should probably bring a book to the mayor and his wife next week, shouldn't I?"

"They might have it already," he said. "Marguerite's a big reader. Remind me, and I'll give them a call and ask."

"I'll do that," I said. "Thanks again for the wonderful lunch."

"It was my pleasure."

"What time shall we meet tomorrow?"

"Why don't I stop by your hotel at nine-thirty and we can have breakfast before we leave for the track? That way I can bring you a copy of *my* book, and assuage my guilt about deserting you this afternoon and evening, considering that I talked you into coming here."

"I'll be happy to meet you for breakfast, but there's no need to feel guilty. I intend to enjoy a leisurely promenade around the French Quarter. I spotted some artwork in Jackson Square I'd like to see again, and maybe I'll even buy myself a straw hat, like yours."

"Till tomorrow then. You know how to get back to your hotel?"

I nodded. Wayne gave me a peck on the cheek, checked the crease of his straw hat, slid the hat on his shaved head, and took off at a brisk pace.

I browsed a few windows en route to my hotel. In one, I saw a familiar face reflected back at me. I turned around. Across the street was mayoral aide Philippe Beaudin in his tan cowboy hat. He was talking animatedly with a muscular man in a black T-shirt, who had a ponytail hanging down his back and a windbreaker slung over one shoulder. I couldn't see the man's face because his back was to me, but he had a distinguishing feature that was hard to miss. Peeking out from his left sleeve, curled around his elbow, was the long tail of some animal tattooed on his arm.

Thinking I could save Wayne a call by asking Beaudin if the Amadours might have my book, I waved at him and called his name. He looked up with a frown and continued talking to the man.

I stepped off the curb. A big green bus advertising "Swamp Tours" pulled in across the street, and the clip-clop of hooves alerted me that a mule-drawn carriage was approaching. I took a step back. The carriage was blue, with purple fringe around the sunshade top. The driver had given his mule a red felt hat, and had cut holes in it through which the mule's ears protruded. Everyone wears a hat in this heat, I thought wryly. That would have to be my first purchase.

The carriage passed and the bus moved out, and I crossed the street only to find both men gone. I looked down the street in one direction, and then the other. I'd only waited a moment to cross. Beaudin's cowboy hat ought to be easy to spot in the crowd, I thought. But he'd disappeared. I stepped back into the street to get a better view. No man with a pony-tail was visible; no tan hat stood out among the bobbing heads.

How strange, I thought. I was sure he'd seen me.

Chapter Four

Room 108 at the Royal Hotel, one of several "Royals" in the city, was a bright but cool haven when I returned there following lunch at Antoine's. I'd stopped at the concierge desk first to learn that my package for Napoleon was still awaiting pickup. But another package, a thick envelope, had arrived for me. It was David Stewart's mystery story. I briefly contemplated reading it right away, but knew I'd prefer to have a stretch of time in which to make notes and give his story my full attention. Airplane trips are perfect for that kind of work. Phones don't ring, neighbors don't stop in, and there are none of the myriad distractions that make it easy to put aside a project. I slipped the envelope containing his story into the same pocket of my airplane carry-on bag where I keep my plane tickets, and returned the bag to the top shelf of the closet.

My accommodations were on the ground floor; French doors opened out to a paved stone pathway, leading to a charming courtyard with a tinkling fountain where breakfast was served each morning. I couldn't see the patio through the glass panes of the doors—a large bush on one side of the path obstructed my view, but also afforded a measure of privacy. Nevertheless, I drew the heavy drapes closed, slipped off the silk dress I'd worn for this morning's book-and-author program and my lunch with Wayne, hung it up, and pulled the terry robe the hotel had thoughtfully provided from its hook on the back of the bathroom door. With the drapes closed, the dimmer light in the room allowed me to see the message light on my phone, which I hadn't noticed when I'd come in.

I sat on the side of the bed and picked up the phone, and the pen and pad next to it. The first message was from my publisher's new marketing director, Paulette Parr, who'd left details about my upcoming book signing at Bookstar. Paulette was a wonderfully organized young woman, supporting four children with the assistance of her mother. How she managed to keep track of all their schedules—after-school soccer, ballet lessons, play dates, pediatrician appointments—as well as the book tours of several dozen authors, never failed to impress me.

The second message was from my good friend of many years, Seth Hazlitt, who called to tell me his nurse's cat had had a litter of calico kittens, and did I want him to put a hold on one for my nephew, Grady, and his new wife, who'd just bought their first house. I checked my watch. Seth would have a waiting room filled with patients now; I'd better put off my return call to a better time. For many years, Seth had been the only doctor in Cabot Cove, and had recently been talking about retirement. Of course, he'd mentioned it before, but there was always a chorus of objections whenever he raised the topic down at Mara's Luncheonette. But he'd finally taken the first step six months ago when he'd asked a lovely young woman, a graduate of Albert Einstein Medical School in New York City, to join his practice. Jennifer Countryman was a native of Maine who'd left home for the first time to go away to college. During her interview with Seth, she'd told him that her years of education, internship, and residency in big-city schools and hospitals made a return to her home state, and a small town medical practice, very attractive. With Cabot Cove only an hour's drive away from her parents, who lived inland, the arrangement seemed perfect for her. And it was a great relief for Seth.

It took a while for a few of Seth's patients to warm up to Dr. Countryman, but her sunny smile and professional competence eventually won them over. Her presence in the office meant Seth could take some much-deserved time for himself to putter in his yard, or steal a few afternoon hours out on a boat fishing, or on the golf course.

I deleted the messages and leaned back. The bed, queen-sized with wrought-iron head and footboards, was covered with a white linen duvet, and the sheets and pillowcases were white as well. I stifled a yawn—big meals make me sleepy—and decided an afternoon nap was just what I needed. I crawled beneath the sheets and fell asleep immediately, the smoothness of the linen pillowcase cool beneath my cheek.

It was nearly four when I awoke refreshed and ready to explore the interesting shops and other attractions of the French Quarter. A khaki skirt and matching cotton blouse were just right for the informal atmosphere of the area, where most tourists wandered around in T-shirts and shorts during the day, and T-shirts and jeans at night. I slipped on a pair of good walking sandals; ran a comb through my hair; put my wallet, room key, sunglasses, and a packet of tissues into a small purse; looped my reading glasses on a cord around my neck; and stepped out into the sunshine.

A proper hat was my first order of business, but a hike over to the Central Business District, where I knew there were department stores, was not appealing. Instead, I found myself strolling back to Jackson Square. With so many vendors at the park, there was bound to be one selling hats.

The square was almost as crowded as it had been at noon, but I was beginning to get my bearings. As I walked, I kept an eye out for Napoleon. A few of his competitors were there—a magician in a black cape doing card tricks on a folding table, and a pair of clowns dressed as Raggedy Ann and Andy. But no clown on skates with a top hat. At the corner, I could see a display of T-shirts pegged up on what looked like a laundry line tied to the square's black iron fence. Were those baseball caps on a stand? I inched my way along until I reached the display.

"Excuse me," I said. "Do you sell any hats other than baseball caps?"

The vendor, a red-headed man in his forties with a handlebar mustache, was folding a pile of shorts with "NOLA," shorthand for New Orleans, Louisiana, sewn on the patch pocket, and stacking them on the table against the fence.

"Yeah, my wife's around here somewhere. She's got a box o' hats."

"Can you point me in her direction?"

"Stella," he yelled. "Stella!"

A short woman in a sundress, her brown ponytail sticking out from the back of her baseball cap, broke away from the customer she'd been helping and turned to us. She hit her husband on the arm, and grinned at me.

"Don't mind him. He loves to do that."

"Do what?"

"Yell for me. Just like the line from Tennessee Williams's *Streetcar Named Desire* where Stanley yells for Stella. He's Stanley. I'm Stella. He's been doing that for seven years."

I thought Stella was remarkably good-natured for being able to smile at a joke she'd been subjected to for so long.

"The play was set in New Orleans, wasn't it?" I said. "I'd forgotten that."

"We even had a streetcar line named Desire at one time, but it doesn't run anymore. There's a bus on that route now."

"A Bus Named Desire doesn't have the same ring, does it?"

Stella laughed, although I was sure she'd heard that comment before.

"Stanley says you have a box of hats somewhere. I was hoping to get some protection from the sun, but I'd like something other than a baseball cap."

"Oh, sure. They're over here."

She bent down, lifted the bottom of the tablecloth, revealing a pile of boxes and packing materials stowed beneath the table, dragged out a big carton, and folded back the flaps.

"I've got some felt hats from the end of the season, but it's too hot for those now. Here are some straw hats. I'll be getting more in next week, but of course that doesn't do you any good right now. Do you like this one?"

She held up a straw hat with a wide brim and yellow checked ribbon around the crown. I tried it on and adjusted the brim so it was snapped down in front and up in back.

Stanley pointed to a small hand mirror hanging on the fence. "You can use that," he said, "but I'll tell you right now, that hat looks great on you."

I scrunched down a little so I could see my reflection in the low-hanging mirror.

"Thank you. I like it, too."

I straightened up. "How much is it?" I asked.

"For you . . ." Stanley said with a wink.

"Oh, Stanley, cut it out. Just give me a hand with this box."

They wrestled the box back under the table and Stella stood, clapping the dust off her hands.

"I don't suppose they change that much," she said, "but it's really last year's hat. I could let you have it for half off."

We agreed on a price and I paid for my purchase, leaving it on my head. Stella clipped the string holding the label, saying, "So you won't walk around looking like Minnie Pearl," referring to the country music singer–comic who always wore a hat with a dangling pricetag.

"Sure you don't need anythin' else?" Stanley asked, waving at his laundry line of colorful shirts. "Got any friends back home who'd like—you know?—a souvenir from New Orleans?" He pointed to his chest, and I noticed for the first time that he was wearing a shirt advertising the Jazz and Heritage Festival. Beneath the dates was the image of a curly haired man playing the trumpet.

"Is that a picture of Little Red LeCoeur?" I asked.

"Stella, we got us a live one here. How do you know about Little Red? You must be a ringer. You're not a tourist after all. Only New Orleanians know about Little Red, New Orleanians or true jazz buffs. Which are you?"

"Neither one actually. It's interesting to me that Little Red is so well known here in New Orleans, but his reputation never carried outside the city."

"He deserves more attention, no doubt about it. He was a musical genius. But he never left his roots, never played nowhere else."

"A good friend of mine is doing research on Little Red LeCoeur," I said, "and looking for recordings he may have made around the turn of the last century."

Stanley shook his head from side to side. "Never happen," he said.

"What do you mean?"

"He'll never find any recordings by Little Red."

"How can you be so sure?"

"Because I'm an expert on Little Red LeCoeur. Been hearin' about him from the old players since I was a little tyke in the bayous, huntin' alligators and trappin' crawdads. Read everthin' I could find about the man. Never saw nothin' about recordings."

"Just because there's nothing written doesn't mean—"

"Oh yes it does." His voice was louder now, and we were starting to attract observers.

Stella tapped her husband on the shoulder. "Calm down,

Stanley. The lady doesn't know what you do. Just tell her quietly, and patiently."

"Yes, Stanley, please tell me what you know."

He took a deep breath, and blew it out.

"Sorry about that. I get a little hot when people challenge my knowledge. Don't have any fancy degrees, but I know my jazz. And I know my Louisiana jazz the best."

"And I don't know much about either. I didn't mean to offend you."

"That's okay. I've got a big mouth. Don't mind me."

"Please continue, Stanley. By the way, my name is Jessica Fletcher, and you're correct. I'm not from New Orleans. I'm from Maine. My friend, the one interested in Little Red LeCoeur, is Wayne Copley, the music critic."

"Well, at least he's a hometown boy. But he ought to know better. I could set him straight."

"Okay. I'll suggest he come here and speak with you. But in the meantime, won't you tell me why you're so certain Little Red never recorded?"

"LeCoeur came from a long line of Rada Houngan, voodoo priests, that's why."

Stanley leaned over to a man looking through his pile of shorts. "What size do you need?" he asked. The customer told him and Stanley turned away from me, pulled out a pair of red shorts, and lay them on top of the table.

I peered over Stanley's shoulder.

"I'm afraid I don't see how that proves—"

He turned around abruptly.

"I don't know if you know voodoo, Mrs. Bletcher."

"It's Fletcher."

"Huh? Oh, right. Mrs. Fletcher."

"You were saying?"

"Voodoo. I don't know if you know it, but it's a very spiritual religion. I guess all of 'em are. But with voodoo, there's lots of variations. It's like each person kind of makes up his own version. You know? Anyway, over the years, some things stay the same, but other things, they just die out. Like LeCoeur's. His kind of voodoo just died out."

"What was different then?"

Stanley's customer had drifted down to the next vendor, and I knew he was anxious to be rid of me.

"Well, for him, music was one of the most important parts of voodoo rituals. Still is, actually. But for Little Red, music was an expression. You know? Of his spirit. It wasn't supposed to be commercial. It was for ceremonies and communing with the loa—those are the voodoo gods. There wouldn't have been recordin's, photographs, drawin's. Anythin' that captured the soul and bound it to the earth was bad."

I pointed to his shirt. "How would you know what he looked like if there weren't any photographs or portraits of him?"

Stanley dropped his gaze to his shirt, pulled the hem down, and angled his head.

"An educated guess, maybe. Ever'one says he had hair like cayenne pepper and a temper to match. Lots of the old timers knew 'im, so this is probably based on their descriptions."

"And you say recording was against Little Red LeCoeur's religion."

"Absolutely!"

"But Wayne's been hearing about these cylinders for years. Couldn't someone have secretly recorded Little Red without his knowledge?"

"Wishful thinking. Equipment in those days was big and bulky. You had to play or speak right into the microphone. You couldn't hide behind a rock and record somebody from a distance."

"Then you've never heard the rumors about these recordings?"

"Oh, I've heard them, all right, but I know they're non-sense. Just another wild-goose chase for the uneducated."

"Well, I don't think Wayne is exactly uneducated."

"Didn't mean to insult your friend. Copely knows his jazz, that's for sure. I read his column all the time. But this time, he's being taken in. Tell 'im not to pay good money for bad karma. He'll never find recordings of Little Red LeCoeur. Not genuine ones anyhow."

"I'll certainly tell him what you said. And thank you for taking time from your work to explain all this to me."

"You're very welcome, Mrs. Fletcher. Jazz is my favorite topic. I hope you'll get a chance to come out to the Fair-grounds Race Track while you're here, and—you know?—listen to some world-class playing."

"I intend to do that very thing tomorrow."

"We'll be there, too. Maybe we'll see you again."

"I'll look for you."

I saw that Stella was busy with a customer, and asked Stanley to say good-bye to her. Leaving their booth, I scanned the work of the artists and craftspeople that lined the park, but my heart wasn't in it. My mind was full of what Stanley had told me.

Was Wayne simply the victim of false rumors, leading him on a vain chase for a prize that didn't exist? I hoped not. He was so sure those recordings could be found. Maybe Stanley didn't know as much as he thought he knew, I comforted myself. But he was acquainted with Little Red's religious beliefs, and if Little Red had been a devout man, as he was assumed to be, then Stanley could be right, and the wonderful music of the famed trumpeter might never be heard by his successors. Even though I was not knowledgeable about jazz, I felt the loss for this generation not to have access to the genius of a talented musician of another era.

Mulling over the possibility of Wayne's disappointment, I walked between the iron filigree stanchions that served as streetlights, and through the open gates into Jackson Square. The peaceful setting inside the park was an odd contrast to the frivolity outside its iron boundary, and I welcomed the opportunity to walk quietly without being jostled by my fellow visitors to the city.

I reached the far side of the park and crossed Chartres Street, entering the flagstone passageway called Pirates Alley, which borders St. Louis Cathedral and the Cathedral Garden. Distracted by my thoughts, I almost missed the vibrant multicolored palette—yellow, red, green—of the brick and wooden buildings with fanlights, iron lacework galleries, and other decorative structural details so unlike the spare New England architecture my eyes were accustomed to seeing. The cheerful aspect of the buildings, and the smiling faces of the young people who passed me on their way to the Square, raised my spirits, and I arrived at Royal Street intent on not permitting Wayne's worries to become mine.

Royal Street was an avenue of beautiful buildings, fashionable boutiques, fine restaurants, and elegant antiques shops. One store in particular appealed to me because among the gold pocket watches, silver candelabra, framed etchings, and snuff boxes arrayed in the window was a highly polished mahogany gramophone. A bell tinkled overhead when I pushed open the door to Simon West's Antiques.

In the center of the shop, a gleaming brass-and-crystal chandelier hung over a walnut table, its surface covered with small decorative pieces. Recessed lighting in the ceiling, obviously on a dimmer, was kept low to allow customers to observe the effect of the antique fixture.

I pulled off my new straw hat and fluffed my hair. My eyes swept the shadowy perimeter of the room, taking in the beautiful seventeenth- and eighteenth-century chests and sideboards, each with its complement of gold-edged china and cut crystal goblets, or silver epergne and other lovely mementos of another age.

A breeze wafted through an open door at the back of the shop, carrying the delicious scent of barbecue smoke. My stomach rumbled. Since it was less than four hours since Wayne and I had left Antoine's, I was surprised to find myself feeling hungry. I followed my nose to the source of the tempting smell and reached the door. Outside was a courtyard of red brick paving on which sat an elaborate wrought iron chair, its peeling white paint revealing the original black of the metal. Nestled next to the chair were large pottery planters filled with red geraniums and trailing ivy.

"Do you need any help?"

"Oh, I didn't see you," I said, startled at the voice.

"It takes a while till your eyes adjust to the light."

"Are you Simon West?"

"I am."

Marking his place in a book and rising from his chair at a highboy secretary tucked in a corner was a thin, dour-faced man who I judged to be in his forties, despite hair that was completely white, although thick eyebrows revealed he'd had dark hair in his youth. He wore a powder-blue shirt, the same hue as his remarkably blue eyes. He pulled a navy jacket from the back of a chair and shrugged into it, frowned, and slipped the book he'd been reading into a side pocket.

"There's a lot more upstairs if you care to look," he said, standing at the desk and pointing to a narrow flight of stairs adjacent to the back door. He didn't move from his place, perhaps hoping that I would disappear above and leave him in peace to continue reading.

"Or did you have something specific in mind?" he asked.

"I saw your gramophone and thought I'd see if you had any old cylinder recordings."

Obviously agitated, he pulled at the cuffs of his shirt, and came to where I stood.

"You're the third customer to ask me that question today," he said. "What in heaven's name is going on?"

I told the irritated store owner about Wayne's announcement that morning and his campaign to bring to light recordings of Little Red LeCoeur.

He huffed softly and tugged on one ear. "I should thank Copely," he conceded. "I sold a fireplace fan and a set of andirons this afternoon to a couple who came in looking for cylinders. By the way, that gramophone plays records. A cylinder player is a different machine altogether."

"I know, but since you had one thing related to old recordings, I thought it was worth asking you about another."

"I did have some old cylinders at one point, but it's been quite a while since I've seen any in the marketplace. Collectors pick those up pretty quickly."

"Do you know if any of them featured LeCoeur?"

"Not that I recall. They were mostly classical compositions or opera singers. Copely should check with local collectors and see if they can help."

"I'm sure he's already done that. He's been searching for these recordings for a long time now."

West squinted at me, and cocked his head to one side.

"Have you been in my shop before?" he asked. "You look familiar."

I introduced myself and we shook hands. I told him that I'd been on the panel with Wayne that morning. "You may have seen my picture in the paper," I offered.

"That must be it," he said, brightening. "I like a mystery now and then myself. Right now I'm reading P. D. James. You know this one?" He pulled the paperback from his pocket, *Cover Her Face*.

"I know both the book and the author. Phyllis is a good friend and a wonderful writer. Practically by herself, she's changed attitudes toward mystery writing, or 'crime writing' as they say in England, and inspired a new level of appreciation."

He smiled for the first time. "Please tell her when you speak with her how much I'm enjoying this book."

"I'll be sure to let her know. She'll be delighted you're reading this particular one. It was her first novel."

West pulled up his cuff and glanced at his watch. "Look, it's just about closing time," he said. "Can you stay awhile? I'd love to talk more about mystery writing. I can offer you some iced tea and cookies. Or a glass of brandy if you prefer. The patio is pleasant this time of day."

I was taken aback by the transformation of West from grumpy proprietor into congenial host, but since I had no immediate plans, I decided to accept his invitation.

"I'll consider staying for tea on condition that you tell me the source of that enticing aroma coming from the back of your shop."

"I'll even introduce you to the chef. He's my neighbor, and his kitchen is just across the courtyard. We can probably talk him into giving us a taste of whatever he's making."

"I don't want to impose."

"No imposition at all. Food is a passion in New Orleans. He's hoping to open his own restaurant and is always eager to try out recipes on his friends. Come, you can sit outside while I lock up."

Simon ushered me out the back door and pulled a second chair next to the one I'd seen earlier. "I'll be right back with the tea. Thanks for agreeing to stay. It's not often I get to meet a famous author, and one whose interests parallel mine. I promise to tell you anything you want to know about wax cylinders if you'll let me quiz you about mysteries."

"That sounds like a fair exchange."

"And then, if you're hungry and can still stand my company, we can walk down to Brennan's."

He went to close the store, and I sat down, enjoying the

warm evening now that the sun no longer beat down on my head. The sound of a saxophone being played somewhere on the street drifted into my consciousness and I sighed at the mournful tone.

West returned a few minutes later with two glasses, a pitcher of iced tea, and a plate of cookies on a small tray table. He dropped into his chair. "Let me ask you a couple of questions, and then it'll be your turn."

"All right," I said, balancing my hat against a flowerpot. "Go ahead."

We chatted for a half hour about writing and the publishing business. His questions were not very different from the ones I regularly encounter on my book tours: Where do I get my inspiration? How much do I write each day? How do I promote my books? What kind of research do I do?

I told him that a location like New Orleans can provide a lot of inspiration. That when I'm working on a book, I start early, write every day, and try to finish ten pages before lunch. That the next morning, I edit my pages from the day before, and that helps me start the new ones. That the publisher is responsible for promotion, but that I help out by going on book tours and talking with readers and booksellers.

"As to research," I said finally, hoping he'd take the cue, "I enjoy learning new things. And one of the ways I do that is by talking to experts like you."

"Ah," he replied sheepishly, realizing I was waiting for the opportunity to ask him some questions. "You've been very patient." He refilled my glass. "So, wax cylinders," he said. "What would you like to know?"

"When were they made? What did they look like? What are they worth? I just want some general information."

You know that Thomas Edison invented the phonograph in the eighteen seventies?"

"Yes."

"His earliest recordings were made on tinfoil wrapped

around a little drum, but I've never seen those, if any of them survive. The foil was very fragile and ripped easily."

"So they started making wax recordings."

"That's right. I believe they became the standard some time in the late eighteen eighties. They were about four inches in length and two inches in diameter, and the earliest ones were brown. Black cylinders came in around nineteen-oh-two."

"Would Little Red LeCoeur have recorded on brown or black cylinders?"

"I'm not sure really." He rubbed his chin thoughtfully. "If he recorded on brown, however, the cylinder probably wouldn't have any identification marks on it. The older ones didn't."

"How would you know what was on them?"

"Well, if you had the original packaging, it was on a slip inside the case. Otherwise, you had to listen to it."

"They didn't use labels?"

"Nowhere to put them without interfering with the recording surface. As the production of cylinders became more sophisticated, the manufacturers began engraving information along the edge."

"If nothing is written on the early ones, how do you know what's on the cylinder and the date it was recorded?"

"You can approximate the age of a cylinder by listening to it. The oldest ones announce the song and the performer at the beginning of the recording. Later on, the announcement included where the recording was made, and sometimes a particular record number, or a description of the performer. Those are the clues to age."

"Are wax cylinders very rare?"

"Not really. But they are brittle, and break easily. And the wax is soft so if they've been played a lot, the quality can be poor. Down here in Louisiana, it's hard to find ones in good shape."

"Why is that?"

"Mainly because of the mold." He waved a hand around. "Feel this humidity?"

I nodded.

"Humidity means mold, and mold eats wax." He dropped his hand. "Once the cylinder is eaten by mold, it's virtually impossible to repair."

"How valuable are wax cylinders?" I asked. "Does it depend on the date?"

"No," he said, shaking his head. "Like all antiques, it depends on the rarity. Standard two-minute black cylinders can go for as little as five or ten dollars. Three-minute cylinders are not as plentiful and their price is higher, maybe sixty or seventy dollars if they're in good shape. But for a rare recording of an artist with historical importance—"

"Like Little Red," I interjected.

"Yes. For that, the value is incalculable."

I sat silently, contemplating the difficult road that lay before Wayne. Even if he found a cylinder Little Red had recorded, it might be cracked or worn or moldy. So many negative possibilities argued against his being able to achieve his dream of bringing the music of Little Red LeCoeur to the public.

Simon West interrupted my reverie. "Jessica?"

"Yes?" I replied. "I'm sorry, I was lost in thought."

He drummed his fingers on the arm of the painted chair. "If you happen to find a cylinder of Little Red LeCoeur . . ." He hesitated, trying to find the right words.

"Yes?"

"I know a collector who would pay *us* handsomely for it," he stated smugly.

"I could never do that."

"Why not?" he demanded. "Do you know what that cylinder would be worth?"

"I believe I just asked *you* that question," I replied. I realized that although I'd received some interesting informa-

tion from Simon West, it was well past time to take my leave
of him. My friendship with Wayne was far more important
than any monetary gain West could offer, and I was offended
that he thought my ethics could be so easily compromised.

I picked up my hat. "This has been very pleasant, Mr.
West. However, I really must leave now. I have another appointment."

West realized he might have made a blunder. "It was just
a possibility," he said. "Something to think about." He
walked me to the door. "We could bring in Wayne as well,"
he added weakly. Changing tacks, he said, "I haven't had a
chance to introduce you to my neighbor."

"Perhaps another time," I said. "Thank you for the information, and the tea." I turned down Royal Street toward my
hotel, and took a deep breath. The humid hot air felt
strangely refreshing.

Chapter Five

"Would you like another beignet, ma'am?"

"Thank you, no. If I'm not careful, New Orleans is going to be the ruination of my figure."

"Then how about more coffee?"

"Yes, please, it's very good."

"I'll bring some right away."

I was sitting in the quiet courtyard at my hotel Friday morning, waiting for Wayne. I'd been up early, taken my exercise in a brisk walk that followed a recommended circuit provided by the hotel, and now, showered and dressed for the day, was reading the morning newspaper. Since Wayne was notorious for being late, I'd gone ahead and ordered the hotel's continental breakfast, which included fresh orange juice, New Orleans's famous chicory coffee, and two beignets—puffy, square, doughnutlike pastries wearing a heavy coating of powdered sugar, a good portion of which had threatened to settle on the napkin on my lap. I'd struggled not to make too much of a mess; the delicate flavor was worth the effort. "I don't know a soul who can eat those neatly," the waitress, a blonde with a big bosom, had said when she'd set the plate in front of me. "Even a knife and fork are no help."

It was another sunny day, only slightly less hot than the one before, with the promise of temperatures approaching ninety, and still no rain in sight. The *Times-Picayune* reported that the drought was causing local farmers concern, particularly so early in the season when water was essential to establishing new crops.

I turned to the police page, which featured an interview with the city's superintendent of police, Jimmy Johnson. A photo accompanied the article and depicted a handsome, African-American man, about fifty, wearing a dress uniform emblazoned with multiple medals on his left shoulder. He was shaking the hand of Mayor Maurice Amadour, and both men were smiling at the camera. The mayor was quoted as congratulating the police department for the continuing drop in the crime rate.

Superintendent Johnson, the article related, had praised the hard work of NOPD's Operations Bureau, in particular the District Investigative Unit assigned to street crime in the French Quarter, and had issued a list of security recommendations for tourists to ensure their well-being during their stay:

> Tourists are advised to travel in pairs; avoid walking alone at night in out-of-the-way parts of the city; keep hotel doors securely locked, and admit no one unfamiliar to the occupants.

I scanned the police blotter along the side of the page. Superintendent Johnson's advice came a day too late for a pair of elderly ladies visiting the city from Tallahassee, Florida. The police report noted that they were attacked when they opened the door to an armed robber, who knocked one down and hit the other on the side of her head when she refused to relinquish her handbag. The latter was in serious but stable condition at Tulane University Medical Center.

Another report announced that teenage suspects had been

taken into custody, accused of being behind a series of hit-and-run muggings of tourists in the French Quarter.

Too, another statue was found missing from a family tomb in Lafayette Cemetery. In its place, the thief had left a lace cross and a purple candle, wrapped up in a green ribbon. Investigators were consulting voodoo specialists for an interpretation.

Finally, there was a list of overnight arrests made for drunken and disorderly conduct.

"That's enough to spoil anyone's appetite," the waitress said, cocking her head toward my reading material. "They keep telling us that crime is down, but there's plenty around to keep you quaking in your sandals."

She filled my cup halfway with coffee and then topped it with hot milk. Eyeing the extra place setting, she added, "Still waiting for someone?"

"Yes. I'm sure he'll be here shortly."

"May I join you?"

I looked up to see Doris Burns. Her face was scrubbed clean of makeup, and a sprinkling of freckles decorated her nose. A large pair of sunglasses were perched on the top of her head, holding her straight hair away from her face. She wore a pink plaid sundress with narrow straps exposing her freckled shoulders, and she could have passed for sixteen years old, a tall sixteen, but sixteen nevertheless.

"Please do. You look fresh and ready for a day in the sun. Are you going to Jazz Fest?"

"I was hoping I could tag along with you and Wayne. I've never been there before."

"Of course. Wayne should be here any minute."

"Did I hear my name being bandied about?"

"Good morning," Doris and I said in unison.

Wayne pulled out a chair, sank into it, and fanned his face with his straw hat. The waitress ambled off to get a third place setting.

"No comments about the 'late' Wayne Copely? You ladies are too good to me. My apologies nevertheless. My sister called just as I was stepping out the door, and love that she is, she does go on and on. Jessica, she has invited you to Sunday dinner, a rare treat since Clarice's cook is superb. She stole her away from one of the cousins in the Long family, and of course, they haven't talked to her since. Clarice promised Alberta her own cottage at the back of the garden, which clinched it. That plus a kitchen that looks like the *Starship Enterprise,* all chrome and stainless steel and enormous burners on the gas stove. Cost my brother-in-law a fortune, may he rest in peace. All the chefs in town have been trying to pry Alberta's recipe for étouffée out of her for years. But she holds tight to it like a waterlogged cat on a downstream log. I have to beg Clarice to let me come over when Alberta makes étouffée, so you must come. These invitations are like gold. And she knew you were in town because I've talked about you. She gets all excited when I mention going somewhere with a woman."

Wayne put his hand on Doris's arm.

"My dear, I'm so sorry to talk of an invitation that doesn't include you. Isn't that like me? So rude! But I'll make it up to you, I promise."

"Think nothing of it, please. As it happens, I already have plans for Sunday."

While Wayne had been recounting the call from his sister, the waitress had returned and set down napkins, utensils, and coffee cups, and handed menus to Doris and Wayne.

"Are the beignets from Café du Monde?" Wayne asked.

"Of course, sir."

Wayne closed his menu and tapped it on the top of Doris's.

"In that case, I recommend the continental breakfast. I hope you're not one of those bacon-and-egg people. You must try the beignets. Jessica, you've already eaten? Yes?"

Wayne didn't wait for a reply. He addressed the waitress.

"We'll have two continental breakfasts with café au lait, and give us a lagniappe on the beignets, please. Jessica, you'll have another, won't you? Have you been down to Café du Monde yet?"

He was in high spirits and there was no point in contradicting his orders. I sat back, amused, and let the Wayne Copely steamroller roll over Doris and me. Wayne was delighted that Doris wanted to accompany us to Jazz Fest. He chatted away about the musicians scheduled to play throughout the day, consumed three beignets, and sent the waitress off for more coffee. Finally, he patted his mouth with a napkin, erasing the last vestige of powdered sugar, and sat back, contentment on his face, and absently brushed the front of his shirt with the side of his hand.

I decided not to spoil his good mood by relating yesterday's disturbing conversation with Stanley in Jackson Square about Little Red LeCoeur. Bad news could wait, and maybe Stanley was wrong. I was still hopeful. Instead, I turned to Doris, who had been an attentive audience to Wayne's monologue.

"Doris, tell us what kind of response you received to your request to tape voodoo practitioners," I said.

"I met with three people yesterday, and I have a few appointments tomorrow. I haven't been able to return two calls, but I'll try again before we leave this morning."

"How did you happen to become interested in voodoo?" I asked.

"I'd been teaching a course on the history of religion, and had to read up on voodoo because I knew so little about it. Voodoo is rich in folklore, but unlike most mainstream religions, it has no uniform infrastructure to maintain it. There's no pope, no central governing body. Every temple does its own thing, so to speak. Yet it's lasted for seven thousand years."

"I didn't realize it was that old."

"Yes, very old," she said. "It's kind of like jazz in the way it developed. Jazz evolved from both the African musical culture brought to this country by slaves, and the European musical tradition, which was familiar to slave owners. New Orleans voodoo is also a mixture, in this case, a blend of at least three separate religious traditions—African from Dahomey, Catholic from the French and Spanish who settled in New Orleans, and Native American, too."

"You've given this talk before, I think," Wayne said, smiling to soften his comment.

Doris blushed. "I have indeed. I'm sorry. I didn't mean to lecture you."

"Please don't apologize," I said. "I hadn't heard it."

"I've been known to go on about a topic till eyes glaze over," she said, chuckling.

"You're just passionate about your work and that's an admirable trait," I said. "Go on, Doris."

Doris cleared her throat. "There are two historical figures associated with the spread of voodoo and its influence in New Orleans in the Nineteenth Century. One was Dr. John, also sometimes called 'the Drummer.' The other was Marie Laveau."

"Now there's a name every New Orleanian is familiar with," Wayne interjected.

"I'm sure that's true," Doris continued. "Voodoo is matriarchal, and the powerful voodoo queens were always more important than the men, even witch doctors."

"Yes, but wasn't Marie Laveau actually two women?" Wayne prodded.

Doris smiled at him. "I'd love to have you in one of my classes. You'd certainly keep me on my toes. Yes, they were two women, mother and daughter, both with the same name. Marie, the mother, reigned over notorious ceremonies that took place in Congo Square and along Lake Pontchartrain, with frenzied dancing and boiling cauldrons of frogs and snakes and the like. That's what became the Hollywood image of voodoo."

"Is voodoo still practiced that way?" I asked.

"Actually, today believers say 'verdoun' rather than 'voodoo' to dissociate themselves from the sinister portrayals of voodoo involving casting evil spells, human sacrifice, and stabbing pins into voodoo dolls to harm your enemies."

"None of that takes place anymore?" I asked.

"I think some of it probably does. Animal sacrifices, but certainly not human sacrifices. There are always fringe elements in religion. But for the most part, voodoo focuses on living in harmony and attaining spiritual balance by serving the *loa*, the spirits."

"Wayne, you mentioned the loa when you talked about Little Red," I said.

"Yes. They're also called the 'mysteries' or the 'invisibles.' They're kind of intermediaries between the human world and the creator."

"Like saints," Doris added. "You can see the Catholic influence there."

"But Dr. John and Queen Marie Laveau are loa," Wayne put in, "and they were not very saintly."

"That's true," replied Doris, "but they were powerful in their day, and are still considered powerful."

I turned to Wayne. "Are they the same loa that are supposed to have possessed Little Red and influenced his music?"

"I don't think so. There are many loa, and Little Red was probably identified with Ogoun. He's associated with metals, so the trumpet fits in, and is also represented by the color red—blood and fire. Little Red's playing was supposed to be very fiery and passionate. Of course, that's an assumption we can't prove until I find those recordings."

His eyes did a quick check of the other tables on the

patio, before he leaned toward us and added in a soft, singsong voice, "And I think that's coming closer."

"Your meeting last night?" I whispered, caught up in his need for secrecy.

He sat back with an enigmatic smile, but said nothing.

Was someone leading him on? I felt guilty for having held back the information I'd learned from Stanley. But I didn't want to approach the subject in front of Doris. There would be time later when I could pass along Stanley's comments to Wayne without an audience.

Leaving Wayne with my morning newspaper, Doris and I returned to our respective rooms to make a few phone calls and ready ourselves for a day at the festival. I called Charlie Gable to confirm our upcoming dinner interview, and checked with the bookstore to verify that my books were in stock before we finalized plans for the book signing. At a quarter to eleven, new hat in hand, I met Wayne and Doris in the hotel lobby.

Chapter Six

"I don't think I've ever seen so many people in one place at one time," I said.

Wayne and Doris and I, along with thousands of like-minded people, were crossing the dirt track of the Fair Grounds Race Track to where a sea of tents, flags, and booths filled the huge grassy oval. Atop a giant scaffolding, a sponsor's sign welcomed us to the New Orleans Jazz & Heritage Festival.

"They do get quite a crowd," Wayne remarked. "Over four hundred thousand last year, plus the four thousand or so putting on the show."

Wayne guided us to the first green-and-white-striped tent on our left, in which a gospel group was warming up. In the shade of the tent, he gave us a fatherly lecture. "You see all those flags?" He nodded toward the kaleidoscope of pennants, flags, and banners dotting the scene before us. Many were homemade with suspended ribbons, bows, and fringe fluttering as their bearers carried them aloft. "People use those to identify themselves, so their friends and family can find them in the crowd. If they didn't do that, they might wander around here for days and never meet up."

"Isn't that clever," Doris said. "Look at that one." Bobbing by us was a feather-bedecked pole with bouquets of ribbon arrayed across three crossbars. It was held high by a tall man who wore one of the ribbon bouquets on his head, and who walked backward, keeping an eye on his flock of teenaged followers.

"We don't have a flag," Wayne reminded us. "And it's easy to get separated in this crush. I'll try to hold on to you, but let's agree to meet in specific places at specific hours. That way if we lose sight of each other, we'll know we've got a regular rendezvous point to reassemble."

Doris and I agreed that making appointments to meet at certain hours was prudent, and we all synchronized our watches as if we were on a military mission.

"What do you suggest we see right now?" I asked, hanging on to my hat when a stiff breeze threatened to carry it away.

"I need to check in at the press tent, but we can use this time just to look around and get our bearings. There's music everywhere. We can just stop in to hear whatever appeals to us." A family carrying folding chairs squeezed by, and Wayne took our arms. "There's no way you can whip through this fair. Get used to strolling. That's the only effective pace."

The air at the festival fairly hummed with the strains of gospel, zydeco, bebop, Cajun, Dixieland, and virtually every other musical variation of jazz and pop and country, the sounds drifting out of the tents and rising on the breeze in a delightful cacophony. A gust of wind blew up, flapping the colorful pennants strung from tent top to tent top, and wafting the smells of spicy cooking in our direction from the food stalls on the other side of the oval. The intermittent breeze was a blissful counter to the blazing sun.

The press tent was abuzz with activity when Wayne flashed his pass and ushered us inside. Large oscillating fans on stands whined in each corner but had little effect on the stultifying air. I blotted my forehead with a handkerchief, and followed Wayne as he dipped into bins that had been set up along two sides. A flustered press aide was attempting to fill the bins as quickly as the press corps emptied them. Wayne studied their contents, retrieving press releases and biographical backgrounds on the acts scheduled for that day, flipped through samples of music magazines, and dropped them back in the bins.

"How nice to see you again, ladies."

I looked up into the clear-blue eyes of Julian Broadbent. Wayne joined us, his hands full of papers.

"Copely." Broadbent nodded curtly.

"Broadbent," Wayne grunted in acknowledgment. He turned his back on the reporter. "Ladies, I'd like to introduce you to some of the musicians who are here." He pushed us across the room toward a series of tables set up for press interviews. The musicians sat against the outside wall of the tent; across from each were two or three chairs, most of which were occupied. A pile of black-and-white glossies for autographing, and a set of black and blue pens, sat at each musician's elbow.

"Say hello to Oliver Jones," he told me. Jones was a short, stocky black man with a sweet face and even sweeter smile.

"Oliver is one of Canada's many gifts to the jazz world, Jessica, Doris. He studied piano with Oscar Peterson's sister, Daisy, in Montreal."

"I have one of your albums," I said. "A friend, Peter Eder—he's the conductor of our symphony orchestra back home—loves your music. So do I," I added hastily. "You play so beautifully."

"Thank you. I hope you enjoy the concerts."

"I know I will," I said.

Doris and I were introduced to a few more musicians—the vibest, Terry Gibbs; a bass player, Ray Brown; and a saxophonist, Bobby Watson.

Julian Broadbent trailed our little party, eavesdropping as Wayne greeted colleagues, and nodding at the musicians as if Wayne were including him in the introductions. When we finally left the press tent, he touched Doris on the shoulder. "Mind if I walk around with you today?"

"Sure. Why not?" she said, taking his arm.

Agreeing to meet us at the gospel tent later on, Julian and Doris went off to explore on their own, while Wayne and I stopped to read the program and choose which performances to see. He craned his neck to make out something off to our right. "I hear one of the brass bands," he said. "Let's catch up with them."

We hustled to get a good look at the small band of performers. Clad in bright-blue suits, gold sashes, and white gloves, they were slowly snaking their way around the field, stopping every so often to allow their leader, who was carrying a matching blue umbrella, to execute a little two-step dance. When we reached them, the players—two trumpets, a trombone, a sousaphone, a tuba, and a drum—were in the middle of a Dixieland tune that had me tapping my toe with the beat and clapping along with the other listeners.

"This is a typical New Orleans brass band," Wayne told me as we applauded at the end of the piece. "They're sponsored by clubs in the African-American community, and have a long history in New Orleans. Brass bands were hired for every social occasion—weddings, funerals, picnics— and it became a wonderful tradition."

The band's next song was one I recognized, "When the Saints Go Marching In." The leader pumped his umbrella above his head and the musicians headed off in another direction.

"I have something I want to talk about," I said to Wayne. "Has anyone come forward with information for you about the cylinders?"

"I have a few leads," he replied, turning his attention to me and twirling a pencil between his fingers. "And the paper mentioned it in the article covering our panel." He pulled a leafed-through copy of the magazine *Wavelength* from under his arm. "I've also got a little ad in here that should churn the waters."

I told Wayne about Stanley and the street merchant's insistence on the futility of searching for recordings by Little Red. "I'm concerned that you'll be terribly disappointed after putting in all this effort," I said. "I know how much it means to you."

He listened intently. Then a smile creased his face, and he patted my arm. "You know, Jessica, I've heard that argument for years. But I'm not the only one looking for them; there was an ad in the paper a few weeks ago. So I think the odds are good. If nothing else, my research may clear up the mystery and determine once and for all if the recordings were ever made. And if they were, what happened to them." He grinned. "Either way, I'll have enough material for another book."

"You devil. And here I was worrying for nothing."

Wayne and I continued on, starting with zydeco, sampling some bebop, and listening to stride piano. Two hours later, Doris, Julian, Wayne, and I exited the gospel tent, our cheeks red and foreheads gleaming. The gospel tent had had rows of folding chairs, but few people had stayed in their seats once the concert had begun. We all stood, swaying, moved by the music, hands clapping, feet tapping. It was a physical as well as spiritual experience.

"What wonderful, talented young people," I exclaimed, fanning my face with my straw hat.

Wayne was smug. "Picked a good one, didn't I?" he said.

"They were terrific," Doris agreed. "Sure got me hopping." She bounced lightly on her feet, holding on to the new gris-gris—a small red pouch suspended from a string around her neck—that she had purchased at a voodoo stall. "This has already brought me good luck."

"Brought me luck, too," Broadbent said.

I saw an intimate look pass between them that caused a blush to rise on the young woman's cheeks, and realized that Broadbent had been on his best behavior with Wayne today so he could pursue Doris. Unlike the cool reception she'd given the mayor's aide, she seemed not to mind Julian's attentions. Wayne was doing his best to ignore Broadbent, and considering that their last meeting had nearly resulted in blows, I was grateful for the truce.

Wayne clapped his hands. "Well, I'm hungry. Anyone else ready to eat?"

We followed Wayne, but we would have known which way to go anyway. The spicy aroma in the air intensified and led the way. At the food stalls, clouds of steam rose from griddles, grills, and kettles used for cooking gumbo, jambalaya, étouffée, grillades, and other Louisiana specialties. Sandwich stands featured muffulettas, made with Italian meat and cheese and an olive spread, and po-boys with a variety of ingredients piled on French bread. A couple walked by, balancing paper plates bearing small mountains of boiled crawfish. Nestled in with the bright-red crustaceans were chunks of yellow corn on the cob and red-skinned potato.

"Want to try some fried alligator?" Broadbent growled, putting an arm around Doris.

"Don't tease," she replied, ducking away from his side. "What's it taste like anyway? And don't say 'chicken.'"

He chuckled. "The all-purpose comparison?" he asked. "No, I don't think it's anything like chicken, and it might be an acquired taste. It's a little bit oily."

"I'll skip it then," she replied.

He turned to me with one eyebrow raised. "Are you game?"

"I'm adventuresome," I said, "but I don't think I'm that adventuresome."

Doris and Julian wandered off to inspect a gumbo stand, while Wayne and I lined up for po'boys, fried oysters for him, crawfish for me. I insisted on paying for our sandwiches, and despite his scowl, he agreed.

"That looks mighty good, Wayne Copely," a hearty voice said from behind as we left the stand with our sandwiches. We turned to see Mayor Maurice Amadour bearing down on us. He wore a well-tailored yellow-and-white-striped seersucker suit, buttoned over an imposing stomach, a straw boater, and a big grin. He clapped a beefy hand on Wayne's shoulder and poked his face toward me.

"You must be that famous mystery writer Phil was jawing to me about." He stuck out his hand. "Nice to meet you, Miz Fletcher."

I wiped my hand on a napkin and placed it in his paw.

"I understand you're going to sample some of our downhome Louisiana hospitality next week," he said, continuing to hold my hand. "My wife Marguerite and I are tickled you can come. She's a big fan of yours, reads all your books."

"How nice," I murmured, withdrawing my hand.

But he hadn't heard my reply. He was on to another topic, urging Wayne to bring his sister Clarice to the party, too. "Haven't seen her since the funeral," he declared loud enough to make heads turn, and Wayne cringe. "Make her come with you. She needs to get back in the social whirl again. Marguerite will take care of her. Even find her a new husband. What do you think? Will she come?"

"It's very kind of you to invite her. I'll let her know."

The mayor grinned at me, and I hoped he wasn't planning to offer to find me a new husband, too. "So, Miz Fletcher, how do you like the Big Easy? Appropriate name, don't you think?"

I nodded, realizing I wasn't going to be able to slip a word in edgewise.

"Crime is down for the third year in a row," he told me, raising his voice so he could be easily overheard. "New police chief has it all under control."

I looked past the mayor and saw Broadbent holding a platter of crawfish with both hands. Amadour caught the direction of my gaze and abruptly left to spread his sunshine on a new prospect, hailing Julian like a long-lost brother, and fussing over Doris.

Wayne heaved a sigh at the mayor's departure.

"He's a bit dramatic," he said apologetically, "but he's got this city moving ahead. New industry's coming in, and the bankers are happy. He's done a good job."

"Do you really think he's considering a Senate race with Lunsford's seat open?" I asked.

"If Phil has anything to say about it, he will," Wayne replied. "He makes no secret of his ambition. With Lunsford out of the way, Maurice stands a good chance of being nominated. No wonder he's such a fan of Broadbent's."

Philippe Beaudin broke through the spectators who surrounded our little party and cajoled the mayor into following him to his next appointment. The mayor waved to us and plunged through the crowd, turning this way and that, shaking hands and bussing cheeks, not missing anyone wanting to touch him.

We ate our lunches in blessed silence, savoring the delicious flavors of the food even though it had gotten cold. Following our meal, the four of us headed toward the main stage for the Marsalis family concert. We passed through a section of the fair devoted to traditional country crafts. Around us were booths displaying a host of handmade items—clothing, jewelry, quilts, soaps, candles, toys, boxes, dried flowers, and clocks. Doris's eyes lit up.

"Been here, done this," Broadbent complained, holding up Doris's shopping bag in one hand and pointing at it with the other.

Wayne tapped me on the shoulder. "We'll go ahead," he said, indicating Broadbent, "and hold some seats in the VIP tent. You ladies shop awhile, but don't be late." He looked at his watch. "You've got twenty minutes."

Doris was delighted. "You've got to see some of this voodoo stuff," she told me. "It's incredible."

We headed for a line of stalls selling an assortment of strange-looking voodoo paraphernalia. Doris stopped at one and greeted its proprietor, a wizened black woman in a striped turban and long purple robe with gold braid at the neck, waist, and wrists.

"This is Ileana Montalvo," Doris announced proudly. "She's a voodoo priestess we met earlier."

The priestess, who had been sitting in a chair shuffling a deck of tarot cards, slowly got to her feet and limped toward me. She was a diminutive woman, her brown eyes bright despite her age, which I guessed to be in the mid-seventies. She studied my face intently.

"Ileana picked out this gris-gris for me," Doris said, fingering the small red pouch that lay against her chest. "To help with the research."

"That's nice," I said, wondering why Doris was so excited about what looked to me to be simply a keepsake sold to tourists.

"And it's already worked," she said, her voice full of laughter. "She's agreed to let me interview her tomorrow."

The woman smiled at Doris. "I be good for your research," she said. "Only give you truth, no nonsense like you see on TV."

Thinking a voodoo charm might be an entertaining gift to give friends back home, I perused the items on the table, including a rack of gris-gris like the one Doris was wearing. They were hanging in groups of colors, red, orange, pink, blue, and white, each cluster identified by a hand-lettered sign indicating the benefit to be derived—Psychic Power, Do Well in School, Peace & Protection, Money & Good Luck, Win-in-Court, Enemy Be Gone, Lucky Lotto & Gambling, Good Memory—I could use that last one myself at times. In a basket were voodoo dolls, their wood and moss bodies covered with dark burlap. On several dolls, colored string tied off the bulge that defined the head. Tiny cowrie shells were sewn on for the eyes and mouth. Others had clay heads with tiny holes for eyes, and painted hair.

The old woman cleared her throat, and gestured to me with her hand. "May I see?"

"See what?" I asked.

"Your hand." She leaned over the table to take my wrist, and cupped my hand with both of hers, peering down at the lines in my palm, her nose inches away. She traced one crease with a gnarled finger, shivered, and looked up.

"You're a good person," she said, searching my eyes, "but sometin' not right here."

"It isn't?" I said, surprised.

"No." She shook her head sadly. "Don't see what it be. Mist over it. But you must take care. There's evil near you."

Despite the heat of the day, I felt a chill creep up my spine. I rubbed the goosebumps on my arms. Was this just a clever act to sell me some trinket?

"Not what you tink," she answered my thought in a raspy whisper. She squinted at her rack of gris-gris, her wrinkled hand hovering near the Enemy Be Gone. Changing her mind, she bent to rummage in a box on the ground, and pulled out a small packet of green felt tied up with raffia.

"Here." She thrust it into my hands. "Take it."

I started to pull out my wallet.

"Put your money away," she insisted, backing away from the table and wiping her hands on the front of her dress.

"What is it?" I asked, turning the packet over to see a small, carved skull sewn on the other side.

"A juju. For protection. Keep it with you."

"Thank you. I appreciate your concern, but I really don't need it." I laid the packet on the table.

She became visibly upset, mumbling and pacing the small space behind the table. "Bad luck. Bad luck to leave it here." She picked up the packet and offered it to me again, her eyes pleading with me to take it. "It be good magic, blessed by the spirits."

"All right," I conceded, taking the juju and reluctantly tucking it in my bag.

Doris had watched this exchange solemnly. "Come on, Jessica," she pressed nervously. "We'd better go. We'll miss the concert.

I thanked the priestess, who seemed relieved, and followed Doris down the aisle toward the concert stage. How strange, I thought. What did she see? I've never believed in psychic powers. Oh, I've had the occasional "female intuition." I've even felt a strong compulsion to be guarded in certain situations which, indeed, became threatening. But caution in those risky cases was just prudent. What you need when you place yourself in danger is not ESP, but good solid preparation and a thorough knowledge of the people you're dealing with so there won't be any surprises. Policemen often tell me that the more they know about a case, the more they find their "hunches" come true. But I wasn't working now, not writing about crime, not investigating cases, not talking to suspects. So what could have influenced the voodoo priestess?

"I hope you're not upset, Jessica," Doris said as we approached the expanse of lawn in front of the concert stage. The area was filled with clusters of people, children chasing each other, and families gathered around their flags, either standing or sitting on blankets and lawn chairs.

"Not at all," I told her.

"Do you think it was an act?"

I hesitated. "I might have thought so," I said, reasoning it through, "if she'd wanted money for the juju, but it doesn't make sense to give it away. She has the booth to sell her merchandise at the fair. That's why she's here. She must have very strong faith in her voodoo beliefs to feel the need to protect me, more than the need to sell me something."

"Faith. Of course," Doris said. "There's so much commercialism in voodoo, you tend to forget that it's a genuine religion."

I hooked her arm in mine. "That's enough of that," I said. "Let's see if we can find Wayne and Julian."

The Marsalis concert was thrilling, and included a lesson in jazz for the children that was appreciated even more by the adults. Mayor Amadour presented the members of the family—Ellis Marsalis and his four sons, Branford, Wynton, Delfeayo and Jason—and posed for pictures on stage, clearly tickled to be associated with the celebrities. That wasn't the last time we saw the portly mayor that afternoon. We met him again when we walked into the tent for the five o'clock performance by Blind Jack, a trumpeter whom Wayne had described as the natural successor to Little Red LeCouer. Taking seats in the front row, we waited to meet the musician, who was deep in conversation with his manager and the mayor.

Wayne crossed his legs and jiggled his foot impatiently. "I want you to meet Blind Jack before he plays. It's always such pandemonium after."

"Your mayor sure gets around," Doris commented.

"It's an election year," Broadbent reminded her. "And this is one of the city's biggest events."

Philippe Beaudin walked up to the mayor and whispered in his ear. Amadour excused himself to Blind Jack and his manager and walked to the back of the tent, Beaudin on his tail, where he greeted an elegantly dressed couple.

"Contributors," Broadbent muttered, rising to follow the mayor. "I'll be right back."

Wayne jumped to his feet and intercepted Blind Jack before his manager could lead him away, or anyone else could gain his attention. Holding the musician's elbow, he took a step toward Doris and me. Blind Jack was an old man, stooped and frail, a fringe of white curls outlining his shiny pate. His hand shook as he adjusted a pair of dark glasses that rested on his nose, but his voice, while low and gravelly, was strong.

"Jack, I want you to meet some friends," Wayne said, waving us over.

"Wayne, my man. Where y'at? Good to see you." He chuckled at his own joke. "Where you been? You haven't written me up in a while."

"Jack, I've written more columns about you than any other player," Wayne said. "You know you're my idol— after Little Red, that is."

"That Little Red, he was a wonder," Jack said, shaking his head from side to side.

Wayne introduced us. "This man is a genius on the horn," he said as Doris and I took turns shaking his hand.

"It's lovely to meet two such charming ladies," he declared.

"We're looking forward to listening to you," I said. "Wayne has been anticipating your performance all day."

"He's a good boy, Wayne is," Jack kidded, groping behind him for Wayne's arm. He held on tight, and leaned into Wayne's side.

"You hear about Elijah?" he asked in a low voice.

"Yes, but let's not discuss it here."

Doris and I looked at each other.

"Jack, I want us to sit down and discuss Little Red's recordings," Wayne said, keeping his voice low.

"Find any yet?"

"Not yet, but I have a new lead to run by you."

"All right," Jack agreed. "Maybe I can help you out. Why don't you meet me after my late show at Café Brasilia. We'll sit on my veranda and down a couple of Cokes together."

"It's a deal."

"Did you know Little Red personally?" I asked.

Blind Jack swiveled his head in my direction. "I was a young pup, Mrs. Fletcher, when Red was an old man, like me today."

"Was he still playing?"

"Oh yes, Red played to the end." He paused, remembering. "Never recorded when I knew him. But he might'a had in his younger days. Wayne, here, will discover it if he did."

Blind Jack's manager put an end to our conversation. "You've got five minutes," he said as he passed us carrying a microphone stand.

"Okay, okay. You got my horn?" Jack shuffled around following the sound of his manager's voice.

"It's next to your chair, where it always is," the manager called back.

Jack addressed us. "I gotta go. It's nice to have met you, ladies. Wayne, I'll see you later."

Age had claimed Blind Jack's fragile physique, but when he raised his trumpet to his lips, the strength of his soul shone through. He played with all the force and vigor of youth, but overlaid with a wisdom and grace youth had yet to discover. Wayne sat next to me, entranced. Sometimes he listened with his eyes closed, nodding at nuances that escaped me. Other times, he rocked from side to side, or tapped his feet, his whole body involved with the music. I concentrated on the melodies and the variations that Blind Jack and his accompanists played, striving to decipher the secret language of jazz, and taking pleasure in the process.

Philippe Beaudin came up to me at the end of the performance. "Mrs. Fletcher, did you enjoy the concert?"

"Very much so," I replied.

He stood next to me, but his eyes kept straying to Doris and Julian Broadbent.

"You've been working very hard today, Mr. Beaudin," I said. "We seem to be seeing you everywhere we go."

"The mayor has a lot of responsibilities in a big event like this," he said, still distracted.

A sheen of perspiration coated his handsome face. He carried his suit jacket over his arm, and had loosened his tie so it hung askew. His collar was unbuttoned and I noticed a thin black leather cord around his neck; my gaze followed the dark line, visible through his white cotton shirt, down his chest to a slight bulge. I looked up, embarrassed to find he'd been watching me.

"You won't ask, but yes, it's a gris-gris."

He reached inside the open neck of his shirt, tugged on the cord, pulled out a small leather pouch, and let it dangle in front of his shirt. It didn't look like the tourist version of a gris-gris Doris was wearing so openly. This one had signs of wear, the leather dark where it had touched and absorbed the oils of his skin.

"Do you practice voodoo, Mr. Beaudin?"

He seemed surprised at my question. "I'm a Cajun boy, Mrs. Fletcher, born and bred in the swamps," he said. "My ancestors were kicked out of Nova Scotia for being Catholic. So we hold pretty tight to our religion."

"But you wear a gris-gris."

"We have a wide and varied constituency here in New Orleans." He let his head sweep the room indicating the multicultural audience that was milling about the tent. "Sometimes the way to signify solidarity is through nonverbal communication."

"For your voodoo constituents?"

He laughed. "People who actually practice voodoo as a religion are, at most, ten to fifteen percent of the population," he said. "Half the city wears one of these, Mrs. Fletcher."

"They do?"

"Sure. It's part of New Orleans life."

"Then this is part tradition, part political strategy?" I posed, indicating the gris-gris.

"Everything is part of our political strategy, Mrs. Fletcher," he said affably. "I'm trying to get Maurice to wear one of these, too." He lifted the pouch and dropped it back inside his shirt. "We can use all the help we can get."

"I thought the mayor was far ahead in the polls."

"Polls can never be relied on." He buttoned his collar and straightened his tie, pulling the knot snug against his neck.

"Does he have a strong opponent?"

"So far, he has the field pretty much to himself. Just a couple of weak wannabes."

"For the mayoral field, or the senatorial field?" I asked, adding, "Senator Lunsford's seat is open."

He laughed. "You're spending too much time with Broadbent," he said. "Please excuse me. I've got to round up the mayor for another couple of stops, before he and Mrs. Amadour go to dinner. Have a good evening, Mrs. Fletcher. I'll look forward to seeing you at the mayor's party next week."

He turned away, bumping into Wayne, who was coming to collect me.

"Sorry, man," Beaudin said, dusting off Wayne's jacket as if he'd knocked him down. His hand grazed the top of one of Wayne's pockets. Beaudin loped away, choosing to slide down a row of empty chairs to avoid the crowds in the aisles, and reached the far side where the mayor was entertaining a party of ladies in flowered hats, whose laughter could be heard across the tent.

"Did he just drop something in your pocket?" I asked.

Wayne looked startled. He slid his hands in and out of his pockets. "Nope," he said, but I wasn't certain I believed him.

He consulted his schedule. "There's plenty of music to

come tonight, but I don't see anything here I'm especially keen on," he said.

"Where are Julian and Doris?" I wondered aloud, straining to pick them out of the throng leaving the tent.

"Broadbent met up with some of his macho buddies and they took off," he said, sounding disdainful. "They said to tell you 'good night.'"

"Why don't we leave now, too?" I coaxed. "I'm going to need some rest if we're to do this again tomorrow."

"Rest? I was planning on taking you chank-a-chanking at a fais-do-do."

"That sounds sinister. What are we doing?"

"We're going dancing, Jessica."

Chapter Seven

"Happened again. Did you see it?" The blond waitress held a coffeepot in one hand and a pitcher of hot milk in the other.

"Did I see what?" Seated in the hotel courtyard for breakfast, I put down the newspaper and picked up my spoon as she poured my *café au lait.*

"The police report. They found another body in the cemetery."

"Isn't that where bodies are supposed to be?" I asked, mock seriously.

"You may think so," she said, "but they're usually entombed, not sitting up out in the open where other bodies can trip over them."

"Is that what happened?" I asked, more soberly.

"Page three. Read it for yourself," she said tartly, and sauntered off to the next table.

I opened the newspaper again, and turned to page three.

NOPD reported finding the body of a white male last night in St. Louis Cemetery Number One. The body was discovered propped up against the tomb of Marie Laveau by teenagers, who alerted police. The man's identity is being withheld pending notification of his family. Police declined to speculate on the cause of death, but homicide detectives were observed at the scene. An autopsy is scheduled.

Police Superintendent Jimmy Johnson would not comment on rumors that a voodoo symbol was found with the body, and said that it was too early to conclude that this death was related to that of murder victim Elijah Williams, a former voodoo priest whose body was found in the same position at Marie Laveau's tomb several weeks ago.

"We're not even sure we have a murder yet," Johnson said. "We could have a prankster who read about Williams and decided to set a body in the same spot."

The superintendent disclosed that he is in "constant communication" with the mayor's office, and said the investigation into Williams's murder was proceeding on schedule. He reminded citizens to call the hotline if they have any information to provide detectives.

Overall, crime in New Orleans has been on the wane for several years. However, recent incidents in the French Quarter and other parts of the city have alarmed residents and business people alike. Superintendent Johnson noted that, thanks to COMSTAT, the city's crime management program, New Orleans led the nation with the greatest drop in violent crime over three years, particularly in Districts 1 and 8. Violent crimes include murder, rape, robbery, and assault. Nevertheless, he said, he's ordered the NOPD to beef up patrols in vulnerable neighborhoods.

I put that portion of the newspaper aside and picked up *Lagniappe,* the weekend entertainment section, and started to read a review of Blind Jack's concert at Jazz Fest. But my mind kept leaping back to the cemetery and the murder of Elijah Williams, and now this second victim who was found in the same place. The location of the two bodies at the same spot in the cemetery was certainly unusual and unsettling. Wayne had told me the cemeteries were dangerous, and to stay away from them unless I went with a tour group. How sad, I thought, that what should be a place for peace and comfort for both the departed and their families had become instead menacing and violent.

"Would you like beignets again this morning?" The waitress was back, pad and pen in hand.

"Maybe tomorrow," I said, picking up the menu I hadn't looked at. "I think I'd like to have something light. I don't know how you New Orleanians can eat such rich food every day."

"We like to keep our nice plump figures," she quipped, patting one hip. "I can get you a fresh fruit platter. How about that?"

"Perfect."

"It's so light, I guarantee you'll be hungry in an hour," she said, walking away, a smirk on her round face.

I reached down and rubbed the top of my instep. Wayne had taken me to a fais-do-do last night, a Cajun dance, and in his efforts to teach me the steps—and my initial awkwardness in learning them—he had tromped on my feet several times with his patent leather spectator shoes. Despite my purple bruise, I'd had a marvelous time. By nine-thirty, however, I was bleary-eyed and insisted on going back to the hotel. Wayne had begged off breakfast this morning—he'd been planning to be out late with Blind Jack following up a lead on Little Red's recordings—but we intended to catch up at Jazz Fest. I was to look for him at the press tent at two. My schedule was filling up. I had a dinner interview with Charlie Gable. Lunch with Wayne's sister tomorrow. And I mustn't forget my book signing—when was that?

Doris Burns entered the courtyard, her eyes skimming over the tables till she found mine. I beckoned her to join me. She pulled out a chair and sank into it. The circles under her eyes suggested that she, like Wayne, had had a late night.

"What a party city," she said, holding her head very still. "I think I'm hung over."

"Are you up to going to Jazz Fest again?"

"Oh, yes," she said, mouthing a grateful thank-you to the waitress, who was pouring her coffee. "Julian insisted I meet him there; otherwise I might have slept in." She sipped her coffee slowly, eyes closed, humming her satisfaction.

I told her of my plans to meet Wayne later in the day.

"I'll call Julian and tell him to meet me there at the same time. We can go together. Between us, we should be able to find the press tent."

"I hope you have a good sense of direction," I said, unzipping my shoulder bag, pulling out a pen and placing it on the table.

"Post cards?"

"No. I always carry a little book for making notes and keeping track of appointments," I said, feeling around in the depths of my bag. "I was just trying to remember when I'm scheduled for the book signing."

"Mine's on Monday," she said.

The notebook eluded my grasp, but my hand encountered an unfamiliar texture. I drew out the juju that the voodoo priestess had pressed upon me. For a moment, I wasn't sure what to do with it.

"I hope you're not worried about that," Doris said.

"I'd forgotten I have it, actually," I said, putting down my bag and examining the packet. It was lumpy under the green felt.

"Do you suppose it's bad luck to open it and see what's inside?" she asked, leaning over to get a better look.

"The priestess didn't say, so I don't know."

"Aren't you curious?" she asked.

"I suppose I am." I knew Doris was.

"If it were mine, I'd unwrap it just to see what it is, and then wrap it up again."

I handed her the packet. "Would you like to do the honors?"

"Oh no, it's yours."

"I don't mind if you open it."

"Okay." She scooted her chair closer to mine, spread her napkin on the table, and placed the little parcel on it. Carefully, she untied the raffia, lay the strands on the table, and unfolded the felt. Whatever was inside was rolled up in a piece of off-white linen. Doris unrolled the cloth, and a black object tumbled out into her hand, along with some powdered material.

"What is it?" She turned in her seat and blew the powder off her palm onto the ground.

I picked up the object to examine it more closely. "It looks like a little alligator head."

"Ugh," Doris said, making a face and dusting the powder, and the idea, off her hands.

"I've got one of those hanging up at home," the waitress remarked as she placed my fruit platter in front of me.

"What's yours for?" I inquired.

"Gator heads guard against evil," she said, sliding a knife and fork next to the plate. "Most people here have one over the door. I'm hoping mine will keep my ex-husband away."

"Is it working?"

"I haven't seen him in three months, so I guess it is."

"Jessica, let me wrap that up again so you can have your breakfast," Doris said. She took the alligator head and began twining it back in its linen swathing.

"I'd like to wash my hands first."

"Here you go," said the waitress, dropping a half dozen packets of wipes next to my cup. "I keep them so folks can clean off the powdered sugar from the beignets."

"Ooh, I'd like one of those, please," Doris said. "The beignet, I mean." She helped herself to a wipe, too. She retied the raffia around the felt, and my juju, a little bulkier than before, was back in its original form.

I returned the juju to my bag and retrieved the notebook

I'd been looking for in the first place. I checked the date of my book signing—it was Monday.

A few hours later, Doris and I joined the throng at Jazz Fest. It was Saturday, and it seemed that all the people in New Orleans and its surrounding suburbs, off from work for the weekend, were trying to cram themselves into the race-track for the festival. We had the advantage of having been there the day before, but even though we were reasonably familiar with the layout, we arrived late at the press tent.

The entrance was flanked by two security guards. "We're supposed to meet some people inside," Doris said to the taller of the two, who might have been a wrestler before taking up security work. His short-sleeved shirt revealed enormous biceps, the sight of which probably prevented many from challenging his authority.

"Your names?" he asked.

He checked his list, moving his index finger slowly down the page. "Well, they didn't leave your names on the list," he growled.

"Does that mean we can't go in?" Doris asked.

"That's right, ma'am. No one gets in without a badge, or their name on my list."

"Is it possible for one of you to check around inside?" I appealed. "Our friends may be worried about us."

"Sorry, but we can't leave our post."

It was another hot day, and I was pleased that I'd purchased my broad-brimmed hat. Doris, who was hatless, fanned herself with a printed program. She was becoming increasingly, and overtly, agitated.

"I guess we'll have to wait till they realize we're not there and come looking for us," I offered.

She scowled at the guard, whose face remained impassive, and started pacing in front of the tent. As I attempted to look past the guards into the tent, Oliver Jones, the pianist we'd met the day before, came out.

"Hello there," he said with a wide smile. "You look lost."

We explained the dilemma, and he agreed to look for Wayne and tell him we were there. We thanked him, and he disappeared inside. A long, hot ten minutes passed before he reemerged, accompanied by a press aide.

"I'm sorry I wasn't able to help you," he apologized, "but maybe Miss Heaney can." He handed me an envelope. "Those are some passes for VIP seating at my concert, just in case you don't find Wayne," he said, and excused himself.

"Hi, I'm Ryan Heaney," the pretty young woman said, "assistant to the director of press relations. How can I help you?"

She led us past the guards and into the crowded tent where she helped us look for Wayne and Julian. Neither was there.

"Did you speak with Julian this morning?" I asked Doris.

"No, but I got his answering machine and told him where we'd be."

"We have a notices board where reporters leave notes for each other. Let's check that," Miss Heaney suggested. But there were no slips addressed to either Doris or me among the many messages posted.

Baffled as to where they might be, we asked Miss Heaney if we could post our own note for Wayne and Julian. She supplied the paper and pushpins and left us.

"Okay, so where do we tell them to meet us, assuming they ever get this message?" Doris asked. She was flushed from the heat, and fast losing patience.

"Since Oliver Jones was kind enough to give us VIP seating for his concert," I said, "that sounds like a good place to connect. If they don't turn up there, we'll just have to keep going on our own."

"That's fine with me," she replied, scribbling the note and jamming it up on the board. "Now, can we get out of this hot tent? I'm dying in here."

Outside was not much better. It still hadn't rained, and the breeze stirred up dust from the oval racetrack. We wandered around the edges of the fair for a while, listening to some of the lesser-known musicians, before we used our passes to find seats in the shaded VIP section at the main stage.

Oliver Jones's concert was the highlight of Jazz Fest for me. His rollicking piano style was the perfect blend of all the music I'd enjoyed. It was mostly jazz, but with ingredients of classical, gospel, Latin, Caribbean, even country. It was complex yet accessible, spirited and moving, and made me forget the absence of our escorts. But when the concert was over, and the ovation had faded away, I was left with the nagging feeling that something was not right. It was not in Wayne's nature to be cavalier about appointments.

Doris and I left the festival after the concert and returned to our hotel, she to do her interview with Ileana Montalvo, and I to my room hoping for voice mail from Wayne. There was none. Dismayed and worried, I showered, dressed, and prepared for my dinner interview with Charlie Gable. Before leaving the room, I called Wayne's apartment and spoke into his machine, explaining where I was going and that I'd try to reach him later.

"Oh, Copely's a bit of a flake," was Gable's assessment over cocktails at Arnaud's, a traditional Creole restaurant he'd chosen for our interview. "Look at that crusade he's on to find LeCoeur recordings." He took a sip of his drink and looked over the rim of his glass. "You know he's gay, don't you? It's probably something simple, like a fight with his boyfriend."

"I don't think Wayne's sexual orientation has anything to do with keeping appointments," I replied stiffly.

"C'mon, Jessica, don't be offended," he coaxed. "Copely and I go back a long ways. We're old friends. And he's a

New Orleans boy. We're very free-and-easy down here, not so rigid in our schedules as our Northern neighbors."

"That's not *my* impression of Wayne," I responded. "I haven't known him as long as you have, of course, but in my experience, he's always been very responsible, and he's passionate about jazz, so I doubt he'd willingly miss a day at Jazz Fest."

"How do you know he wasn't there?" Gable was more consoling now. "You said yourself you were late getting to the press tent. He could've reckoned he just wore you out yesterday, and you couldn't reach him to cancel. So when you didn't show, he decided to go on without you."

"He could have," I agreed, "but he wasn't at the Oliver Jones concert, and I know he's a big fan."

"Jones plays again later this week. Copely may have gone to one of the other concerts, thinking he could catch Oliver another time."

"Yes, that's possible."

"Anyway, it's tough to find anyone in that crowd," he said, spearing a bit of shrimp remoulade on his fork. "You'll both laugh about this tomorrow."

"You're probably right," I said, forcing myself to relax. I spooned up a taste of oyster stew. "This can take your mind off anything," I said, savoring the creamy flavor.

"Isn't it wonderful? One of my favorites, too."

Though, every table was occupied, the atmosphere in the restaurant encouraged relaxation. The décor was decidedly old New Orleans with mosaic tile floors, crystal chandeliers, potted palms, lead-glass windows, and ceiling fans lazily circling high above our heads. And the food was of the delicious, stick-to-your-ribs variety. When we'd sat down, Gable had asked permission to record our conversation— "Saves me trying to write and eat at the same time"—and I'd given it. He'd placed a small tape recorder on the table, reset the counter to zero, and made a note on a small lined pad at his right hand.

"Whenever you make a particularly *bon, bon mot,*" he explained, "I jot down the topic we're discussing and the number on the tape counter, so I can find where your quote is later."

"And then you don't have to listen to our entire conversation all over again?"

"That's it. Although sometimes I get hungry all over again," he joked, "reliving the meal."

Gable's interview was wide ranging. Once we'd put aside the topic of Wayne Copely, we chatted during appetizers about the success of his Book Club Breakfasts. Over entrées, we moved on to changes in the publishing industry, particularly the impact of the Internet on bookselling, discussing the many websites authors now use to promote their works.

"Anne Rice has a good one. Have you see it?" he asked.

"Oh, yes. I visited her site before my first trip to New Orleans."

"So, is there a jessicafletcher.com in the works?"

"Not yet." I hesitated, refolding my napkin in my lap. "A section of my publisher's site is devoted to my books," I continued. "That's sufficient for now."

"Are you a fan of cyberspace?" he asked. "Many writers are,"

"I'm happy to use the Internet for research, especially when the weather is bad and it's difficult to get to the library," I replied. "And I have to admit I've fallen in love with e-mail. It's a wonderful way to stay in touch with far-away family and friends, and I use it for business correspondence as well."

"I hear a 'but' in there, Jessica," Gable said, raising his eyebrows and making a note on his pad.

I sighed. "*But* I also find the Internet can steal my time.

It's too easy to get lost in front of the computer. Before you know it, hours go by and you're not getting anything done. So I use the Internet sparingly, and mostly when I'm working and need information I can't find anywhere else. It is a great springboard for research."

The waiter cleared our places, and I glanced at my watch, wondering if Wayne had gotten my message and left one for me at my hotel.

"Don't be in a hurry," Gable chided. "They have wonderful desserts here. Besides, I have a few more questions."

He ordered a *crème brûlée,* and at his suggestion, I opted for the bread pudding.

"I enjoyed *Murder in a Minor Key*, as I have all your books," he started, "but I was surprised you didn't use any voodoo material in it. It would seem a natural for a New Orleans setting."

"This particular story didn't lend itself to voodoo," I explained. "Sometimes a book takes you where it wants to go, and you just have to follow it along."

"How can that be?"

"It's a strange phenomenon." I paused, trying to find the right words. Gable was writing on his notepad. "Lots of writers create outlines for their books; some are more detailed than others. I use an outline, too, but often I'll finish a chapter and reread the section of my outline I was supposed to be covering, and find that I've gone off in a different direction."

"What do you do then?"

"If I like the new direction, I'll follow it and rearrange the plot," I said. "Sometimes, though, much as I may like what I've written, I'll have to rewrite the scene and wrestle the story back into its planned structure."

"It's kind of like a fight with your subconscious."

"That's a good analogy."

"So the last book took you in a different direction?"

"Away from the voodoo, yes." I thought about Ileana Montalvo, and the juju in my bag, and about Little Red and his voodoo beliefs. "For some reason, on this visit, I seem to be more aware of voodoo than I was the last time I was here, and even though I'm not currently working on a new book, I'm thinking of doing some research anyway."

"Well, if I can help in any way, let me know."

I was torn. I wanted to get to a phone and call Wayne. He was on my mind all the time now. But I also wanted to use this opportunity to question Gable about voodoo. As both a native New Orleanian and a journalist, he would have a lot to offer, not only in factual information but perhaps in interpreting situations—like the juju in my bag, or the deaths in the cemetery. I couldn't shake that image of a seated corpse leaning against a tomb.

"You can, actually," I said, moving my spoon around the bread pudding. It was superb, but my appetite had flown. "Tell me about Marie Laveau, and the tomb where she's buried."

"Ah, the infamous voodoo queen." He smiled. "You should visit her tomb before you leave. It's one of our more colorful sites, in a city full of colorful sites."

"I plan to get there soon."

"Make sure you go with a tour group," he cautioned. "It's not in the safest part of town."

"So I understand."

"You want to know about the mother, of course. Her daughter had the same name and was a queen, too."

"Yes, I think it's the mother I want to know about."

"She was a tall woman of mixed race, supposedly the daughter of a white planter and mulatto mother, although some say she had Indian blood as well. She married a man named Paris, from Santo Domingo, but he disappeared soon after, and no one knows what happened to him."

"Did she practice voodoo on him?"

"Hard to say. She considered herself a devout Catholic. His disappearance and her involvement in voodoo may not have been connected. Anyway, she became a hairdresser, and was very popular with white aristocratic ladies who told her all their secrets, which, I'm sure, she put to good use. Later, she lived with a man called Glapion—and by the way, that's the name on her tomb."

"Glapion?"

"Right. She had more than a dozen kids with him. They lived over on St. Ann Street, here in the Quarter, but the house is long gone now."

"What made her so powerful?"

"It must have been the influence she held over people," he replied. "Supposedly, she had the police and city officials in her pocket, and she managed to eliminate all her rivals, using spells and deadly gris-gris."

"Remarkable."

"Well, that's what people believed anyway. Who knows what's true?"

"And her tomb?"

"Lots of voodoo practitioners—and the tour industry for sure—say both she and her daughter are entombed in the Glapion crypt in St. Louis Number One. Other cemeteries lay claim to the daughter."

"What do you think?"

"What do I think? I think if both Maries are in the same tomb, that's a lethal concentration of voodoo spirits in one place."

"Lethal?"

"Just a turn of phrase," he said, lifting the check the waiter had left on the table. "The tomb is definitely a voodoo shrine, a place of magic, maybe black magic. You should see some of the fetishes people leave there."

I felt a chill that had nothing to do with the air conditioning.

"Would you please excuse me a moment?" I pulled the napkin from my lap, gathered my bag, and stood.

"Certainly. Anything wrong?" he asked, rising from his seat.

"No, no. I'll be right back." I swiftly made my way out of the dining room to find a public telephone. I emptied my wallet of coins, and dialed my hotel. No messages. I searched my bag for my notebook, feeling increasingly nervous. Gripping the receiver between my shoulder and my chin, I held the notebook open with one hand, and with the other, dropped more coins into the phone. I punched in Wayne's number and held my breath.

"Hello?"

"Oh, Wayne, I'm so relieved. I've been trying to get you all day."

There was silence on the phone.

"Wayne?"

"He's not here," said a man's voice that didn't sound like Wayne at all.

"Where is he?"

"You'll have to call back later," he said, and hung up.

Furious at his rudeness, I contemplated calling again, but changed my mind and returned to the table.

"Charlie, this has been a wonderful dinner, and I really appreciate all your attention, but I must run."

"What's the matter?"

"A strange man just hung up on me at Wayne's apartment. I'm going over there to find out what's wrong."

The waiter handed Gable his credit card and the bill on a tray. Gable signed his name and stood. "Would you like me to go with you?" he asked, pocketing his fountain pen.

"Thank you," I said quickly, "but that's not really necessary. But you can help me get a cab if you would. Are you ready to leave now?"

We stood on the sidewalk outside the restaurant and my

stomach clenched. The street was full of cars, but they weren't moving.

"Saturday night traffic," Gable grumbled. "Where does he live?"

I gave him Wayne's address.

"It's less than ten blocks," he said, looking down the street. "You can walk it if you want, and probably make better time than waiting for a ride in this mess." He waved his hand at the gridlocked cars. "Are you sure you don't want me to go with you?"

I nodded. "Which way do I go?"

He pointed. "Down to Bourbon Street. That's the next corner. And turn left." I thanked him, and rushed away.

Bourbon Street may have been the most direct route to Wayne's, but it certainly wasn't the easiest. I walked as quickly as I could, but the throngs of people spilling out of buildings onto the street kept my progress slow. There were bars and nightclubs lining the street, as close to each other as the beads on a necklace. The piano music emanating from one club melded with horns from another, merged with the banjo and guitar from a third, and all were punctuated by the horns of cars and taxis trying to negotiate the intersections. Barkers urged pedestrians to sample the entertainment inside the clubs, which in addition to the jazz, rock, blues, honky-tonk, and country, included topless, karaoke, and even can-can shows. From the open doors, the smell of alcohol was pervasive, mixed with the spices and smoke of restaurant kitchens. I dodged a group of young people, singing, clapping, and drinking from plastic cups, and skirted two children tap dancing on a piece of hard, thick plastic. They were no older than ten, and danced to music played on a boombox, the volume competing with the shouts of revelers and the cacophony of sounds from the nearby nightspots. Above me, the balconies were jammed with more people, their voices and laughter adding to the din.

I had worn a silk dress and pumps to dinner, never anticipating a long walk, and was aware of being observed by some of the street's more disreputable denizens. Determined not to look like an easy mark, I adopted what I'd learned in other cities, and walked purposefully, my expression staunch and fearless. I fished in my bag for my key ring. Not a very effective weapon, I thought, but at least it gave me something to hold on to. I closed my fist around the ring with the keys poking up between my fingers like the spokes of a wheel, and held my bag close to my side.

Finally, the crowds began to thin, and as I turned down Wayne's street, the noise of Bourbon Street faded behind me. It became eerily quiet. I increased my pace, the only sounds the click of my heels on the stone paving, and the skitter of plastic cups rolling in the gutter.

I checked my address book for the number of Wayne's apartment house. An old brown Ford was angled into the curb under a NO PARKING sign in front of the building. A streetlight illuminated the soft pink façade. Iron lacework outlined the balconies that ran the length of each floor; on them was a profusion of green plants and a series of tables and chairs, demarcating the individual apartments.

Surprisingly, the double doors leading inside were open. I checked the directory for the number of Wayne's apartment, climbed the stairs to the third floor, and pulled on a brass knocker in the shape of an alligator. The door swung open and a man in a brown suit frowned at me.

"Who're you?" he asked gruffly.

"Perhaps I have the wrong apartment," I said, taken aback. "I'm looking for Wayne Copely."

"What's he to you?"

"I'm a friend, and I haven't heard from him. I was concerned. Are you an acquaintance of his?"

I knew the answer before he gave it, and felt my stomach drop. Men like him have a certain look. It's in the eyes, a world-weariness, a cool appraisal, an unbending attitude worn like a carapace on their backs meant to protect them from the brutalities of life.

"I'm a cop."

"What's happened to Wayne?"

"He's dead."

Chapter Eight

"You look a little pale. Come in and sit down."

Numbly, I entered Wayne's apartment and slumped down on his green damask sofa. The officer remained standing on the other side of the glass-topped, painted wooden box that served as a coffee table. He tugged at his belt, trying to draw the waistline of his trousers over a protuberant stomach.

"Did you call earlier?"

"Yes," I said. "Was that you who answered?"

"Yeah."

"I heard your voice and I just knew." I sat up, trying to regain some semblance of control.

"Knew what?"

"That something had happened to Wayne."

"How did you know?"

His question was like a slap, startling me back to conscious thought. I straightened my shoulders, alert.

"I didn't *know,*" I said briskly, "but I had an uncomfortable feeling all day, and when I heard your voice, it intensified."

"Is that why you came here?"

"Yes. And then when I saw you, I really knew."

"What do you mean?"

"It's obvious," I said impatiently, "that if the police are here and Wayne's not, then something is drastically wrong."

"You knew I was a cop?"

"Yes.

"I'm not in uniform."

"You look like a policeman."

"I do?"

I nodded.

"And just how is it I look like a cop?" he asked irritably.

I took a deep breath, but before I could tell him that there was something in his eyes and his body language, he interrupted me.

"Forget I asked that," he said. "I don't think I want to know." He raised his eyebrows. "Do you always get these 'feelings' about things?" There was a tinge of sarcasm in his voice.

I ignored it. "Not that I'm aware of."

He was a heavyset man in his forties, with bushy eyebrows and tousled brown hair. His suit was wrinkled and his brown shoes looked like they hadn't been polished in a long time. I studied him as he debated what to do with me. Finally he asked, "When did you last see Copely?"

"Friday. Yesterday. When did he die?"

"Sometime last night."

I looked up. "I was with him last night, till just before ten."

He grunted but said nothing.

"How did it happen? He seemed perfectly healthy."

"I'll ask the questions."

"Go ahead," I said wearily.

He must have taken pity on me, because his tone changed. "Why don't we start over? I'm detective Chris Steppe, NOPD." He flipped open a leather wallet revealing his badge. Pocketing the wallet, he pulled out a pencil and a small black binder with lined paper, and looked down at me. "And you would be?"

"Jessica Fletcher."

"Why do I know that name?"

I explained to him why he might know who I was.

"A mystery writer, huh?"

"Yes."

"A famous person." He smiled, wet his pencil point on his tongue, and wrote in his book.

While Detective Steppe scratched away at his notes, I looked around the room. Wayne's living quarters were spare but with an innate elegance that was difficult to define. It might have been the warmth of the wooden floor, a broad-planked relic from an earlier era, the scars on which only enhanced its appeal. Or it might have been the diaphanous curtains that billowed over the open French doors, which looked out on the black night beyond the balcony. The furnishings were simple: the sofa, coffee table, a small Oriental rug in front of what I was sure was a decorative fireplace, a line of low bookcases on one wall, and a delicate round table of highly polished dark wood with two matching chairs. An efficiency kitchen occupied one corner. No bric-a-brac, no clutter. There was a calmness to the apartment that I could sense, despite my agitation, a calmness that must have been restful for a high-strung personality like Wayne's.

A door from the living room opened into another part of the apartment, and I could hear someone shuffling around in there, opening doors and drawers.

"Where did Wayne die?" I asked Detective Steppe.

"We found his body at the cemetery."

"The cemetery!"

"Yeah, ironic, isn't it?"

"Which one?" I was almost afraid to ask.

"St. Louis Cemetery Number One. He was sitting up against a tomb."

I shivered. "In the paper this morning," I whispered to myself.

"Yeah, tough to keep that stuff out of the paper." Steppe combed his hair with thick fingers, which made the unruly thatch even more disheveled. "It'll be all over the news tomorrow, now he's been ID'd, and seeing who he is and all."

"Who identified him?"

"His sister, I think." He riffled through the pages of his book. "Yeah, Clarice Copely-Cruz. Know her?"

"No. We were supposed to have dinner at her house tomorrow. Wayne wanted me to meet her."

"How well did you know him?"

"Not very well," I admitted. "We were just recent acquaintances, really."

"You're not from here, so how did you meet him?"

"I got his phone number last year from someone we both know. I was researching a book, and his name was suggested as a resource. He gave me an education in the music of New Orleans. When I knew I was going to be here for an authors' panel, and in time for Jazz Fest, I called him."

"And?"

"And he got Charlie Gable of the *Times-Picayune* to add him to the panel, and we took up where we'd left off in my musical studies." I smiled at the memory of Wayne thrilled at having an acolyte to introduce to the joys of jazz. His enthusiasm had been contagious, and his knowledge of the history of this art form was encyclopedic.

I shook my head to clear it. "What was the cause of death?" I asked.

"Are you sure you want to discuss this?"

"Detective, I make my living writing murder mysteries. I read case histories, interview coroners, pore over police photos. I think I have a pretty strong constitution by now."

"No doubt," Steppe said, pushing his notebook back down in his jacket pocket. He hesitated a bit, considering what to tell me, then decided not to. "Well, we're not really sure," he said. I didn't believe him. "We won't know officially till the autopsy report comes in."

"But you have an idea, right?"

"I might." He fiddled with his pencil.

"Why don't you want to tell me?"

Steppe's eyebrows flew up. "You ask a lot of questions, don't you?" He retrieved his pad. "Where did you say you were yesterday?"

"I didn't," I replied stiffly. "You didn't ask me. But I was at Jazz Fest most of the day with Wayne, and I can supply you with the names of our other companions. In the evening, Wayne and I went to a fais-do-do, and then he dropped me off at my hotel at about nine forty-five."

Steppe took some more notes, and I got up and paced the room, trying to get a glimpse of the layout of the rest of the apartment, and to see who was in the other room.

"You didn't answer my question," I said.

"Don't really know," he replied. "I'm not the medical examiner. Now tell me, Mrs. Fletcher, in your estimation can you think of why anyone would want Copely dead?"

I whirled around. "He was murdered?"

"I didn't say that."

"Your question implies it."

"You don't see any crime scene tape here, do you?"

"No, but you're here, and your partner is, too." I flung out my arm, indicating the other room.

"Just covering all the possibilities till the medical report comes in. So, do you?"

"Do I know why anyone would want to kill Wayne? No!"

The face of Julian Broadbent materialized in my mind. I wondered again where he'd been today, and why he hadn't left an explanation for Doris. Still, I was convinced Julian's absence had nothing to do with Wayne. He wouldn't have had any reason to hurt Wayne, even though he didn't particularly like him. Julian was prickly, yes, and macho, and there was no love lost between the two men. But no, I wouldn't bring up his name.

"Do you know why Copely would have been in the cemetery at night?"

"No, unless it had to do with his research."

"What research?"

I gave Steppe a brief rundown of Wayne's interest in the recordings of Little Red LeCoeur. "But he hasn't found any so far," I added, and then remembered sadly that "so far" was as far as Wayne would be able to go.

"Who else knew about this research?"

"Everyone, I guess."

"Who is everyone?"

"He made a public announcement of his intent to find the recordings at the Book Club Breakfast on Thursday, and it was mentioned in the paper on Friday. And he told me that he'd placed an ad in a music magazine asking for information about the cylinders."

"What magazine?"

"I believe the name is *Wavelength*."

"What would have happened if someone else found the recordings, not Copely?" Steppe asked. "Would he have been angry? Would he go so far as to fight for them?"

"In my opinion, Wayne would have been delighted if anyone found them, so long as they were willing to let them be copied."

"Why's that?"

"The actual physical cylinders themselves were not really important, only what they contained. He desperately wanted this generation—and himself as well—to be able to hear the playing of a musical genius. He kept stressing how rare LeCoeur's style was, a musical missing link between modern jazz and its beginnings."

"Hmmm. So he wouldn't have gotten into a fight for them?"

"Wayne wasn't a very big man," I said. Remembering his confrontation with Broadbent, I added, "I don't think he frightened easily, but he was more accustomed to using his brain, his powers of verbal persuasion, than his fists."

"So he was smart?"

"Oh, yes. Very smart."

"Mr. Copely was a native of this city, Mrs. Fletcher. Everyone in New Orleans knows not to go to those cemeteries alone. *That* wasn't very smart."

"Maybe he wasn't alone."

"Why do you say that?"

"He was supposed to meet the trumpeter, Blind Jack, last night after Jack finished his last set. When Wayne left me, he was going to the club where Jack was playing. They'd planned to have a drink together to discuss Wayne's latest lead on the recordings. You should ask him."

Steppe wrote down Blind Jack's name. "Where was he playing? Do you remember?"

I wracked my brain for the name of the club, but it escaped me. "I'm sorry I don't, but I'm sure it would have been in yesterday's paper."

"Never mind," he said. "That's easy to find out."

"I remember something else, though."

"What's that?"

"At lunch on Thursday, Wayne mentioned something about death threats."

Steppe stared at me. "Death threats? You're just now remembering that he *mentioned* death threats. I wouldn't think that would be easy to forget."

"I didn't forget," I said, flaring at his tone. "And I don't appreciate your sarcasm, Detective Steppe. I was not withholding information. I've only just learned of Wayne's death, and didn't consider till a moment ago that he might not have died of natural causes. You, of course, never said that directly. In fact, you seemed to deny it."

He held his palms up. "Sorry, Mrs. Fletcher. You're right to be annoyed. It's been a long day, and I get nasty when I'm tired." He hung his head for a moment and then drew a deep breath. "Just tell me what Copely told you about the death threats. Try to give me every detail you can think of."

Mollified, I relayed what Wayne had told me over lunch about the vicious letters and phone messages he'd received over the years, about how he thought his career as a critic left him open to the rantings of those who took issue with his columns, and about how the police had not been able to help him when he'd reported the first few incidents.

"So he didn't report the latest ones?" Steppe shook his head. There were lines of strain around his mouth.

"Not this time, no," I said, feeling guilty that I hadn't pressured Wayne into calling the police again. "Did he die in the cemetery?" I asked abruptly.

Steppe ignored my question, and asked one of his own. "What do you know about voodoo, Mrs. Fletcher?"

I thought of tonight's conversation with Charlie Gable. "Barely anything at all. Why?"

"Copely was found sitting up against the tomb of Marie Laveau, the famous voodoo queen." He paused, waiting for my reaction. "But you know that," he added. "It was in the paper today."

"I read about it, of course, but I don't know how it relates to Wayne."

"Think, Mrs. Fletcher," he pressed. "You remembered about the death threats. Maybe something else will come to you."

I frowned at him. "He must have known something about voodoo," I said, "but that would be true of anyone raised in New Orleans."

"Did he ever wear a gris-gris, Mrs. Fletcher? You know about them, don't you, those pouches on a string meant to bring good luck or ward off evil?"

"I never saw one on him. He did say he should buy one to help him find the recordings. I thought he was kidding. As far as I know, he wasn't wearing one when he left me last night."

"Well, his corpse wore one. There's more." He was eyeing me closely now.

"Yes?"

"We don't have the autopsy report, so this is just a guess on my part."

I said nothing.

"His hand, Mrs. Fletcher. I saw two puncture marks on his hand. Wasn't easy. His hand was all swollen."

"Does this have something to do with how he died?"

"Possibly." He was stalling.

"What could have made those marks, Detective?"

"There's only one thing I can think of, Mrs. Fletcher." He stared into my eyes. "I think your friend died from a snakebite."

Chapter Nine

I was beginning to feel like Alice falling down the rabbit hole. Wayne was dead. Bitten by a snake? How? He'd been in a dangerous cemetery at night that he'd warned *me* against visiting during the day. Had he been meeting some-one? Had he simply sat down to wait, and disturbed an un-seen reptile he wasn't expecting to be there?

"Are there usually snakes in the cemetery?" I demanded of Steppe.

"There are snakes all over Louisiana, so I guess there could be snakes in the cemetery."

"But has anyone else ever been bitten by a snake in the cemetery?"

"Lady, I don't have the slightest idea. I don't know a lot of people who hang around the cemetery at night to start with, unless they're involved with some bizarre voodoo rit-ual."

"I don't believe for a second that Wayne was involved with voodoo rituals," I said indignantly.

"Hey, you never know about some people. He led—what's it called?—an 'alternate lifestyle,' and those people do strange things."

He was baiting me, but I wasn't sure why. "Are you try-ing to be offensive?" I asked, watching him closely.

He tried to hide a smirk, but the curl of his lip gave it

away. "So tell me, Mrs. Fletcher, did Copely ever introduce you to any of his lovers?"

"I don't know that he had a lover. Are you implying that he had many?"

"Hey, I didn't know this guy. He could have one; he could have fifteen. You tell me."

"I've already told you that our friendship was of recent vintage. Although I'm—was—very fond of Wayne, I didn't know him well."

"He never introduced you to any friends?"

"The only friends of his I met were musicians at Jazz Fest."

"Their names?"

I paced the room as I dictated to Steppe the names of the musicians I'd met at the press tent and elsewhere at the festival. I continued to leave out Julian Broadbent. I was sure Wayne wouldn't have considered him a friend, but that was no excuse. I pondered my motives. I wanted to talk to Julian first, before I gave his name to the police. I needed to know his whereabouts today, to hear him explain why he was incommunicado after having made a date to meet with Doris.

"Anyone else?"

"No."

I found myself standing in front of Wayne's efficiency kitchen. It was no more than a high counter with two stools. Across from the counter were two narrow cabinets, one with a sink and the other with a low refrigerator of the kind you find in college dormitory rooms. Open shelves on the wall above displayed beautiful porcelain plates and cups, and crystal glassware.

"May I have a glass of water?" I asked.

"Yeah. Go ahead."

Steppe was disappointed with me, I could see. I wasn't able to give him any leads on Wayne's murder—if it was a murder. I walked around the counter and pulled a cut-glass tumbler from the shelf. On a hunch, I opened the refrigerator. There were several bottles of water, as well as a half-consumed bottle of wine, an unopened bottle of champagne, a box of crackers, and a wedge of cheese. No wonder Wayne was so knowledgeable about his city's restaurants. He obviously didn't eat at home very often. There wasn't even a toaster-oven or microwave in view, much less a full stove. I took a bottle from the refrigerator and filled my glass. Standing behind the counter sipping my water, I followed the detective with my eyes as he ambled along Wayne's bookcase, scanning the titles and scrutinizing the few items displayed on top—a vase of lilies, a silver bowl, a small figurine. Steppe picked up the silver bowl, turned it over, squinted at the bottom, and put it back in place. He looked up to see me watching him.

He turned toward the opening to the other room. "Teddy," he yelled.

A tall, young man with light-brown skin and freckles leaned into the room. "Yo! Chris," he said.

"Find anything?"

"Nah. Nothing to speak of," Teddy said, spying me and easing the rest of his lanky body through the doorway. He pushed a pen into his shirt pocket.

Steppe pointed at me. "Teddy, this is Mrs. Fletcher, a friend of Copely's. Mrs. Fletcher, my partner, P.O. Teddy Bailin."

"How do you do," I said.

The young policeman glanced toward Steppe, and a silent message passed between them. "Ma'am, sorry about your friend," Bailin said to me. His eyes held mine for only a second, and then dropped to his shoes, which, I noticed, were more carefully tended than Steppe's. In fact, the young officer's entire appearance was well turned out, in distinct contrast to his older colleague.

"Thank you."

"Teddy, why don't you go wait in the car," Steppe said. "We're just about finished here anyway."

"Sure, Chris." He nodded at me and strolled out of the apartment, his long limbs giving him an ungainly gait. Steppe watched the door till Bailin's footfalls on the stairs were barely audible.

I had to move quickly. I put down my glass. "Detective Steppe," I said, drawing his attention back to me, "Wayne borrowed a book from me that I very much would like to have back. Mind if I see if it's inside?"

"Huh? Oh, yeah, go ahead."

I walked out of the living room slowly because I didn't want him to see how eager I was to examine Wayne's bedroom. The hallway angled to the left; a door to the bathroom on the right stood open. Wayne's bedroom was ahead of me. I stood for a moment taking it in. A double bed with an ornate headboard was neatly made up, but there was an indent on the ocher coverlet, where someone had sat down on the edge. To one side of the bed was a low fruitwood nightstand, with a broad front, curved legs, and a half-open single drawer, revealing a jumble of blank pads, pens, tissue packets, and business cards strewn across a divided tray. On top of the nightstand was Wayne's combination telephone–answering machine, next to which were a pad and pen, and my book. A marker stuck out beyond the pages, indicating Wayne had already started reading it. I grabbed the book, tore the top page off the pad, and put it inside the front cover. I checked the wastebasket on the other side of the cabinet, but it was empty.

My eyes roamed the room. Wayne's closet door stood open, and all the drawers on his antique bureau were ajar. I peeked in the top drawer to see a hodgepodge of shorts, socks, bow ties, and handkerchiefs. As quietly as I could, using the skirt of my dress to avoid leaving my fingerprints,

I pushed in the top drawer, and slid the second drawer farther out to expose another untidy heap of clothing.

I crossed to the open closet and peered inside. Half the closet contained Wayne's hanging clothes, most of them still on the hangers, and several pairs of shoes that looked like they'd been tossed in. The other half was shelved and held an elaborate sound system, with multiple decks of recording and playing equipment. One shelf was lined with rows of cassette tapes arranged in alphabetical order. I glanced at my watch. I'd better get out of here, I thought, before the detective comes looking for me.

Reentering the living room, I spied Steppe standing in the small kitchen, a dishtowel flung over his shoulder. He was placing my glass back on the shelf.

"Detective?"

"So you found it," he said, eyeing the book I clutched to my chest.

"Yes, thank you very much," I said, unzipping my bag and depositing the book inside.

"Good. We have to go." He folded the towel and placed it back in the drawer from which he'd taken it.

I smiled sweetly. "Would you mind terribly if I used the bathroom before we leave?"

"No, of course not. I'll wait in the hall."

I locked the bathroom door behind me, and turned on the sink faucet to mask any sounds I might make. The room was tiny; a claw-foot tub took up most of the space. I opened the door of the old-fashioned medicine cabinet and perused the items. Wayne had grouped all his shaving materials on the end of one shelf, and his toothbrush, toothpaste, and floss on the other. Apart from a large selection of colognes, there was nothing but mundane boxes and bottles one would expect to find. A narrow linen closet on the opposite wall was crammed in next to the tub. The door squeaked when I opened it, and I froze, hoping Steppe couldn't hear it. The closet contained only the usual items. I flushed the toilet, closed the closet door, washed my hands, dried them on a linen towel, and turned off the water.

Detective Steppe was standing in the hallway outside the apartment, bouncing a set of keys in his hand. "C'mon, c'mon. It's late."

"Yes, thank you for your patience."

Steppe locked the door, and we clattered down the stairwell to the ground floor.

"Do you need a ride to your hotel?" he asked.

"That would be very kind," I said gratefully, suddenly aware that my feet, unaccustomed to long walks in heels, were aching, and that a pervasive sorrow was consuming me. I climbed into the back seat of the brown Ford—brown seemed to be Steppe's color—and told Teddy where I was staying.

"How long are you going to be in town, Mrs. Fletcher?" Steppe asked.

"I'm not sure now," I answered honestly. "At least until after Wayne's funeral, I expect."

"We may have to interview you again," he said. Teddy glanced at him with a strange expression, but Steppe was looking back over his shoulder at me. "I'll need your address and home phone number."

"Certainly," I said. "If you give me your book, I'll write it in for you."

Steppe opened his wallet instead and took out two business cards. "Here," he said, passing them to me. "Keep one in case you think of something helpful, and put your vitals on the back of the other."

I did as he asked and returned one card to him, just as Teddy pulled up in front of the Royal.

The bright glare of the hotel lobby was painful coming from the dim lighting of both Wayne's apartment and the unmarked police car. I stopped at the front desk for my key.

"Good evening, Mrs. Fletcher," the night clerk said. He studied my face. "Are you feeling all right?" he asked, sliding my room key over the marble counter.

"Just a bit of a headache," I said. "I'll be fine after a good night's sleep."

But sleep was not on my agenda that night. Visions of Wayne kept me awake. I saw him giddily dragging me from one musical experience to another. I relived our conversation in the restaurant when he told me about his death threats.

Images of people I'd met in New Orleans clouded my brain—Julian Broadbent, Doris Burns, Charlie Gable, Simon West, Mayor Amadour, Philippe Beaudin, Napoleon DuBois, Detective Steppe, and Police Officer Bailin. And Wayne's sister, Clarice. We hadn't met yet, but now I'd be paying her a condolence call on Sunday, instead of a social visit.

Why did Wayne go to that cemetery? What happened there? Was he the victim of some voodoo curse? Was he getting too close to the cylinders for someone's comfort?

And the police. There was something strange there, something bothering me that I couldn't quite put my finger on. In Wayne's apartment. Why would Steppe, obviously unconcerned about his appearance and who wore sloppy clothes and scuffed shoes—and who allowed Wayne's drawers and closet to be ransacked—why was he so careful to wash my glass and put it back on the shelf?

Chapter Ten

"Jessica, what in the deuce is going on down there?"

"Seth?" I groped for the clock on the bedside table. It was eight-thirty. How did it get to be so late? I couldn't recall the last time I'd slept past seven. Then I remembered what had kept me awake most of the night. Groggy, I sat up, swung my legs over the side of the bed, and tried to concentrate on my friend's voice.

"Got the *Bangor Times* this morning. There's a small story on the national page about a body being found in the cemetery. Turns out to be that critic friend you went to visit. That right?" He sounded agitated.

"Yes, Seth, that's right." I sighed.

"Are *you* all right?" he asked, the sympathy in his voice comforting. Seth can be overbearing at times when he worries about me, but I've always appreciated his concern.

"I've been better," I said.

"So, why don't you catch the next plane, and come home where you have your friends around you."

"That's very tempting," I said, rubbing my eyes.

"Lorna's still got one of those kittens left over. Cute little thing, orange and black and white. Would be perfect for you. Dr. Jenny took one. Nice gal, that Dr. Jenny. Mara's grandkids gave her that name. Now all the little ones are calling her Dr. Jenny."

He prattled away, giving me all the Cabot Cove gossip

from Mara's luncheonette. I smiled fondly as I listened to his stories. I knew they were meant to entice me to come home.

"And Mort," he said, finishing up, "has got Mrs. Treyz on a campaign to raise money for his new patrol car. She's already got the Ladies Auxiliary to promise the proceeds from the fashion show and bake sale, and got Dave Ranieri down at Charles Department Store to donate a toaster oven for the raffle. She even put one of those collection cans on the counter in Doug's office, and everyone who comes to see him for a toothache has to plunk in some coins before they can leave."

I laughed softly. "She'll do it, if anyone can," I said.

"Ayuh. So when're you coming home?"

"I can't leave just yet, Seth. For one thing, I'd like to be here for Wayne's funeral."

"Of course. I suppose you would."

We talked for another ten minutes, and when I finally put down the receiver, I was feeling better. The news from home was good to hear, a sign that in Cabot Cove, for the moment at least, all was orderly and peaceful, the myriad details of small-town daily life the main concern of residents far from the turmoil and anxiety of the big city. I ordered coffee and a slice of melon from Room Service, and switched on the radio as I prepared to start my day. Detective Steppe had been right. Wayne's death was all over the news.

". . . and the city's medical examiner has ruled that Copely's death was an accident, although it's still unclear why he was in the cemetery the night he died. According to the mayor's office, the recent drought has reduced food supplies for reptiles, causing them to expand their habitats. WWL News spoke with the mayor's spokesman, Philippe

Beaudin, and he had this to say about recent reports of snake sightings in the city . . ."

The jingling of the telephone interrupted the report. I turned down the radio and picked up the phone.

"Yes?"

"Jessica, oh my word. I'm so sorry. I just heard about Wayne on the radio."

I recognized Charlie Gable's voice, higher pitched than it normally was, reflecting his agitation.

"You were right last night," he said. "Something *was* wrong. Are you okay?"

"Yes, Charlie. I'm all right."

"Were you there when they found his body?"

"No, of course not. Don't you remember? I told you about the strange voice on the phone at Wayne's apartment."

"Yes, I remember now. That's what sent you running out of the restaurant."

"I went to his apartment. The man I spoke to was a police officer. He told me about Wayne."

"You poor thing, learning about it that way. Bitten by a snake. I can't even begin to imagine such a thing."

"Nor can I."

"Why was he in that cemetery? Do you think it had anything to do with the Little Red recordings?" He started to ask another question but I interrupted him.

"Charlie?"

"Yes?"

"I'm just listening to the report myself," I said. "Can I call you later?"

"Yes, of course, but it's not necessary." His voice was calmer. "I just wanted to make sure you're okay. You'll let me know if there's anything I can do for you."

"Thanks so much for thinking of me. I'll give you a call

soon." I hung up and turned up the radio, hoping to catch the
end of the report.

". . . accidental death from snakebite. Police Superintendent Johnson and Mayor Amadour have scheduled a press
conference for later this afternoon. But you don't have to
wait that long to find out where y'at in the Big Easy. Coming up in five minutes, *New Orleans Live.* Here's your
chance to tell us your drought stories. The phones are open
now . . ."

I fiddled with the dial until I found some soothing music.
Accidental death from snakebite. I shivered, and forced
away an image of Wayne dying alone and in pain in a desolate cemetery. I'd missed a part of the report. Had there been
any mention of the gris-gris, or of the fact that another body
had been found in the same position less than a month ago?
How could they call this an accident? All my experience argued that it couldn't be a coincidence, two bodies found at
the same tomb. Not only that, but the tomb was considered
the resting place of one, possibly two voodoo queens, what
Charlie had said might be a "lethal concentration of voodoo
spirits." There had to be a connection. But what was it? Perhaps something would come out at the press conference. I
hoped it would be televised. I was interested to see if the reporters would pick up on what was not being said. Surely,
the police had an explanation for why, of two deaths in the
same spot, one was being labeled a murder, and the other an
accident.

The home of Clarice Copely-Cruz was uptown, in the
Garden District, a fashionable neighborhood of elegant
homes and lavish gardens. A taxi had dropped me in front of
a narrow, three-story white Georgian Colonial Revival
house that was set back from the street. Four enormous

columns rose from the porch, past a second-floor balcony to support the eaves over the third floor, where peeling paint revealed that the color of the house had once been saffron. A wrought-iron picket fence ran along the front of the property and ended on either side with a hedge of privet that bordered the lot. The rusted gate squealed when I pushed it open. I walked down a graveled path to the front steps. This was to have been a pleasant Sunday dinner with Wayne and his sister. Now I would meet her under the worst of circumstances.

An elegantly dressed woman in her sixties answered my knock.

"I'm Jessica Fletcher. I'm here to see Mrs. Cruz."

"Oh, Mrs. Fletcher, please come in," the woman said. "I know she wants to meet you." She held out her hand. "I'm Marguerite Amadour, a friend of Clarice's."

"How do you do," I said. "The mayor's wife. I've met your husband."

"Yes, he mentioned he'd met you." Mrs. Amadour was small and delicate, the opposite of her bearlike husband. Her blond hair was pulled back into a chignon at the base of her neck. She wore a white crepe blouse with a frilly front under a navy knit jacket with matching skirt. "We're expecting you at the big party next week," she continued with a wan smile. "I was hoping to persuade Clarice to come, too. She's been so housebound since Steve died. But now, I don't suppose she will." Her words trailed off as she led me through the vestibule, past dark front rooms, down a narrow hall to the side of a flight of stairs, to a large open sitting room in back. The modern décor was a surprise after seeing the classical dimensions of the outside of the house. Light flooded in from skylights in a cathedral ceiling. Sliding glass panels led to the garden in back. To the right, a marble tabletop, laden with cakes and casseroles, sat on iron legs. High-backed chairs had been pulled away and lined up along the wall. To the left, a pair of Barcelona chairs faced a white leather sofa. Large tropical plants reached up toward the light, giving the spacious room the appearance of a conservatory.

Sitting on the sofa between two women who held her hands was a short, stout woman with red eyes. She sent a questioning glance to Marguerite Amadour.

"Clarice, this is Jessica Fletcher," Mrs. Amadour said softly. One of the women rose to give me her seat.

"Yes, yes," Clarice said, her eyes filling up. "Wayne's friend. Please, Mrs. Fletcher . . ." She motioned to the empty spot beside her. The other woman patted Clarice's shoulder, murmured in her ear, and gave her seat to the mayor's wife.

"Mrs. Cruz, I'm so sorry . . ." I began as I sat down.

"It's Clarice," she said, her voice quavery. She put her hand on my arm. "And you must let me call you Jessica. I feel like I know you already. Wayne was so excited about your coming to New Orleans again."

"Your brother was a wonderful teacher, so generous with his time and knowledge," I said. "We were on our way to becoming good friends, I know."

"Oh yes, I think so, too." There was a trace of a smile on her thin lips. "He loved to share his passion for music." Her eyes filled again. "But then, I think that's what may have killed him."

"What was?"

"His love of music. That's what killed him. Those stupid recordings. If only . . ." She dabbed at her eyes with a lace handkerchief, and crushed it in her hand. Marguerite Amadour placed a packet of tissues on her lap.

Clarice gazed at them sadly. "My hankie isn't up to the job today, is it?" she whispered, pulling out a few tissues as tears slid down her face. "My mother always insisted that a lady must carry a hankie." Marguerite put her arrn around

Clarice's shoulder, and drew her against her side. "It's okay, sweetheart, ladies use tissues, too."

"First Steve, and now Wayne," she moaned.

"Perhaps I should come back another time," I said, conscious of Clarice's need to express her grief without an audience. Her misery brought back a bitter reminder of when I'd lost my husband, Frank, so many years ago, yet the pain, although duller now, was still present. I understood the hollow feeling, the chasm that could never be filled, only the edges of it softened.

She turned back to me. "Please stay," she said, gulping down a sob. "I need to talk about Wayne, and you were with him last, I understand."

I took a deep breath and nodded. "He took me dancing."

She gave me a watery smile. "Oh, wasn't that like him. Where did you go?"

I sketched a verbal picture for her of the fais-do-do Wayne had taken me to, exaggerating a bit as I described his skills in teaching me the steps, but accurately noting his delight in having me join in the festivities, and his enthusiasm for the dance.

"He was always a good dancer," she said, eyes downcast, remembering. "Even when we were children. He would learn the latest dances, and teach the rest of us." She seemed calmer now, her thoughts turned inward to the happy times in their childhood. I hesitated to intrude on her reverie.

Glancing around the room, I noticed there were others evidently wishing to express their sympathies, but who'd held back, waiting for a signal to approach. Marguerite had noticed them as well. "Clarice, dear," she said, "Allen and Patricia want to say hello."

I caught Marguerite's eyes. "I'll come back another time when there aren't so many people," I said.

Clarice looked up abruptly, and took note of the rapidly

filling room. It seemed to steel her, to remind her of her duties as a hostess. "Marguerite, do I look terrible?" She ran her hands over her hair, tucking stray strands behind her ears, then straightened her shoulders and her skirt. The three of us rose. She took my hand. "Please come back, Jessica," she implored. "Tomorrow, come tomorrow. I have something of Wayne's for you, just a little memento. I promise I won't be so weepy."

"Why don't I call you later and see if there's a convenient time. Will that be good?"

"Archer takes care of all my appointments," she said. "He's Wayne's assistant." She looked around the room. "Is he here?"

"He was a moment ago, but you sent him to Wayne's apartment to pick out funeral clothes," Marguerite reminded her, "and to the mortuary to make arrangements."

"That's right." Clarice squeezed my hand. She seemed to gather her restraint around her like a mantle. Her eyes, dry now, met mine. "Talk to Archer; he'll have the schedule," she urged. "And you must go to Marguerite and Maurice's party on Wednesday. Don't let this stop you. Wayne would have wanted you to go. He loved parties."

"Clarice, you don't have to think about that right now," the mayor's wife said softly.

"Marguerite, she must see your beautiful garden. It's one of the secret splendors of New Orleans."

"Thank you, dear. I do love my garden," Marguerite said, "although it's difficult to keep at it, especially when some people have no respect for others' hard work."

"Did your neighbor's dog get loose again?" Clarice asked.

"No. This time some teenagers trampled my prized coleus. It must have happened when we were out the other night. I found beer bottles on the ground. What a mess they made. It'll take me some time to clean it up."

"I'm sure it will be even more beautiful than before," Clarice said. She turned to me. "Before you go, you must have some dinner. Alberta has been cooking all morning. She's a famous cook, and she'll be upset if you don't stay and eat. Marguerite, please tell Jessica what the dishes are." She ushered us toward the table, and then turned, in full control, to greet a group of people awaiting her attention.

"She'll be fine now," Marguerite told me as she led me around the table. She handed me a plate, indicated various dishes, and insisted I try Alberta's étouffée, if nothing else. I hadn't planned on eating, but realized that I was actually quite hungry, the melon slice the only food I'd had, and that was hours ago.

The mayor's wife excused herself to speak with more new arrivals, and I waited as two women next to me surveyed the food on the table before spooning up portions of a rice and shrimp dish I planned to sample as well.

"Do you think she'll inherit?" the shorter of the two asked her companion in a low voice.

"I think so. Who else is there? Not that twerp Archer."

"He was with Wayne a long time."

"Maybe. But Clarice is blood after all."

"True, but Archer's been her walker for years. Wayne might've wanted to reward him."

"Walker," I knew, was a term used in the South for men who escort older women to social occasions. Wayne's assistant apparently assisted the family in many ways, though I wondered why Clarice would have needed a walker when her husband was alive.

"She certainly can use the money," the first woman commented. "Steve gambled away everything they had."

"I know. They never finished paying for this addition, and the rest of the house is falling down around her."

"I can't figure out how she managed to get Alberta. She must have promised her a bundle."

"It was probably that lovely cottage in the garden, because she didn't get a penny when he died. His life insurance had lapsed because he never paid the premiums. Besides, you know how persuasive Clarice can be."

"How do you know Clarice's husband didn't leave her any money?"

The other woman tipped her head toward the center of the room, in the direction of Marguerite Amadour. "I heard he was into the mob for a small fortune."

"I hadn't heard that."

The women carried their plates to chairs along the wall. I took some étouffée and a little bit of salad, and tried not to look too obvious as I trailed them around the table, taking a seat two chairs away and pretending to concentrate on my plate.

"How much do you think she'll get?"

"Who knows? Wayne must've had insurance, and it's double indemnity, isn't it, when it's an accidental death. She'll get twice as much."

"Accidental? Do you really believe that? What was he doing in that cemetery?"

"Doesn't matter. Probably up to no good. Even so, he got bitten by a snake. It's not like he had a heart attack."

There was silence as the women chewed their food in contemplation.

"Eleanor Hawes had a snake in her laundry room last week," said one. And they were off onto snakes and other vermin in unexpected locations, the topic of Wayne and Clarice exhausted for the time being. I mulled over their comments, and experienced a wave of sympathy for Clarice, who in addition to being bereaved was the subject of speculation regarding her finances. How humiliating.

"Mrs. Fletcher, I believe you've met my husband." While

I'd been staring at my plate and eavesdropping, I hadn't seen Mayor and Mrs. Amadour approach. I stood.

"I'll take that," Marguerite said, whisking my plate from my hands and heading for the kitchen.

"It's a sad day in New Orleans, Mrs. Fletcher," the mayor said, shaking his head. "Dreadful accident."

"Do you really believe Wayne's death was an accident?" I asked. "I'm not convinced that it was."

The mayor took my elbow and ushered me toward the sliding glass doors. "Let's not talk of this in here," he said.

We stepped outside into the hot air, and paused under a palm tree.

"I know how upset you must be, Mrs. Fletcher. Wayne was a friend to us all."

"I certainly am upset, Mayor Amadour," I said, feeling a different kind of heat rising in my blood. "I'm particularly upset that the police department made such a quick decision on the nature of Wayne's death. I really can't believe it."

"I don't find it unbelievable, Mrs. Fletcher," he said, turning so his back was to the door and blocking my view. "The superintendent laid it all out for me this morning, and the coroner is convinced it was an accident. How else does one get bitten by a snake?"

"I'm not saying it wasn't an accident," I argued. "I'm just questioning why the decision was made so fast. Wayne warned me only days ago never to go into the cemetery alone. Would he really have gone there himself, willingly? At least, it's a question that should be pursued."

"Now, now, Mrs. Fletcher." He took my hand between his and patted it. "I knew Wayne for many years, and he was a bit of an odd duck."

"I don't think . . ." I started to say, but he wouldn't let me speak.

"He was an obsessive man, always going off half cocked on some project or other," he said, squeezing my hand hard and catching my ring in the vise of his grip. "No telling what he would do if he took a mind to it. I believe if you think about that for a little while, you'll come to the same conclusion."

I yanked my hand away, and suppressed the urge to rub my finger where the ring had made a dent in the skin. "I *have* been giving this a lot of thought," I said. "I'm not in the habit of making snap decisions. I just wish the police had the same inclination."

"Watch our press conference this afternoon."

"I intend to," I said.

"Good," he said, smiling. "You'll learn something." He guided me back into the house, adding in a low voice, "I hope you'll resist sharing your opinion on Wayne's death with Clarice. She's suffered enough."

"I would never say anything to hurt her."

"Thank you, Mrs. Fletcher," he said. He walked to where Wayne's sister stood and put his hand on her shoulder. Her arm came around his back, and she leaned into him.

As I watched him, I reviewed in my mind the conversation we'd just had. Was he simply protecting a family friend? Or did he have another motive? I studied the group that had assembled to support Clarice Copely-Cruz in her grief. Apart from Clarice and Marguerite, the only other faces I recognized were those of the mayor and his aide, Philippe Beaudin. While Marguerite ferried soiled plates and glasses into the kitchen, and clean ones back to the table, the mayor continued hugging Clarice to his side and talking animatedly with other guests. Beaudin, on her other side, offered her a plate of food. It was good, I thought; they were distracting her. I remembered how grateful I'd been to my friends, who chattered about commonplace items and cleaned up after the visitors who'd paid condolence calls while I struggled not to focus on the hole in my life where

Frank had been. There would be plenty of time to cry. There always was.

I checked my watch. I wanted to be back at the hotel this afternoon to catch the mayor's press conference on the news channel, but first there was a stop I wanted to make, and I knew I had to leave quickly, or miss it.

The double doors into Wayne's building were locked this time, and, at midafternoon, the sun blazed down. A fly had discovered me, and I swatted at it ineffectively as it dive-bombed my head. The street was deserted, and I held out little hope of catching some tenant on the way in or out. I briefly considered pushing the button for another apartment and hoping someone would buzz me in, but decided that if Archer was still in Wayne's apartment, there would be little difference in his surprise at my appearing at this door, or the one upstairs. I pushed the button.

"Who's there?" a crackly voice came over the intercom.

"It's Jessica Fletcher. I'd like to come up."

The voice was replaced by a high-pitched hum, and I let myself into the building.

Archer was waiting in the hall when I reached the top of the three flights, keeping the apartment door propped open with one foot.

"No one told me you were coming, " he said.

"I know," I replied, drawing a deep breath and hoping my heartbeat would slow after the climb. I was in pretty good shape, but most of my exercise was taken on level ground. "I knew you would be here," I improvised, "and Clarice wanted me to consult you about the arrangements you're making." It wasn't very far from the truth.

Archer grunted and held the door open wide.

"We haven't met," I said. "I'm Jessica Fletcher."

"I know who you are," he replied. "Archer Levinson, Wayne's associate." He held out his hand, and I shook it.

Archer had a pleasant face with no outstanding feature. He was of medium height and had a medium build. I estimated his age to be early thirties. Even with his fashionable attire, and a haircut from the hands of a skilled stylist, he was a man who could be easily overlooked in a crowd.

I noticed that the sun was streaming in through the French doors, but otherwise the apartment was unchanged since my last visit, its simple décor still a serene haven. I felt close to Wayne here, imagining him moving about this room and relaxing in his home.

"Can I get you anything?" Archer asked. "Water? Wine?"

"No, thank you," I replied. "I'm fine." I perched on the edge of the sofa.

He walked to the bookcase, ran his fingers lightly across the top, and stared out the French doors. I saw his Adam's apple bounce up and down as he swallowed, working to contain his emotions.

"How long have you known Wayne?" I asked gently.

"Sixteen years." He turned around and sank down on one of the two straight-back chairs next to the round table.

"You must have been quite young when you first met him."

"I was just a dumb teenager on the streets. My father had kicked me out when he found out I was gay. Wayne took me under his wing, taught me all there was to know about music, writing, how I should dress, behave. He was like a father to me, or older brother. He was all the family I have." He was silent a moment. "And Clarice, of course," he added as an afterthought.

"I'm sorry. He was obviously very important to you, and I know you'll miss him."

He slumped in the chair and stared down at his hands clasped between his knees.

"What do you do for Wayne?" I asked, realizing I was still speaking in the present tense.

"Whatever he wants," he said, rising and pacing to the window. "I type his manuscripts, buy his clothes, order his tickets. Or I did anyway." He circled the room, touching items, pausing to study the dishes on the shelf, the mirror over the false fireplace. He seemed restless, unable to hold still.

"I came here to get clothes for his funeral, but I just can't go into his room, you know?" He pinched the bridge of his nose and shook his head from side to side.

I nodded. "I'll help if you want."

"No, I'll do it. I just need a minute."

"Archer, I was here the other night with the police."

"You were? I didn't know the police were here." Agitated, his eyes examined the room, looking for something amiss. "How did they get in?"

"They had keys," I said. "I assume they took them from Wayne's body."

"What were they looking for? They said his death was an accident." He started to pace again.

"I don't know," I said. "I thought maybe you could tell me. They went through his bedroom." I nodded in its direction.

Archer immediately went there. I followed, more slowly, and stood in the doorway as he inspected the damage.

"Oh my God, look what they did to his clothing," he cried as he drew out the drawers on Wayne's bureau. He crossed the room. "And his closet." He moaned when he saw the mess, knelt down, and angrily began pairing shoes, stamping them down in a row. He picked up a shirt that had fallen off its hanger, and turned to me. "Wayne was always so careful about his clothes. Why did they do this to him?" He slammed the closet door.

"I'm not sure it was the police who did this," I said. "Police are usually very careful not to disturb a place, particularly if they think it might provide evidence."

"Then who?" Archer's gaze fell on the bureau again, and the steam went out of him. "Do you mind if I clean it up? I know he's not here to see it, but it would upset him to know someone had trashed his things."

"Go ahead," I said. "But while you're doing that, please think about what someone could have been looking for. What did Wayne have that someone might have wanted desperately?"

He looked at me sharply. "What do you mean 'desperately'? Do you think his death wasn't an accident?"

I was withholding judgment on the nature of Wayne's death, but I didn't want to tell that to Archer. "I mean desperately enough to search his apartment," I said.

The task of refolding all of Wayne's clothing was comforting to Archer. His breathing slowed, and his movements became less jerky. After a while, he answered my question. "The only thing I can think of were his notes on Little Red's cylinder recordings."

"Where would he keep things like that?" I asked. "There's no desk in this apartment."

"He has an office at Clarice's. That's their home, you know, from when they were kids. It's been in the family for over a hundred years."

"I hadn't realized that," I said. "I thought the house belonged to Clarice and her husband."

"No, Dr. Cruz never made enough to buy a house. Or never kept it long enough. I always thought that was why he married her, so he could have a place to live. The bastard." He raised his eyes to the ceiling. "I know I shouldn't speak ill of the dead. Wayne was always telling me that." He shook out a sweater vest and folded it on the bed, picked up another sweater, folded it, and stacked it on top of the first.

"What kind of doctor was Dr. Cruz?"

"Something to do with the heart," he said, "but he wasn't

a surgeon. I know that. He couldn't have kept his hands from shaking long enough to pick up a scalpel."

"Did his hands really shake?"

"Oh yes," he said derisively. "I was never sure what it was, alcohol, prescription drugs, illegal stuff. I think he tried them all. Whatever it was finally killed him a couple of months ago." He looked up at me. "I assumed you knew. Wayne never told you?"

"About that? No." In fact, Wayne had never discussed any part of his private life with me until he'd mentioned the death threats. I'd never even heard Archer's name before today, and only knew that Wayne's sister was a widow, nothing more than that. But I wasn't about to admit to Archer my limited knowledge. If he thought I was Wayne's confidante, he'd be more forthcoming with information, which was already proving to be the case.

"Did Wayne share with you what he'd found out about the cylinders?"

"You know, that's funny. Actually, he didn't," he said, continuing to fold the last pair of boxers and laying them lovingly in the drawer. He pushed it closed with his hip. "I know he was planning to use what he found out about Little Red in a book, but he never told me what the topic of the book was. I got the feeling it wasn't only about jazz. He used to say he loved mysteries—that's why he was so tickled to be friends with you—and that there was a mystery about the cylinders, whether they really existed, and if they did, where they were, and why they hadn't been found before."

"Archer, would information on the cylinders have been enough to entice Wayne to go to the cemetery at night to meet someone?"

"No way!"

"How can you be so sure?"

"I know him, that's why," he insisted. "Whenever people

he knew came to town, he was always warning them not to go there unless they went with a tour group or other crowd. Not all the cemeteries, just the St. Louis ones."

"How do you think he got there?"

"I don't know. Maybe someone drugged him and left him there so that when he woke up he'd be scared. Only the snake found him first."

"Why would anyone want to do that?"

"As a prank?" Archer raised his eyebrows. "New Orleans is full of pranksters."

"'That would be a pretty mean thing to do."

"Wayne wasn't the most popular guy in town. He had some enemies."

"Who would they be?"

"I'm not going to name any names, but Wayne had a sharp tongue in print. There were people who didn't appreciate that."

"Archer, if you seriously think anyone left Wayne in the cemetery as a practical joke, you really should tell the police."

"I'm not saying that's what happened. All I'm saying is it could have happened that way. I know one thing, Mrs. Fletcher. Wayne would never have gone into that cemetery under his own power. He must have been drugged, or murdered, or God knows what else."

"Murdered? Do you think that's a possibility?"

"Anything's possible. Don't you think?"

"By the way, did you see Wayne the night he died?" I asked.

"No, absolutely not. I thought you were with him most of the night. Why would you ask that?"

"It's not so surprising. You were close. You might have seen each other later that night."

"Well, we didn't," he said coolly. "We had totally different social lives."

"I see." I wasn't sure if I believed him. "Is the cemetery where Wayne was found the same one in which he's going to be entombed?" I asked, changing the subject.

"No, the family crypt is in Lafayette." He pulled open the closet again, remembering the task he'd been assigned. As he sifted through suits looking for the right one, he muttered to himself, "I have to bring his things to the funeral home. Then Clarice wants Wayne to have a jazz funeral. That's another trip. Do you know how long it takes to make those arrangements? When am I supposed to be able to do all this? There's only so many hours in the day."

I listened as Archer griped about his duties, and wondered whether he was as attached to Wayne as he said he was. Where had he been when Wayne was dying in the cemetery? What did he know about the recordings Wayne had been seeking? What was his relationship to Clarice? How did they both know I'd been with Wayne the night he died? There were too many questions, and I recognized my compulsive need to find answers. If there's a gene for inquisitiveness, I've got it. Seth always scolds me about my curiosity, warning me that it will get me into trouble. And I have to admit that it has at times, although fortunately I've always been able to get out of tight spots in which I've found myself. I'd been looking for an excuse to stop at the funeral home, and Archer was giving it to me.

"Let me help," I said pleasantly. "You've got so much to do. I'll go to the funeral home and bring them whatever clothing you pick out for Wayne." I held my breath, hoping he'd take me up on the offer. The funeral home might hold some of those answers I sought. Wayne was presumed to have died from snakebite, but were there any other marks on his body, marks that got overlooked when the cause of death was so obvious? I doubted they'd let me see Wayne's body, but perhaps I could talk to the undertaker, learn something that would shed light on why Wayne was found, in death, in a place that troubled him in life, a place he'd cautioned his friends about visiting.

"Would you really do that?" Archer asked. "That would save me so much time." His face lit up, and I let out the breath I'd been holding.

"Of course," I said. "I'd be happy to help out."

"That's fabulous. Tomorrow or Tuesday, either day is fine. I'll get the address for you."

He hummed his satisfaction, opening drawers and retrieving items he'd put away not ten minutes ago. He laid socks, shorts, bow tie, and handkerchief on the bed.

"You said Clarice wants a jazz funeral for Wayne," I continued. "Is that where the musicians walk in front of the casket on the way to the cemetery?"

"That's right," he replied, hanging up a suit and shirt on the closet door, and kneeling down to pick out shoes. "They used to play sad songs on the way into the cemetery and happy songs on the way out," he explained. "But these days, the bands play upbeat songs pretty much the whole time."

"I thought those funerals were only for musicians."

"They used to be, but then they extended the definition to anyone associated with music. Of course, Wayne qualifies." He opened the top drawer of the bureau, and replaced the bowtie that had been on the bed, selecting another to go with the suit. "However," he continued, "money can accomplish anything, so if you want a jazz funeral and have the dough, you can have it, even if the only thing you know about music is how to turn on the radio."

We carefully packed Wayne's "going-away outfit," as Archer termed it, in a garment bag he'd found on a shelf in the closet. We tucked shorts, socks, and other accessories in the bag's pockets. Archer wrote down instructions on where to find the funeral home, and checked his calendar for a good time for me to visit with Clarice. We parted, knowing we'd meet again at the funeral. I would have liked some time alone in the apartment to examine more of Wayne's things, but obviously it wasn't going to happen today. Although I was satisfied with the information I'd learned, there were still so many nagging questions. But as I carried Wayne's suit down three flights of stairs, I was convinced I had at least one answer. My fastidious friend, Wayne Copely, had not died an accidental death.

Chapter Eleven

"Mayor Amadour," the reporter shouted, his voice heard above those of his colleagues, "is Copely's death related to the investigation of Elijah Williams's murder?"

The press conference was being carried live on a local news channel. I sat on the bed in my hotel room, focused on the TV screen. Philippe Beaudin stood behind and to one side of the mayor, who'd made an opening statement. Also in the camera's view were New Orleans Police Superintendent Jimmy Johnson and another man I didn't recognize.

"I believe Superintendent Johnson has the answer to that question," Amadour said smoothly, stepping aside from the microphone to allow his police chief to address the press.

Deaf to the barrage of questions aimed at him, Johnson laid a sheaf of papers on the podium, put on a pair of half glasses, and gripped the edges of the wooden top as he read a prepared statement. "New Orleans resident Wayne Copely, fifty-one years of age, died Friday in St. Louis Cemetery Number One," he said in a deep voice. "According to the medical examiner's office, Mr. Copely's death resulted from a rattlesnake bite. We regret Mr. Copely disregarded public warnings not to visit the area alone, and was on the grounds when the cemetery was officially closed."

"Why did he go there?" a reporter shouted.

Johnson peered over the top of his glasses. "We're not sure," he said, his response setting off another volley of questions. He continued reading, speaking loudly to be heard over the press until the roar of voices settled down. "During the time he was in the cemetery, Mr. Copely was bitten and subsequently died from snakebite. Dr. Jacob Renshaw of the medical examiner's office has prepared this chart." A drawing of a hand, and lines representing the circulatory system, filled the screen. "The bite that Mr. Copely sustained was right here between the thumb and forefinger of his right hand, piercing the main artery, and causing the venom to directly enter the bloodstream. Death would have occurred relatively quickly, giving him no time to seek help."

Another spate of questions assaulted the superintendent.

"NOPD's investigation found no connection between Wayne Copely and Elijah Williams, whose body was found in the same location in the cemetery last month. There is no record of the two men ever having met, nor is there any indication that they corresponded in any way. Our investigation into Mr. Williams's death is ongoing."

I pondered the superintendent's confident statement. Had a police investigation actually been conducted? The police hadn't taken very much time to probe Wayne's death before concluding that it was an accident. The speed of their decision made me uneasy. It wasn't as if they routinely acted so quickly. They'd been keeping the Elijah Williams case open for a month. Something about that murder flickered at the edge of my memory. I concentrated on the television again, to see if the press corps had the same misgivings.

"Superintendent?" several reporters called out at the same time. "What about the voodoo connection linking both deaths?" "What is the city doing about snakes in the cemetery?" "Where was the NOPD unit that's supposed to be patrolling the cemetery?"

Johnson held up a hand to quiet them down. Ignoring the stream of questions, he continued his prepared remarks.

"NOPD called in Mr. Robert Pinto to set traps in the cemetery. To date, six snakes have been caught, including . . ." He picked up a piece of paper and squinted at it. "A Louisiana milksnake, a kingsnake, a black ratsnake, two eastern garter snakes, and a canebrake rattlesnake. Only the rattlesnake is poisonous, and we believe that to be the type of snake involved in Mr. Copely's death.

"We've invited a herpetologist, Dr. Steven Caplan, a visiting professor at Tulane, to give you information about snakes. He is a worldwide authority on reptiles, and can answer all your questions." Johnson's exit was accompanied by more shouted questions, but he stepped quickly from the podium. A young man, with a shock of black hair, and wearing rimless eyeglasses and a photojournalist's vest, took his place.

"Good afternoon," he said, his amplified voice carrying above the grumbles of the reporters. "I've handed around a sheet which contains some information on species of snakes native to Louisiana. There's also some brief biographical material on me. I'm Dr. Steven Caplan. I'd like to explain my findings and then answer any questions you may have."

A close-up of Dr. Caplan's face filled the screen as he described the myriad snakes resident in the city and its surroundings. "The reptile population has been particularly hard hit during the drought this spring," he said. "The lack of rainfall, and thus less standing water, means that the snakes' usual prey have curbed their reproduction. With fewer aquatic animals like toads and frogs that form the basis of their diets, many reptiles in the region tend to leave their accustomed habitat to search for food. In addition, recent construction in the Treme neighborhood has disturbed the habitat of some rodents. The combination of these two factors has caused an increase in the numbers of snakes in the cemetery, and around the city for that matter."

There were a dozen questions simultaneously aimed at Caplan. "I'm sorry, I didn't catch that?" he said.

A reporter in the back raised her voice. "What was the snake that bit Copely?"

"We believe Mr. Copely was the victim of a canebrake rattlesnake bite." He spelled the name of the snake for the reporters. "Canebrakes are especially dangerous because they don't always rattle to let you know of their presence. It's probable that Mr. Copely stepped near the snake, without even knowing it was there."

"How big was the snake?"

"The one Mr. Pinto trapped was a six-footer; that's not uncommon," said Caplan. There was a nervous rumble of voices as the press corps pictured the killer snake. "Of course, I can't say with certainty that that's the snake that bit Mr. Copely."

"How long could he have lived with a rattlesnake bite?"

"These snakes are particularly venomous," he replied. "Dr. Renshaw estimated that because the venom went directly into Mr. Copely's bloodstream, he probably was dead within minutes. However, in general, a man his height and weight, bitten on the hand, could have lived as long as three hours or more. You can see why getting a snakebite victim to the hospital is urgent."

The reporters aimed another torrent of questions at him. Instead of replying, he flicked a switch at the podium and said, "I'd like you to take a look at these, because the common assumption—that to treat a snakebite you have to lance the wound and suck out the poison—is exactly the wrong thing to do." Behind him, a list of first-aid measures were projected on a screen.

- **Immediately call for help in getting victim to the hospital.**
- **Remove victim from vicinity of snake to prevent additional bites.**

- Note appearance of snake to describe to medical personnel later.
- Have patient lie down and keep as calm as possible.
- Remove watches, rings, or any confining jewelry.
- Do NOT incise the wound and attempt to suck out venom.
- Do NOT use a tourniquet, ice, electric shock, or suction.
- Do NOT give the victim anything to eat or drink.
- Do NOT administer an antivenin unless advised to do so by a physician.

Several reporters called out questions, until Dr. Caplan called on one of them. "How often are people bitten by rattlesnakes?"

"Rattlesnakes are responsible for two-thirds of all reptile bites in the United States, and there were more than seven thousand such bites reported last year."

"Were they all fatal?"

"Not at all," Dr. Caplan responded. "You're more likely to die from a dog bite or getting hit by lightning. Only six or seven people die from rattlesnake bites each year."

"Sir, I've always heard you should use a tourniquet. Why do you recommend against it?"

"Stopping blood circulation above the wound simply increases the blood pressure to the limb with the venom, forcing the poison through the blood vessels and increasing the chances of losing that limb."

Another reporter shouted from the back of the room, "Dr. Caplan, why nothing to drink or eat?"

"Eating and drinking increase the heart rate. The key is to keep the victim's blood pressure and pulse as low as possible so as not to allow the venom to spread quickly. The last thing you want a snakebite victim to do is get up and start running."

As the herpetologist answered questions, the camera

pulled back, revealing the lone figure of Dr. Caplan at the podium. The mayor, his assistant, and the police superintendent were gone. The camera slowly panned around the room, across the rows of reporters, most of whom were furiously taking notes, and along the bank of cameras and technicians. Leaning negligently against one wall, watching the proceedings with a bored look, was the familiar face of Julian Broadbent.

I picked up the telephone and punched in the number for Doris's room. There was no answer. Then I remembered that when Wayne had been apologizing for not including her in the dinner invitation at Clarice's, she'd said she had previous plans for Sunday.

I pulled open the drawer of the nightstand looking for a New Orleans telephone directory, but found only my own book, the one I'd given Wayne. I had stored it in the drawer when I'd emptied my bag last night. Placing it on the nightstand, I went to the closet. Thankfully, a telephone book was on the shelf, but I was disappointed to find no Broadbents listed in New Orleans. Of course, he could make his home in one of the city's suburbs, but Julian had struck me as a man who'd live in the center of activity. I dialed Information for New Orleans: "We're sorry. The telephone number you requested is unpublished," a recorded voice informed me. I hung up, returned the directory to the closet, and noticed that commercials had replaced the press conference on the television. I pushed a button on the remote and the TV screen went black.

Murder in a Minor Key. The lamp on the nightstand illuminated my latest work. I stared at the cover illustration, admiring the way the artist had taken a colorful picture of New Orleans and added drops of blood, as if the victim in my story had bled onto the photograph. I sighed and lifted the cover, intending to reread my inscription to Wayne. A piece of white paper clung to the title page for a second, and then drifted to the floor. I bent down and picked it up. I remembered putting it in the book. It was the blank top sheet I'd torn from the pad next to Wayne's telephone. I held it up in front of the lampshade. Only a watermark shone through. But when I angled the paper under the light, I could make out slight indentations. I found a pencil, laid the paper down and lightly ran the side of the lead across its surface.

The letters emerged from the black, rising to the surface like a body from the depths of the sea. ELIJAH.

Drawing a card from my shoulder bag, I picked up the phone again and dialed.

"Charlie?"

"Jessica, how are you doing?"

"'I've thought of something you *can* do for me, Charlie. Is it too late to add a short item to your newspaper column for tomorrow?"

Chapter Twelve

"I know it's late, but by any chance, do you still have a copy of today's *Times-Picayune*?"

I heard a clunk as the concierge put down the phone, and then the rustle of paper before he picked it up again.

"I have a slightly used one, Mrs. Fletcher. It's the only newspaper I have, but you're welcome to it. I hope you don't mind that it's already been read."

"I don't mind at all," I said, relieved. "Would you please be so good as to have it delivered to my room."

"With pleasure, ma'am. I'll have a bellman bring it right over."

I had remembered why the name "Elijah" stirred something in my mind during the press conference. At Friday's Jazz Fest, the trumpet player, Blind Jack, had asked Wayne if he'd heard about Elijah, and Wayne had hushed him up. Of course, it was possible they weren't talking about the man who was murdered. The name "Elijah" is not that unusual, and the police were convinced—so they said—that there was no connection between Wayne and Elijah Williams. But since the bodies of both men had occupied the same seat in death, I suspected that, with a little work, a connection could be found. I wanted to ask Blind Jack if he knew what it might be, and whether he knew whom Wayne was supposed to meet the night he died. The blind trumpet player had said he was playing in a club; its name should be listed somewhere in Sunday's paper.

There was a sharp rap on my door, and I peered through the peephole. Surprised, I opened the door to find Philippe Beaudin holding my newspaper.

"You don't look like a bellman to me," I said with a smile.

"I intercepted him," he said, returning my smile. "I hope that's all right. I was coming to see you anyway."

"You were?"

"Yes." His face took on a serious expression. "I missed you at Mrs. Cruz's house. You were there, and then you were gone."

"I had another appointment," I explained, "but I plan to visit her again tomorrow."

"She'll appreciate that. This is a rough time for her, and for you, too, I imagine. I'm sorry for the loss of your friend."

"It's considerate of you to think of me, but you didn't make a special trip over here just to express your condolences."

"Not precisely."

"Why did you wish to talk with me?"

"I have a message from the mayor, but I'd rather not discuss it here, standing in the hall."

"We can go to the lobby if you like, but let me put that away first." I held out my hands.

"I have a better idea," he said, relinquishing the newspaper. "Can I buy you a drink in the lounge? I would offer you dinner but I have to meet Maurice in an hour."

"That's very nice of you," I said, juggling sections of the paper that were about to fall out, "but I'm afraid I've got so much to do right now. Perhaps another time?" I was eager to read through the news to see what had been written about Wayne's death. I also planned to look up where Blind Jack was playing. I wanted to speak with him and find out if he knew who Wayne had intended to meet Friday night, and if he'd been asked the same question by Detective Steppe.

"I won't keep you long. Surely you've got time for one drink."

"Can't you just give me the message?"

"I see this looks like a bad time for you," he said, a note of contrition in his voice. "I'm sorry for the interruption. Why don't I come back tomorrow morning. We can have coffee together. Would that be more convenient?"

"Actually, tomorrow might be worse," I said. If I went to see Blind Jack, it could end up being a late night. Jazz performers often didn't go on till late, and if I had to wait for him to finish two sets, it could be 1 or 2 A.M. before I got to speak with him. It would be better to sit down with Beaudin now, and listen to what he wanted to tell me. And truth to say, I was curious to know why he'd come to my hotel. A message from the mayor could easily have been conveyed on the phone, or a note dropped off with the reception desk.

"Well, I suppose I can manage one drink," I said. "Can you give me five minutes? You go ahead. I'll meet you there."

"Thank you. I promise it'll be a quick one." He checked his watch, gave me a sharp nod, and disappeared down the hall.

I closed the door and put the newspaper on the dresser. I freshened up, and pulled a light cardigan sweater from a drawer; the hotel's air conditioning was sometimes too cool for comfort. I glanced around the room, pocketed my key, switched off the overhead light, and went to meet the mayor's aide.

Beaudin had taken a table in the corner. The room was dark, small halogen lights illuminating only the center of each table, on which sat a bowl of salted nuts and a small plastic stand advertising the specialty drinks of the evening. Beaudin was already nursing a glass filled to the brim with ice cubes and a golden-brown liquor. He stood when I approached.

"Thank you for joining me." His smile was warm.

"Thank you for inviting me." We sat down, and I pulled the cardigan around my shoulders. The air was frigid.

"Are you too cold? I can ask them to turn up the temperature."

"There's no need," I said. "That's why I brought the sweater. I'm sure as the room fills with people, it will warm up." I picked up the plastic stand. The featured drink was the Hurricane, a New Orleans favorite, a concoction of rum and passion fruit and lime juice, too strong for my empty stomach. I ordered a glass of seltzer with lime.

Now that he had my attention, Beaudin seemed in no hurry to explain his presence. He asked about my book. "How's *Murder in a Minor Key* doing?"

"As far as I can tell, it's doing very well," I said. "This is the last stop on my promotion tour, and the books have been selling out wherever I've gone. I'll find out more when I get home and speak with my publisher."

"It takes place here, doesn't it? Sorry, but I haven't read it—yet."

"Yes. I used jazz as the theme. Wayne was a great help to me."

"New Orleans has a great literary heritage, you know. It's been the setting for a lot of famous stories, and many writers have worked here. Anne Rice, of course. She's our most famous citizen right now. But also William Faulkner, Jack Kerouac, F. Scott Fitzgerald, Truman Capote, Tennessee Williams. And going back some, Mark Twain and O. Henry. I'm sure I'm leaving out some well-known names."

"The city has a unique atmosphere," I said. "That's always appealing to writers. I know it was to me."

"We try to take advantage of that. We host a writers' con-

ference every September, and a literary festival in March.
Perhaps you'll come back for one of them."

"Perhaps."

Beaudin continued his mostly one-sided conversation.
He was comfortable talking, an articulate, ambitious young
man. I'd seen people like him before, making their careers
by advancing the fortunes of those who possessed more
charisma. Riding their coattails, it used to be called. But
today, political promotion was a specialty all by itself. And
Beaudin looked tailor-made for the part. I gauged him to be
in his forties. He was handsome, intelligent, able to take the
measure of a crowd and advise his boss what themes to es-
pouse at what time. I wondered what had drawn him to such
a self-effacing career. Was it the competition that stirred his
blood? Or was I being too cynical? He was now telling me
all about New Orleans, about how it was a mecca for artists
of every kind, not just musicians and writers, but also actors,
painters, sculptors, and dancers. He seemed to be evading
the one topic that sat between us like a hulking, uninvited
guest.

". . . If you're in New Orleans another week, I'd be delighted to take you there," he said, referring to a performance by the Southern Repertory Theatre that had
enthralled the critics. "It's playing not too far from here. The
theater is in Canal Place, a shopping complex that's too elegant to call it a mall. If you haven't been there yet, you
should go. It puts other malls to shame. There's so much to
see in the city. I'd be happy to make other recommendations."

"I'm not sure how much longer I'll be in town," I said.
"I'll probably return home after Wayne's funeral." If he
wasn't going to raise the subject of Wayne's death, I would.

"Of course. I didn't mean to be insensitive. When will the
funeral be?" he asked. "Have you heard?"

"I don't think it's been decided yet," I replied. "I understand Clarice wants Wayne to have a jazz funeral, and apparently that takes some time to arrange."

"If they have a specific brass band in mind, it might have to be worked around their schedule," he said. "I'm sure Archer is on top of that. I assume you've met him."

"Yes, I have."

"I didn't see him at Mrs. Cruz's house today. Was he there?"

"I believe so. At one time, anyway."

"Have you met other friends of Wayne's?"

I had the feeling I was being delicately grilled. "Only the musicians in the press tent at Jazz Fest," I replied, pausing for a beat. "And Julian Broadbent."

"Julian. Of course," he said. "He was at the festival with you." He stared down at his half-full glass and used his fingertips to twirl it in slow circles. "I hadn't realized he and Wayne were friends." His eyes met mine. "I seem to recall they were at each other's throats the other day at Gable's book program. You were there."

"Artistic temperaments, that's all," I said. "It was forgotten pretty quickly." I was pressing to see if he would buy the idea of Wayne and Julian being friends. He seemed uncomfortable with the notion, but why? I watched a muscle pulsate on the side of his jaw, and wondered when he would get to the purpose of his coming to see me. I took a sip of my drink.

"The mayor is concerned about you," he said finally.

"Why?"

"Well . . ." He hesitated, weighing how to put his words politically. "With Wayne gone, you have no one to escort you. The mayor wants to be sure you're comfortable—and safe."

"Is he offering you up for the job of my escort?" I asked, amused. "Is that what you're trying to tell me?"

"No, of course not." He gave me a boyish look—he must

be very popular with the ladies, I thought—and cocked his head. "Maurice merely wants to offer you the use of one of his cars and a driver to take you wherever you want to go. He feels it's the least he can do."

"What a thoughtful gesture," I said. "But there's no need. I'm perfectly capable of looking after myself. I've been doing it for years."

"Maurice is a Southern gentleman of the old school," he said. "He feels it's his duty to make sure that ladies are taken care of."

"I did get that impression when I saw him today. He was very protective of Mrs. Cruz."

"He may act a bit old-fashioned," he said, "but he's got a good heart."

"Gentlemanly behavior never goes out of style," I said, wondering how to turn down this generous offer without offending Beaudin—or the mayor.

"He's definitely a gentleman, Mrs. Fletcher. He'll be so pleased you've agreed. I've arranged for the car to be outside the hotel whenever you need it." He looked at his watch. "In fact, it should be there as we speak."

"But I don't need it. Really, I appreciate this offer, but it's totally unnecessary."

"There are so many tourists in the city right now. He doesn't want you to have to worry about transportation around town."

"That hasn't been a problem at all," I replied. "I'm able to walk most places I want to get to, and I can just ask the hotel to call for a taxi for anywhere out of my range."

Beaudin suppressed a laugh. "If they've come when you wanted them, you've been lucky so far," he said, his voice full of mirth. "The Big Easy didn't get its name for nothing. We like to take life as it comes. Slowly. Taxi drivers down here are very laid back. I don't think any of them even wears a watch. This city is never in a hurry. It can drive Northerners crazy when they visit. You must be a patient lady if you haven't noticed."

"I guess I have been lucky, and I would say I'm fairly patient," I said. "Please thank Mayor Amadour, but . . ."

He chuckled. "You would be helping me, too, you know."

"What do you mean?"

"You're a well-known author. The mayor wants me to make sure you see the best of the city, since you've had such an unfortunate experience so far."

"Unfortunate? Yes, that's certainly true."

"You see?" He sighed. "This is purely good public relations, putting our best foot forward for a celebrity. You've probably had drivers in many cities you've visited."

"I have, indeed, but they were never supplied by City Hall. My publisher usually provides them."

"New Orleans has a reputation for generosity and hospitality, and we need to keep that up." He reached into his pocket and withdrew a card. "This has the number of the driver's cell phone. Just call him whenever you need to go anywhere, and he'll be at your door in minutes." He handed me the card and smiled broadly when I tucked it in a pocket.

I'd decided it wasn't worth continuing to argue with a man who'd made up his mind. I simply wouldn't call for the car, and that would be that.

Beaudin paid for our drinks, apologized for keeping me from dinner, and left with effusive compliments on how honored New Orleans was to have me as a visitor, and how he hoped I enjoyed my remaining time in the city.

Puzzled as to why the mayor, or at least his assistant, was so keen on ferrying me around, I made my way back to my room, past a housekeeping cart, and down the long corridor. I slid the key in the lock, and pushed open the door. A brisk breeze snatched at my hair and slammed the door behind me, jarring me out of my reverie. My bed had been turned down, a piece of chocolate left on the pillow, and the spread neatly folded on a rack. I saw with consternation that the French doors had been left open, and the warm humid air was heating up the room. That's careless, I thought, pulling the doors shut and locking them. Though the doors faced an interior courtyard, I was conscious of security, and kept them locked even when I was in the room. I looked around and saw that nothing was amiss. I went to the nightstand and opened the cover of my book. The note from Wayne's pad was where I'd left it. The newspaper was as I'd placed it on the dresser. My drawers were closed. I opened one. My clothes were still as I'd put them away, all neatly folded.

I'll have a private word about the doors with the house-keeper in the morning, I thought, picking up the *Times-Picayune* and settling in the armchair. I slipped on my glasses, kicked off my shoes, put my feet up on the ottoman, and sifted through the sections of the paper till I found the one I wanted. I dropped the rest of the paper on the floor next to my chair and opened the special report on Jazz Fest. It was filled with colorful photos from the first two days—there was one of Oliver Jones—and on pages four and five, a calendar of events for both the coming week and following weekend. I scanned the columns looking for Blind Jack's name and found it under Monday at Café Brasilia. I checked Sunday's listings, too, but he was not scheduled to play. I was grateful. I'd not slept well last night, and the prospect of going out to a nightclub was not attractive. I would have a pleasant, easy room-service dinner, and get to bed early.

A slight rustling sound seized my attention, and caused my heart to skip a beat. I looked over the arm of the chair and saw that one section of the newspaper had slid off the others in the pile. I laughed in relief, chiding myself for being so skittish. Finding the open doors must have jump-started my imagination. I padded over to the telephone and ordered a Caesar salad with blackened chicken, and a cup of herb tea. Covering a yawn, I sank back in the chair and read through the rest of the paper.

Wayne's demise was a page-one story. The reporter noted the mystery surrounding his presence at Marie Laveau's tomb, the rarity of death by snakebite, and the concern of city fathers that the continuing drought would draw more reptilian intruders into the urban environment. There was no mention of the gris-gris, and only a passing reference to Elijah Williams and his unsolved murder. The superintendent of police was quoted as saying the medical examiner had ruled the death an accident, and the mayor decried the "tragedy of losing such a star in the cultural firmament" of the city. Next to the article was a long obituary on Wayne, citing his family's deep roots in New Orleans, and his illustrious career as a critic and authority on jazz and its origin as New Orleans's unique musical art form.

Twenty minutes later, my dinner was wheeled in on a linen-covered table, and set in front of a straight chair. I signed for the meal, locked the door after the waiter, gathered the sections of the newspaper and replaced them on the dresser, turned on the television set, and sat down to eat. I'd had enough of the news, so I flipped around the channels till I found an old movie, *Gaslight* with Ingrid Bergman, Charles Boyer, and Joseph Cotten. I'd seen the suspenseful drama before, but it was still entertaining to watch Boyer as the villainous husband trying to convince his innocent young wife that she was a victim of insanity. Despite the gripping story, I found myself struggling to stay awake until a soft noise in the corner of the room intruded on my consciousness. I picked up the remote, turned off the television, and sat rigidly, my ears straining to hear it again. Nothing.

This is ridiculous, I thought, and pushed the table away. I tiptoed to the corner and peered around the back of the armchair. Nothing there. I picked up my shoes and put them on. With my knee, I nudged the ottoman; it rolled toward the wall, leaving faint tracks on the carpet. I pulled aside the curtains on the French doors. It was dark out now, but the lamp in my room cast a pale light on the empty stones outside. I drew the curtains again, and studied the armchair. It had a skirt. I wasn't happy with the idea of kneeling down and lifting it up, and perhaps coming face to face with a mouse—although, truth to tell, over the years, I'd had my share of little visitors move in at home in Cabot Cove when the weather got cold. Come to think of it, maybe Seth's offer of a kitten wasn't such a bad idea.

Irritated, but resigned to the possibility of a mouse, I wheeled my dinner table into the hall, and positioned it next to my door. The hallway was deserted now. I carefully locked the door, and rechecked the French doors. My earlier weariness had flown. I was determined to get it back and get a good night's sleep. I knew if I didn't, I would be exhausted tomorrow. I got ready for bed, but left my shoes on. I brushed my hair and my teeth, washed my hands and face, slathered a bit of cream on my skin, kicked off my shoes, and climbed into bed. Sleep came quickly.

Sometime later—I didn't know how long it had been since I'd turned out the light—I found myself wide awake and wondering why. My eyes barely open, I took inventory of what might have awakened me. The room was dark. Only a faint light from the other side of the courtyard cast a weak glow against the curtains. All was quiet, the thunder of my own heart audible only to me. I took a shallow breath, unwilling to move the air with my respiration. There was another presence here. I could sense it. The blood hummed in my veins. The skin on my arms, neck, and scalp tightened. I felt a stirring of the bedcovers near my feet. I sat up swiftly and fumbled for the switch on the lamp. The bright light had me blinking, but I wasn't the only one. Curled up at the bottom of my bed, its head rearing back, tongue flicking in and out, was a red-and-black snake.

Chapter Thirteen

"It's only a little milk snake, Mrs. Fletcher."

The hotel's night-duty engineer was holding a burlap bag that contained my earlier bed partner. "They're pretty common, and totally harmless, although I'm sure it gave you quite a start."

"You're a master of understatement, Mr. Gonzales."

"It was probably just looking for some food or water. We got a drought on now. Lots of these little guys out of their usual habitat." He bounced the bag up and down a few times.

"So I've heard."

"You can kind of feel sorry for them." He looked sideways at me.

"Perhaps another time," I replied.

"Well, we got it now." He grinned. "You're safe."

A small crowd had assembled in my room: Mr. Gonzales; Duncan Frey, the hotel's overnight manager; Police Officer Monica Macdonald; and Mrs. Penta, head of housekeeping.

"I apologize on behalf of the hotel, Mrs. Fletcher," Mr. Frey said, gripping his hands together. "We'll have an exterminator out here tomorrow to go over the courtyard. But you can rest easy now. There's nothing else in here, I promise you. Al and I looked everywhere, under the bed, behind the dresser, under the chair, in the closet. We checked all the possible hiding places. I even looked in the toilet tank."

"That's right," echoed Gonzales as he wound a cord around the top of the burlap bag. "Room's absolutely clean."

"Thank you, gentlemen," I said. "I appreciate your thoroughness."

Mrs. Penta cleared her throat. "Mrs. Fletcher, I want to assure you that I will talk with Maria tomorrow, but I don't believe it was the housekeeper who left your doors open." She handed me a sheet of paper. On it was a long, numbered checklist. My room number was at the top, and tick marks had been made next to each of the numbered lines, including the one that said, "Doors and windows closed and locked?" "You may question her yourself if that would make you more comfortable."

"That won't be necessary, Mrs. Penta," I said, handing her back the paper. "I know the door was closed when I left the room this evening."

"Yes, but was it locked?" asked Officer Macdonald. "If you forgot to lock it, the wind could have blown it open, or someone could have opened it from the courtyard."

"Our doors require a key to open them from the outside," the night manager inserted, as Officer Macdonald lifted her clipboard to make a note.

"These kinds of doors are fairly easy to open," she said mildly.

Mr. Frey became visibly upset at that suggestion. "Officer, the Royal has the best-quality locks on its doors."

Macdonald ignored him. "But there's no sign of a break-in," she said, talking to me.

"You checked?" I asked.

"Yes, ma'am. Nothing is broken. There are a few scratches around the lock, but that's not unusual. Are you missing anything?"

"Not that I'm aware of."

"When you came in, did you notice anything different? Did it look like anyone had gone through your things?"

"No. The housekeeper had turned down the bed. Everything else seemed to be as I'd left it—with the exception of the doors."

Macdonald shrugged. "Locking doors is easy to forget."

"I realize that," I said, "but I make sure it's locked every night, and I don't believe I opened it in the morning before I left, or in the afternoon when I returned."

"But are you a hundred percent sure?" The walkie-talkie on her belt crackled to life, and a deep voice filled the room: "We have a possible B-and-E on Iberville." Macdonald shoved her clipboard in front of me and thrust a pen in my hand. "Mrs. Fletcher, would you please sign the report now? I'm sorry to rush you, but I have to go."

I scribbled my name. Macdonald handed me a copy of the report and was gone. One by one, the others excused themselves, and after assuring them I was fine, and no, I didn't want a cup of tea or a glass of brandy, I closed the door and fastened the chain.

The room wore signs of this latest visitation, the furniture slightly askew where Mr. Gonzales and Mr. Frey had moved it out from the wall to check for more snakes. The armchair and ottoman had been shoved to one side, and the drapes in front of the French doors were drawn back to allow for an examination of the locks.

I walked across the room and unlocked the doors. The night air was cool and moist. I stepped out onto the stone walkway. The moon was half hidden by clouds, and the light from my room provided poor illumination for seeing much of anything other than shadows. To my left was a large bush. I couldn't tell if any of its branches had been bent or broken. I'll check again in the morning, I promised myself. I drew a deep breath and listened to the night, half expecting to detect a slithery noise to indicate the presence of other reptiles.

The sighing wind rustled the branches of the bush, and muffled music could be heard in the distance, but no other sound reached me.

I returned to the room, locked the doors, and drew the drapes. I pulled the chair and ottoman into place and circled the bed, smoothing the dust ruffle down where it had been pulled up to accommodate the search for snakes. Satisfied that my quarters were once again as they should be, I got back in bed and turned off the light, my pulse quiet but my mind still racing.

I've lived in or near small towns my entire life, and been exposed to wild creatures before, although there aren't any venomous snakes in Maine. I remember Seth telling me once that Maine was one of only three states without them, the others being Hawaii and Alaska. I know we've got little garden snakes, of course, but I can't recall ever actually seeing one. Moose, well that's another story. They wander in from the woods every now and then. Wildlife is a part of country living. I didn't expect it to be part of urban living, too. In all my travels to cities around the world, I'd never met up with a snake.

Yet, here I was in a major American city, where a friend had been killed by a snake, and I'd awakened to find one in bed with me. Coincidence? I was hard pressed to think so. I wondered if my midnight guest was in any way related to my earlier visitor. Why had it been so important for Philippe Beaudin to invite me for a drink? Had he been trying to lure me away from my room, so someone else could jimmy open the doors and leave me a reminder of Wayne's death? Still, if this was a warning, what did it mean? Was someone trying to scare me away, send me running home? There had been no note, no message on my phone, nothing to indicate this snake was associated with the other. The mayor had been the only one to whom I'd voiced my doubts about the circumstances of Wayne's death. And I hadn't even begun to ask about the cylinders Wayne had been seeking. But I decided it was time to get started, time to see who'd get upset if I poked a stick into a few snake holes.

Chapter Fourteen

"I'm sorry about your friend." The waitress's eyes were full of sympathy.

"Thank you," I said. "How did you know?" I folded the *Times-Picayune* I'd been reading and set it on the breakfast table.

"Recognized his picture in the paper," she said, filling my coffee cup and sliding a plate of beignets in front of me.

"I didn't order these," I said, looking up.

"I know," she said. "They're my treat. He was so darling, making such a fuss about them the other day. I figured he would have wanted you to have them, kind of in remembrance." Suddenly embarrassed by her own presumption, she added, "I'll be right back with milk for your coffee," and hurried away before I could say more.

I was having a late breakfast. Following the events of the previous evening, I'd tried to sleep, but it was not to be. After making a knot of the bedcovers, I'd turned on the light and retrieved the story given to me by David Stewart, the student who'd attended Charlie's Book Club Breakfast. I'd intended it to be airplane reading on the trip home, but I needed some distraction, and didn't want to disturb my neighbors with the sound of television. David's story was clever, about a ventriloquist whose skill at disguising his voice ensnares his victim, but whose conceit about his unique talent causes his downfall. His writing showed a lot of promise, I was pleased to see, simply needing a better ear for dialogue, which I was sure he'd develop as he continued to write.

By 3 A.M., my eyelids were drooping, and I turned off the light again. Doris woke me at seven. She'd learned of Wayne's death last night when she returned to the hotel after a day of taping, and wanted desperately to talk. Between Wayne, and my incident with the snake, we'd stayed on the phone for a long time. I'd tried to get back to sleep after hanging up, but other calls interrupted my rest, and at ten, I'd finally given up and gotten up.

Strangely, I wasn't tired. I now had a purpose, to find out what really happened to my friend and musical mentor. Whom was he meeting the night he died? Had he been bitten during some ceremony? Had he even been in the cemetery, or had someone brought him there after he died? Who'd been leaving him death threats? Did they have to do with Little Red? Questions crowded my mind. There was so much to find out, and to do. I reached into my bag for my appointment book. Today's book signing was at noon. Doris would be there as well because her signing was scheduled right before mine. Maybe I could talk her into waiting till my session was over so we could have a late lunch. I had a few questions for her, too.

The waitress returned with a pitcher of steamed milk. "I read about you in Charlie Gable's column this morning," she said, pouring the milk into my coffee. "That's so sweet, what you're doing, continuing the search for the recordings in your friend's memory."

"I hope I'm successful."

"If they're around, you'll find them."

"How can you tell that?"

"You look like a determined lady, and a hard worker."

I smiled. "I am that, but hard work and determination don't always yield success."

"Then you'll have to have a bit of luck, too," she said, placing a tiny orange pouch next to my cup. "A friend of mine has a shop not too far from here. She makes good-luck charms. This one has been very lucky for me. I want you to have it."

"Do you really believe in good-luck charms?" I asked.

"I believe in having all things working for you," she said. "It can't hurt, right?"

"I suppose so," I replied, picking up the miniature orange bundle. It made a slight crackling sound.

"What's in it?"

"Oh, just some special herbs and roots, like Johnny the Conqueror—that's a powerful one—and probably a few drops of jojoba oil."

"I thought these things were mostly souvenirs for the tourists."

"They are, but that doesn't mean they don't work. You don't have to believe in magic to have it work for you."

"There must be lots of people in New Orleans who feel the same way you do," I said. "There are quite a few shops like your friend's."

Three men at a table across the courtyard were trying to get her attention, and I pointed them out to her. She waved to them, and continued talking to me. "It's probably the voodoo influence. People in New Orleans believe in magic," she said. "We don't always call it that, but we use it all the time."

"What do you mean?"

"Well, take St. Joseph, for instance. If you want to sell your house, you bury St. Joseph upside down in the garden."

"You do?"

"Everybody does. And it works. Your house gets sold."

I laughed. "Wouldn't it get sold anyway?"

"Maybe," she smiled. "But I wouldn't take a chance by not following tradition." She gave me a friendly squeeze on the shoulder. "You may not need my charm, but keep it anyway. It'll help you find what you're looking for, I know."

I hoped she was right. But what exactly *was* I looking for?

Contemplating the circumstances of Wayne's death, and what I considered the police department's precipitous action in reaching a conclusion in one day, I returned to my room. Detective Steppe had given me his card. I called the number, and asked to speak to him.

"Steppe's not in the station this morning," the desk sergeant informed me. "You wanna talk to anyone else?"

"Do you know where or when I might be able to reach him?"

"Sorry, I don't keep track of his schedule. Try calling back tomorrow."

I could hear telephones ringing in the background. "Who else would know about a case he's working on?" I asked.

"Lieutenant Wisenberg's his supervisor. I'll put you through." He sounded eager to get rid of me.

The lieutenant was polite but unhelpful. "Dr. Renshaw's the ME, Mrs. Fletcher. He's the one made the determination. It says right here, 'Cause of death: snakebite; Manner of death: accidental.'"

"Lieutenant, I understand that was the medical examiner's finding," I said. "What I don't understand is why the ruling was made so quickly."

"He must have been certain that's the way it happened."

"Don't you think there should have been a more thorough investigation?"

"Doesn't matter what I think, ma'am." He was losing patience with me. "The ME says it's an accident, it's an accident. I'm not a doctor. I don't challenge the ME."

"What could Wayne Copely have been doing at Marie Laveau's tomb? Don't you want to find out?"

"Mrs. Fletcher, I know he was a friend of yours, and you

don't like to think of him there, but that crypt is a very popular place. People visit it at all hours of the night and day, whether the cemetery's officially open or not."

"Wayne wouldn't have," I insisted.

"Be that as it may, he was there, he got bitten, and he died."

"Did you ever suspect his death was a homicide?"

He sighed. "No, ma'am."

I pressed him again. "So you never assigned any officers to interview his friends or check his apartment," I asked.

"No, ma'am, we knew right away it wasn't necessary," he said.

"When did the medical examiner make his ruling?" I asked.

"Saturday."

"When on Saturday?"

"Sometime in the morning, the word came down—accidental death—case closed. Here, I'll give you the wording." He read Dr. Renshaw's official conclusion to me.

"Can I speak with Dr. Renshaw?"

"I'll give you his number, but I don't guarantee he'll talk to you."

The lieutenant put me on hold and after a long wait, came back on the line and gave me the ME's number.

The doctor wasn't in, or he wasn't picking up the phone. I left a long message on his voice mail and requested a return call.

A loud knock on my door made me jump. Mindful of security, I looked through the peephole before opening the door. An elderly bellman held out two baskets, one filled with fruit and the other with flowers. "This is from the management," he said with a grin.

"Why are they sending me gifts?"

He shrugged. "There's a card, but it's probably to make up for your snake experience."

"Oh, so you know about that?" I took the baskets and put them on the dresser.

"Whole hotel's been talking about it this morning."

"And what are they saying?"

"That you left your courtyard door open and a snake came to visit."

"Well, it was not quite that way," I said, fumbling in my bag for a tip. There was no point in arguing with him about my supposed carelessness. I thanked him, closed the door, and quickly crossed the room. The French doors were locked. I opened them and stepped outside. The late-morning sun bounced off the gray stone. The heat made the air shimmer. I shielded my eyes as I examined the paved walkway leading to the doors from the courtyard. I peered at the earth beneath the large bush, and inspected its branches for signs of someone having brushed past, possibly breaking a twig or leaving a thread, but the closely trimmed plant revealed no such clues. Finally, I knelt down to look more carefully at the doorknob and lock. Only minor scratches marred their surfaces. If someone had been here, he or she had left no evidence to prove it.

"Please write 'To Gertrude and Harold, Happy Fortieth Anniversary.'" The dapper gentlemen held out my book, his thumb holding it open to the title page.

"I'll be happy to," I said, smiling up at him. "Are you Harold?"

"Yes," he said. "This is for my wife. She's a big fan of yours. And I am, too."

"That's very nice of you to say so," I said, changing pens to one with a full barrel of ink. "Are you going anywhere special for your anniversary?"

"We thought we might take one of the evening cruises on a steamboat. Get in a little gambling," he replied as the bookstore manager took his money and handed him change.

I passed him his purchase. "Congratulations to you both. I hope you enjoy your evening, and the book."

"Thank you, Mrs. Fletcher." He moved off, and a young woman took his place.

Nancy Ortiz, the manager, pushed another book in front of me along with a slip of paper on which she'd written the names for the next dedication. After forty-five minutes of signing books, I could finally see the end of the line of people holding copies of *Murder in a Minor Key*, as well as other books of mine. My hand was tired and my stomach was grumbling, hopefully not loud enough for Nancy or anyone else to hear.

"This one's for Doris," a familiar voice said, placing my book on the table. Doris Burns winked at me.

"Doris!" I chided. "I would have given you a copy. You didn't have to buy it."

"Oh, no," she said. "All authors should insist their friends *buy* their books. If I gave books to all my friends, my sales figures would be cut in half."

I laughed. "How would you like me to sign this?"

"Just sign J. B. Fletcher. That way I can read it first before I give it to my sister."

I eyed the line. "Shouldn't be too much longer," I said.

"Great," she said. "Let's grab a bite. I've been hanging around the cookbook section and I'm famished."

"There's an excellent sandwich shop right across the street," Nancy suggested. "Terrific muffulettas."

"Perfect," said Doris. "Look for me in the travel aisle when you're done."

A half hour later, having sold out the store's complement of *Murder in a Minor Key*, I sat down with Doris to two cups of tea and a huge muffuletta shared between us.

"Did your signing go well?" I asked.

"Very well. They ran out of my books, although the store

hadn't ordered nearly as many of mine as they did yours. History can't compete with fiction by a famous author."

"History is popular these days, too," I said. "And an author's name builds. You'll see. Your next book will be even bigger."

"Speaking of the next one, I taped a real weirdo yesterday. He could be a chapter by himself."

"Who was that?"

"Now that I've said that, I'm not sure you'll want to hear about him," she said. She tried to take a dainty bite of the huge sandwich, gave up, and picked up her knife and fork.

"Why wouldn't I want to hear about him?"

"He's a snake broker," she said reluctantly. "Given how Wayne died, and your experience in bed, it just occurred to me you might not want to talk about snakes."

"On the contrary," I said. "I was hoping to pump you for information about how snakes are used in voodoo rituals."

"Do you think that's what happened?" she asked. "That he was participating in some ceremony?"

"I can't be certain," I replied, "but I'm uncomfortable with the idea of an 'accidental death,' especially in a cemetery he was cautious about."

"This guy I taped is the one who set the traps in the cemetery and captured the snake that might have killed Wayne. His name's Bobby Pinto; he's got hair down to here." She indicated the middle of her back. "And he's covered in tattoos. He was on one of the television stations yesterday. The crew had just left when I arrived, and he was bragging about being on TV."

"I didn't see the news," I said. "What exactly does a snake broker do?"

"He raises snakes, catches snakes, sells them, milks them for venom, and sells that. I guess he's a kind of exterminator, too. He'll get rid of them for you if they get in your house, but I don't think he kills them."

"Why do you say that?"

"Because there's a pen with hundreds of them on his property," Doris said, eyes wide at the memory.

"Must be an interesting place."

"If you can stomach it, it's worth a visit." She shivered.

"Does he sell snakes for voodoo ceremonies?" I asked.

"Yes. And he supplies snakes to the pet shops that sell them for voodoo ceremonies."

"What kinds of snakes are they?"

"Constrictors, mainly. They grow to around twelve or thirteen feet, but they're not venomous."

"Is that why they use them, because they don't have venom?"

"Probably. Once they're fed, he says, they're fairly docile. They only eat a couple of mice or rats once a week." She looked down at her sandwich. "Not exactly dinner table conversation."

"I don't mind," I said. "Are those the only snakes they use?"

She shook her head. "No. Those are the ceremonial ones that represent the spirits, but they could use almost any kind of snake for sacrifices."

"So animal sacrifices are still part of voodoo?"

"In some forms, yes, and rarely seen by the public. Pinto says the animal rights people are always trying to stop them. They visit his place almost every month, he said, demanding to see his customer list and checking on how he cares for his snakes. He said he doesn't show them the list and doesn't tell them about the sacrifices. He must be staying within the law because no one's closed him down yet. Of course, I doubt the authorities would want to take his place over. Then they'd have to deal with all those snakes."

"I think I'd like to talk with him."

"I'll give you his number. I have it back at the hotel."

"Why are snakes so important in the voodoo religion?" I asked. "Did you talk to him about that?"

"Not really," she said. "But remember, voodoo originally comes from West Africa, where there are a lot of snakes, so it's not surprising they've been incorporated into the religion that started there. Why did you want to know? Was Wayne into voodoo? He didn't seem the type."

"I doubt it very much," I said, "but where his body was found is strange. If I went on the basis of my limited experience as his friend alone, I would have said no, he absolutely wasn't practicing voodoo. But we didn't know each other long enough, or well enough, for me to be so definite."

"His sister would know, wouldn't she?"

"I assume so. I'm going to stop in on her this afternoon. I'll ask."

Clarice greeted me at the door of her home in the Garden District. Lines bracketed her mouth and divided her brow, but she was dry-eyed and neatly coifed. A trace of red marked her lips. Despite the heat, she wore a gray knit suit and a black blouse.

"I'm so glad you could come back today," she said, ushering me indoors. "I wasn't fit company yesterday."

"No one expected you to be a hostess then, or now," I said. "I hope you don't feel you have to entertain me."

"I'm not ready to entertain anyone," she said, leading me into a dim front room and turning on a table lamp with a fringed shade, "but I did want a chance to talk with you. Yesterday wasn't the time. Please sit down."

I sat on the off-white slip-covered sofa, and immediately regretted it. The cushion on the sofa was so old and soft, I was afraid if I leaned back, I'd never be able to get up again without help. I pushed myself forward and perched on the edge, where I could maintain my balance.

The room was slightly musty, as if it hadn't been used for

some time. The walls were a faded blue. I noticed several lighter rectangles where pictures had been removed. The oriental carpet was ancient and threadbare along the edges. An ebony grand piano sat in one corner, its closed lid covered by a paisley cloth which was, in turn, covered with framed photographs, most of them black-and-white, and obviously taken years ago. Opposite the piano was a hand-painted wooden cabinet. Arrayed on its top was what appeared to me to be a small altar. Candles of different heights and colors flickered and dripped their wax on the bare wood. Rosary beads hung from a standing metal cross. Various bottles surrounded the cross, feathers poking up from one. In a bowl, three small plastic skulls lay nestled together.

"Alberta will bring us some tea in a moment," Clarice said, settling in a lyre-back chair to the side of a walnut table with cabriole legs. She clutched a lace handkerchief in one hand, her white knuckles betraying her tense mood. "Wayne's death has been such a shock," she said.

"It must have been," I agreed.

"I never expected it. And so soon after my husband. I feel as if I've been deserted." She attempted a smile, and swallowed hard.

"You seem to have many friends who are eager to support you."

"Yes, well, they all flock around in the beginning." She sniffed. "They did when Steve died, too. But after a while having a widowed friend gets boring, especially if she doesn't recover as quickly as they'd like. They stopped inviting me, and eventually stopped calling altogether."

I breathed a small sigh, grateful my friends had not been so shallow when I'd become a widow.

Her eyes caught the figure of the cook standing in the doorway holding a tray, and she straightened in her seat.

"Right over here, Alberta," she said, resting her fingertips on the walnut table.

Alberta was a large woman, well over my height, with steel-gray hair tightly pinned back. She wore a freshly pressed apron over her housedress, and would have looked like a stereotypical servant except for her footwear—brand new, bright-blue-and-orange running shoes with thick white soles and laces up to the ankles. The sight was so incongruous, I had to work not to stare at her feet.

She slid the tea tray on the table next to Clarice and left the room, returning almost immediately with a small bench, no more than a foot high, which she positioned in front of me. Clarice poured the tea and gave the cup to Alberta, who placed it on the bench along with a plate of cookies, a sugar bowl, and a pitcher of cream.

"Do you take lemon?"

"No, thank you. This is fine," I replied.

Alberta left the room as silently as she'd come. The whole scene was perfectly choreographed, as if they'd performed this dance many times.

We sipped our tea companionably. "Would you mind if I asked you a personal question?" I said.

"I don't know," she said, smiling. "Why don't you try and I'll see."

"I noticed the altar you have in the corner. Was Wayne a religious person?"

"Not at all. He went to church as a child. My mother insisted. But as soon as he was able, he slept late on Sundays, and only attended services when he was forced to escort me."

"Did he share your interest in voodoo?"

"You're thinking about my skulls over there." She chuckled, and it was good to see her relax for a moment. "Those are more of a decorating fillip, a little gesture to intrigue my friends, if that's possible. Stay around New Orleans for any length of time and you'll find the whole population is caught up in the exotic nature of our city. We have all kinds of traditions that probably stem from voodoo and we don't even know it. I have no special interest in voodoo, and neither did Wayne. He doesn't have an altar at his place, does he?"

"I didn't see one," I said before realizing that she didn't know the only times I'd been at his apartment were after he died. But she took no note of my comment, assuming, I suppose, that I'd been an invited guest at my friend's home.

"Speaking of Wayne's apartment," Clarice said, putting down her cup, "I wonder if I could ask a favor of you."

"Certainly, if I'm able."

"I'd never ask if I didn't feel as if we've known each other for a long time. Wayne was so fond of you."

"I was fond of him as well," I said. "What would you like me to do?"

"There's a box in Wayne's apartment. I want you to pick it up for me. I just can't bring myself to go there yet. You know how it is? So many memories."

"Oh, of course," I said. "I understand. Where did he keep the box?"

"It's an antique, hand-painted, from China. Have you seen it?"

"I'm not sure," I said. "I think I remember him mentioning it. Does it have all kinds of drawers and compartments?"

"Yes, that's the one." Clarice sat up straighter. "Ordinarily, I'd ask Archer, but I've put so many burdens on him recently."

"I don't mind at all."

She patted her pockets. "I'll have to get you the key. Wait here, will you?" She murmured to herself, "There's also his candlesticks, and the crystal clock." She halted at the door and turned around. "Do you have a car?"

"I'm afraid not."

"I'll get someone else to pick up the other things," she

said impatiently, and disappeared. She returned momentarily, handed me the keys to Wayne's building and apartment, and sat down again. "I'm so grateful to you. That box belonged to our father, and has great sentimental meaning for me."

"Naturally."

"I'm just so afraid when word gets out that his apartment is empty, someone will break in and steal things. Thieves read the obituaries these days. Did you know that?"

"I wasn't aware that was a problem in New Orleans," I said.

"It's a problem everywhere, my dear."

"I'll make certain to get the box and safeguard it for you."

Clarice sighed, and leaned back in her chair. "Tell me how he was when you saw him," she said, picking up her tea again. "We'd planned Sunday dinner for yesterday, but I hadn't seen him all week."

"He was very excited about Jazz Fest," I said. We sat together like old friends as I diverted her with stories of the musicians who were Wayne's friends, of the concerts we attended, of his pleasure in educating my palate at New Orleans's famous restaurants, and of his obvious fondness for her.

She responded with memories of his youth, his passion for music, and his frustration that he had no talent to play an instrument, or so he thought. "You can see how we use the piano," she said, looking at the rows of photographs. "My mother insisted upon lessons, but neither of us was any good, although Wayne was better than I was." She talked of how Wayne had turned that frustration into an obsession to know everything about jazz, and how he'd kept notes on every recording and musician he listened to until he finally found a way to use his expertise, writing about his first and only love.

"He kept all his work here, you know. He said there wasn't enough room in his apartment to sing a song. Would you like to see his office?" she asked, rising with difficulty. "I need to move around a little."

"Yes. I'd like to see it very much," I said, grateful to get off the sofa.

I followed her up a narrow staircase to the second floor, and then up another flight to a small room under the eaves overlooking the front balcony. Bookcases lined one side of the room; the center one was filled with narrow books with black bindings. File cabinets took up the other wall. A small desk and chair stood in front of the windows.

"Wayne was much more disciplined than I," she said. "He always did what he said he would do." She walked to the center of the room and paused. "Of course, after Steve died, Wayne said he'd always take care of me." Her voice was quavery. "And now he's not here to support me at all, is he?" She turned to me, her eyes vulnerable.

"No, he's not. But perhaps he provided some insurance to help you financially." I was uncomfortable with the turn the conversation had taken. Clarice was in the throes of grief, her moods erratic. I'd been through the experience. You never knew what would set you off. One minute you were laughing, and the next dissolving in tears.

"I don't know," she whispered. "Archer was here this morning and went through all of Wayne's drawers. He took away piles of papers. He wouldn't tell me what they were, only that Wayne would want him to handle such things."

"Did Wayne leave a will, or other instructions in the event that he died?" I asked.

"He never told me."

"You're entitled to ask what's in those papers Archer took," I told her gently. "This is your house. You shouldn't let him take over, unless you want him to."

"You're right," she said, clearing her throat. "Archer's al-

ways tried to boss me around, even when Steve was alive."
She started to pace. "He thinks all Wayne's things are his.
But they're not. They're really mine, aren't they? He does-
n't know that Wayne was getting ready to let him go."

"Are you sure about that?" I asked.

"Oh, yes," she nearly crowed. "Wayne was annoyed with
Archer's arrogance, always telling him what to do. He'd had
it up to here." She swiped her hand under her chin. "He was
going to tell him to find another job."

"Did Archer know this?"

"I doubt it. Wayne told me he was waiting for the right
time."

"That would have been difficult for you, too—wouldn't
it?—if Wayne had let Archer go. Archer's been very helpful
to you."

"Oh, no, I've got Alberta now. She helps me when I need
her."

Archer would be very disappointed, I thought, to find out
all his years of service to Clarice were valued so little. He'd
obviously been high-handed this morning taking away the
papers, but perhaps he wanted to spare Clarice more pain.
Or if he'd sensed a change in his position in the family, he
might have been afraid she'd keep information from him.
Alberta had been hired as a cook. Would she have been willing to step in as social secretary and save Clarice the burden
of having to make funeral arrangements?

"Let me show you Wayne's pride and joy," Clarice said
brightly. She walked to a row of painted bookcases and
withdrew a notebook with a black-and-white marbled cover,
the kind I remembered using in school. "Look at this," she
said. "There must be hundreds of these."

The notebook was written in a youthful hand. It contained a description of a concert the young Wayne had attended, who the musicians were, what instruments and
songs they played, and his impressions of the quality of the

performance. "Even then he was a critic," I said, smiling as I read a few lines.

"Yes. He always kept such good records."

I jumped at the opening. "Do you know where his notes are for the book he was planning on Little Red LeCoeur?"

"Archer asked me the same question this morning," she said, and sighed. "I don't know. They're probably in his apartment somewhere. He was very secretive about whatever he was working on until it was published. Then he transcribed his notes into another of these books and added it to the collection here."

"Didn't he work on a computer?"

"Only when his publisher insisted. I think there's a laptop in his apartment."

I didn't remember seeing one there, but I couldn't be sure. I wondered if Archer had carted off Wayne's papers, hoping to find his notes on Little Red among them. Was he planning to finish Wayne's work for him? Or would he want to take the credit for himself?

"Mrs. Cruz, are you up there?" Alberta's voice floated up the stairs from the floor below.

"Just let me see what she wants," Clarice said, walking to the door.

"Do you mind if I look around?" I called after her.

"Help yourself," her voice came back from the stairwell.

I walked to the bookcase that held Wayne's notebooks and pulled out the last one on the bottom shelf. It was dated in April, and was only half full. I flipped through the pages, hoping Wayne's propensity to keep good notes extended beyond music to other areas of his life. But if I was disappointed not to find anything personal, I was amazed at what he'd collected. There were reviews of new compact disks, features on established artists, and an analysis of why successful jazz prodigies drew the harshest criticism from his colleagues. On page after page, in Wayne's careful script, was a collection of impressions of jazz. They ought to be in a library, I thought.

I heard Clarice's footsteps on the stairs, and I pushed the notebook back into place. Maybe when the pain of Wayne's death was not so sharp, she could be persuaded to part with these books. What a wonderful memorial to Wayne it would be if his cherished notebooks were made available to other lovers of music, in a public library or at a university.

"More people have arrived," she told me. "Would you like to join us in the parlor?"

"No, thank you," I said. "I really must go."

"You've been very kind to spend so much time with me." She fluttered her hands in front of her face as if something annoyed her. "I can't believe I forgot to thank you. Archer told me you volunteered to bring Wayne's clothes to the funeral home."

"I have the bag with his clothes at my hotel," I said. "I'm going to drop them off tomorrow morning."

"How could I be so forgetful? You must think I'm a terrible ingrate."

"What I think," I said, walking with her to the stairs, "is that you have a lot to think about at the moment. I was pleased there was a way I could help."

She turned to me. "You know, Jessica, I think we could be friends."

Chapter Fifteen

The late set at the Café Brasilia had already started when I slipped into a chair near the back of the room. In the front, a young man in his twenties, wearing sunglasses and a Jazz Fest T-shirt under a black jacket, was playing trumpet, accompanied by three much older musicians on piano, bass, and drums. The placard on my table announced the performance of the Blind Jack Quartet, but the featured player was not the man whose concert I had attended at the festival.

I attempted to hail a passing waitress.

"Be right back," she called out, lifting her tray high above the heads of incoming patrons as she angled her way toward the bar. She disappeared into the crowd, and I waited impatiently for her to resurface.

The quartet was playing, but people around me weren't reacting, except to raise their voices over the music. At the table next to mine, a businessman in his fifties, his tie askew, was clinking glasses with a young woman in a tight tank top. I doubted she was his daughter. From the empty glasses on their table, I assumed they had been at the club for some time. "Excuse me," I said, tapping the man's shoulder.

"Hello!" he boomed, reaching out to put an arm around my shoulder. "Would you like to join us?" His nubile companion didn't appear too pleased at his offer.

"Oh, no thank you," I said, shifting my chair just far

enough away to put me out of reach. I held up the announcement for the Blind Jack Quartet, and cocked my head toward the performers, "I came to see Blind Jack, but that young trumpet player isn't Blind Jack."

"He isn't?" Had I realized how inebriated the man was, I would have buttonholed someone else.

"No, he's not. Did they make an announcement earlier? Have I missed him?"

"Heck, I don't know." He turned back to his table mate. "Vera, did you hear anything?"

The young woman leaned over the table toward me, displaying a clear view of her well-developed cleavage. "Yeah. Don't you remember, Elliott? They said he was sick or something. This guy is, like, the next generation, they said."

"Who said?" I asked.

"That guy over there." She pointed to two men standing under an EXIT sign. "The one in the striped shirt. I think he's the manager."

"Thank you," I said, standing and pulling my bag over my shoulder.

"Hey, honey, aren't you going to stay?" Elliott swayed in his seat, tipping in my direction.

"I'll come back later," I said, swerving to avoid his grasp. I circled the table and edged around several others, apologizing as I forced people to pull their chairs in to let me pass. The manager had turned down a short hall and was holding a door open to an office to let the second man enter.

I hurried after them, knocked on the door, and opened it without waiting for an invitation.

The manager looked up in surprise, and both men rose from their seats. "This is a private office, ma'am. Is there something I can help you with?"

"Yes, I'm Jessica Fletcher," I said, crossing the room and extending my hand. "My apologies for barging in, Mr. . . . ?"

He shook my hand. "I'm Harvey Willauer, the manager, and this is—"

"Detective Christopher Steppe," I filled in for him.

Steppe held out his hand. "Nice to see you again, Mrs. Fletcher."

"Oh, you two know each other," Willauer said.

"Yes, we've met," I said.

Willauer waited for an explanation, his gaze switching back and forth between us as though watching a tennis game.

I turned to the manager. "Actually, I came to see you, Mr. Willauer," I said. "To ask why Blind Jack isn't playing tonight. I hope nothing has happened to him."

"You two are on the same wavelength," Willauer said, pointing to a pink-and-green sofa. "Go ahead, sit down."

Steppe sank down on the sofa, and I took a wooden chair catty-corner to it.

"Jack phoned me a couple of hours ago and said he couldn't make the gig. I was pissed, of course. Oh, sorry, Mrs. Fletcher."

"That's all right."

"Anyway, he came up with some lame excuse, something about personal problems. He said somebody was after him."

"Oh?"

"So he said he was sending in this hotshot player with his regular guys. It was two hours before the show. What was I to do? I gotta have a show. I've got paying customers. But I'll never offer him another gig. Unreliable, that's what he is. And the kid. He's not too bad, but he doesn't have a name. This crowd only wants to listen to a name like Blind Jack. I always fill up with him. This kid doesn't have a following." He wound down like a spring that had slowly uncurled. "That's all I know."

"Do you have a phone number for Blind Jack?" I asked.

"Sure, it's in my Rolodex here," he said, tipping his chair back to pull it off his desk.

A waitress opened the door and leaned into the room. "Willy, we got a drunk at table fifteen yelling for the manager. Cotter's already there, but we need you, too."

Steppe and I both stood.

"On my way." Willauer twisted a card out of his file. "Just leave it on my desk," he said, handing it to me as he left the room and slammed the door behind him.

I withdrew my appointment book and groped around the bottom of my bag for a pen.

"Here," Steppe said, holding out his pencil.

I took it and jotted down the number Willauer had for Blind Jack.

"What are you doing here?" Steppe asked.

"Probably the same thing you are."

"I'm the cop," he said. "You're not. Leave the investigations to the police."

"The police aren't investigating Wayne's death," I said. "I am."

"What are you talking about?"

"You weren't even supposed to be in his apartment," I charged.

"How do you know that?"

"Because I checked with your lieutenant. He said the medical examiner ruled the death an accident on Saturday morning. You were in Wayne's apartment Saturday night. The case was already considered closed by then."

"You called the station?"

"That's right."

"You shouldn't have done that, Mrs. Fletcher."

"Why?"

He slumped on the couch, and shook his head. "Because you put me in a lousy position, that's why."

"How? I merely called the lieutenant and asked if

Wayne's death had ever been considered a homicide. He assured me it had not, that it was a clear case of accidental death by snakebite. Although Wayne was in a dangerous area, his death was just a 'confluence of unfortunate circumstances,' I believe was the phrase he read to me from the report, 'a tragic result of his being in the wrong place at the wrong time, the drought a major factor in the presence of snakes in the city.'"

Steppe took a deep breath and let it out.

"So now that I know you weren't in Wayne's apartment on official business, I want to know *why* you were there."

He stood up and paced. "I didn't buy it," he said. "Neither did Teddy."

"Buy what?"

"That accidental death garbage."

I felt a surge of pleasure. I wasn't alone in questioning how Wayne died. "Why not?" I asked.

"It's just too convenient."

"What is?"

"The drought."

"Why?"

"Because there were too many odd elements along with it."

"Give me an example."

"Where his body was found," he said. "It's not like he took a walk in the country and stepped on a snake."

"No, it's not."

"Marie Laveau's tomb is a spot with a lot of meaning in this city."

"And?"

"The gris-gris was another. The few people I talked to never saw Copely wearing a gris-gris. Why would he be wearing one for the first time on the night he died?"

"The gris-gris was never mentioned in the news."

He shrugged. "I didn't put it in the report we gave to the press."

"Anything else bother you?"

"Yeah, the snakebite itself."

"You don't think he died of snakebite?"

"Oh, he died of a snakebite, all right. I'm just not so sure it was an accident."

"Why not?"

"They use snakes in voodoo. Taken together, the whole thing looked like a setup, like a giant arrow pointing to his death as part of some voodoo ritual."

"And it wasn't?"

"That's what I want to know," he said.

"So the ME said it was an accident, but you decided to follow up anyway?"

"After we got off duty, we thought we'd take a look around Copely's apartment to see what we could find."

"And you found me."

"Yeah. Teddy was reassigned yesterday to another partner, and I've been put on desk duty till they have another guy to pair me with. Somebody got upset with our questions Saturday morning. If they found out we'd continued the investigation against orders, we'd really be wading in quicksand."

"I'm sorry," I said. "Did you find anything in the apartment?"

"Nothing to take home to Mama, but we knew someone else had been there before us."

"I thought so, too. Police don't usually make such a mess of drawers and closets."

"Thanks," he said, smiling at me for the first time. "You know, Copely could've been a slob."

"Wayne was meticulous about his appearance, and the rest of his apartment was immaculate. It made no sense that he would be sloppy in just one area. Everywhere else was perfectly neat."

"That's true."

"Is that why you washed and dried my glass, and put it back on the shelf?"

He laughed. "You've got a good eye."

"I'll tell you one thing, Detective," I said, sitting down in the seat he'd recently occupied, "if it was a ritual, Wayne was a victim, not a willing participant."

" A human sacrifice?" He grimaced at the thought.

I grimaced, too. "Whoever killed Wayne—and I don't believe his death was an accident—wanted you to think he'd been participating in a voodoo ceremony. What we have to find out is: Was it really a voodoo ritual, or simply set up to look like one?"

"Do you think this ties in with Williams's death?"

"I think whoever killed Wayne wanted to link his death to the earlier murder; otherwise, why leave the body in the same place?"

"And they wanted to tie Copely to voodoo."

"Maybe that's what the killer expected," I said. "Voodoo is so much a part of New Orleans life, it was easy to say Wayne had dabbled in it."

"But any good investigator will discover that's a lie," he said.

"Perhaps," I said, "but not if the investigation is closed down."

He nodded somberly. "When Teddy and I raised the question in our report the morning after the body was discovered, we were told in no uncertain terms to drop it. Case closed. We couldn't even talk to the medical examiner. He was off the case, too."

"So when you told me the medical examiner hadn't made a determination about Wayne's death, that wasn't true."

"Well, the determination had been made, but whether the

ME was pushed to make it, or just took the path of least re-
sistance because he's overloaded with work, I don't know. It
seems to me he would wait to get the toxicology reports
back."

"Were they sent out?"

"I'm sure they were."

"Let's assume he was pressured to come up with the accidental conclusion," I said. "What I can't figure out is why
the police department would want to cover up Wayne's murder."

Steppe snorted. "There could be lots of reasons."

"Like what?"

"Like a major blunder, for one thing. Ever since
Williams's body was found in the cemetery, there's been a
police patrol that's supposed to be on duty in the area. They
weren't in the vicinity the night Copely was supposedly
wandering around St. Louis Number One."

"Where were they?"

"You tell me. Some false alarm, I heard."

"So you think there would be a lot fewer questions about
where the officers on that patrol were if the death on their
watch was ruled an accident."

"Not only that, if you've got snakes in the cemetery—
and apparently we do—it's easy for the city to be a hero,
calling in exterminators to safeguard the citizenry. The cops
don't look bad, either. But if it's another murder, this time of
a prominent citizen—when the administration is bragging
about how we've reduced the crime rate so much, and the
mayor is up for reelection—the city would bite down on the
department like an alligator on a duck."

I winced at his image, but the analysis made sense to me.

"Why aren't they pushing for you to solve Williams's
murder? Is it because he *wasn't* a prominent citizen?"

"You mean is this a bias on the part of the department?
No. Doesn't work that way. But I'll tell you, it's a funny

thing," he said, combing his fingers through his hair. "The scuttlebutt is that the voodoo community, which ordinarily would be screaming at us to find the murderer, is shut up tighter than a clam. Our guys are out there, but no one's talking. I'd like to know why."

"There's another thing I'd like to know," I mused.

"What's that?"

"I keep wondering if Wayne actually died in the cemetery, or if his body was moved to Marie Laveau's tomb."

"It's a little late to find that out," he said.

"If we had his clothes, we might be able to find some evidence."

"They probably went with the body to the funeral home."

"Then they might still be there."

"I don't know, Mrs. Fletcher," he said, rubbing the back of his neck. "Copely, he wasn't a pretty sight. There was a lot of blood. Snake venom creates lots of blood. Funeral homes usually burn bloodied clothing, like from road accidents. The families don't want it back."

"The funeral hasn't taken place yet," I said. "There's a chance they may still have his clothes."

"Do you know which mortuary firm his sister is using?"

"I have it at my hotel. I wrote it down."

"All right, let's assume we're right, that Copely wasn't accidentally bitten," he said. "Tell me why you think someone might've wanted Copely dead."

"I'm convinced it has to do with the cylinders."

"You think someone didn't want him to find them, and killed him when he got too close?"

"Yes."

"But why is it so important to keep them from being found? It doesn't make sense. If they're worth a lot of money, wouldn't it be smarter to bring them out?"

"If I knew why someone is going to such trouble to conceal them, I'd be a lot closer to finding the murderer."

"That item in Gable's column this morning announcing that you've taken up the search for the cylinders in Copely's memory. Did you arrange for that?"

"I thought it might be a way to shake up whoever killed Wayne."

"Very clever," he said sarcastically. "Did you also consider that it could make you a potential victim?"

"I think the killer is probably not anxious to make any more news."

"Maybe, but I wouldn't count on that. You'll need my help."

"I'll be happy to have it, Detective Steppe."

He sighed. "So now I have my new partner. Unofficially, of course."

"Yes, unofficially, of course."

"All right, where do we start?"

Chapter Sixteen

Jackson Square was quiet early Tuesday morning, but there were signs it wouldn't remain that way. Folding tables, yet to be set up, leaned against the iron fence surrounding the park, and cardboard cartons were piled here and there, some in the process of being unpacked by their owners. A sidewalk artist was on her knees, drawing a scene on the pavement in colored chalk. Behind her, a stack of pictures teetered on a folding chair. Across from the entrance to the park, an elderly woman leaned over a small table covered with a black cloth, and peeled cards off a deck, laying them carefully in a pattern. The chair opposite hers was empty for the moment.

I'd walked over from the hotel, killing a little time till the funeral home opened. I'd called earlier to make an appointment. An answering machine had informed me that business hours started at eleven, unless a funeral was scheduled that day. A number in case of emergency had been given. I left a message saying that I'd be there shortly after they opened, and requested fifteen minutes of the undertaker's time.

I adjusted my hat against the sun's rays, and wandered to where the old woman was studying her cards. She wore a red-and-maroon tie-dyed dress and a white turban. Something in her manner was familiar. She held the unexposed cards in her left hand, and slid the top card off with her right, making a wide circle with the card before she lay it face-

side-up in front of her. She glanced up from her task, and her
eyes lit with recognition. She left the deck of cards on the
table and approached me. It was Ileana Montalvo, the
voodoo priestess I'd met at Jazz Fest.

"You still have my juju?" she asked.

"As a matter of fact, I do," I said, patting my bag, and realizing for the first time that I'd been carrying the little package with me everywhere.

"Good." She took my hand in hers. The fingers that
pressed mine were calloused and dry. She looked at me for
what seemed like a long time. "Sometin' has happened," she
said. "I see it in your eyes."

"That's true," I said. "A friend of mine died."

"I'm sorry for you."

"Thank you."

"Was it a natural death?"

"I'm not sure," I admitted, for some reason not surprised
at the question. "He died of snakebite."

She closed her eyes and concentrated on some inner vi-
sion. "Danger has not yet passed," she said, squeezing my
fingers tightly. "You are wise, but you are also impulsive. Be
careful."

Her accurate portrayal of my personality made me uneasy. "Wise" might be flattering, but "impulsive" was a
crime I'd been accused of before. I preferred to think I took
advantage of opportunity. Meeting the voodoo priestess
again was an accident of fate, but it was also an opportunity
knocking at my door, and I wasn't about to let it slip by. I
was still weighing the idea of Wayne's death as part of a
voodoo ritual. The location of his body at Marie Laveau's
tomb, the gris-gris the police had found on him—someone
wanted that connection made. I was sure Ileana Montalvo
had heard about Wayne, maybe even knew more than I did
about how he'd died. Even if she'd never been exposed to
the deluge of newspaper articles or television or radio re-

ports on where the body was found, she would have heard about it on the street; news of that kind would have swept through the voodoo community like a swift-flowing current.

"Would you mind I asked you some questions?"

"About?"

"About your beliefs," I said. "I'm trying to understand the significance snakes have in voodoo."

She released my hands, and turned back to her table. "The snake is a powerful life force," she said.

"In the practice of voodoo, you mean?" I asked, following her.

"Yes. Serpents have much magic." She sat down again and started gathering up her cards.

I took the other chair. "What kind of magic do they have?"

"They be old spirits, goin' back all the way to the birth of verdoun." She paused. "The first man and first woman, they were blind till the serpent gave them sight."

"Like Adam and Eve and the serpent in the Garden of Eden?" I asked.

"Just so."

"Is that why they're magic?"

She fanned the cards in front of me and indicated I should make a choice. I pulled one from the deck. She studied it and lay it on the table. I recognized the colorful illustration as a tarot card.

"We honor the snake. They intercede for us with the Supreme Being," she said, fanning the cards in front of me again. I drew a second card and then, at her signal, a third. She placed them next to the first.

She tapped her finger on a card. "This one's not good," she said. "The Devil."

I stared down at the three cards I'd picked from her deck. The card she was touching showed a grimacing fiend, its horns pointing toward its winged back. "What does it mean?"

"The Devil is bad. His is a world of darkness." She glanced up at me for a moment. "He also stand for the ties that keep you there, in the dark. Someone may be concealing the truth from you."

"What about this one?" I asked, pointing to a picture of a narrow building with an explosion erupting from its top; yellow flames rained down on two figures that were falling to the ground.

She frowned. "The Tower. It signifies trouble, sometin' very wrong. It will come quickly. You need to be prepared."

"Oh!" I shifted in my seat, suddenly uncomfortable. "And that one?" I asked, nodding toward the third card.

"The Two of Wands," she said.

I thought I saw a brief smile cross her lips.

She picked up the picture of a man, dressed in medieval costume, standing between two leafless trees. "You will face great difficulty, maybe even danger, but you possess the power to prevail. The Two of Wands shows your strength." She sat back with a sigh.

"Thank you," I said. "I think."

She pulled the three cards toward her and placed them at the bottom of the deck.

"We were talking about snakes," I reminded her.

"You want to know about the Sacred Snake?" She seemed more relaxed, as if her reading of my future removed a burden from her shoulders.

"Yes, that's what I was asking about before."

"The snake be the symbol of our faith, Damballah, the Great Serpent, and Aida-Wedo, the Rainbow Serpent. She is his consort."

"And are living snakes used in your ceremonies to represent them?"

"Yes, but they are special snakes. They swallow. They do not bite."

"Do you mean snakes that bite aren't part of voodoo ceremonies?"

"The Sacred Snake takes its prey whole, stretching its body to swallow it all." She flung her arm out to demonstrate. "To be voodoo, you must stretch your soul, to learn, to take it all in." My eyes followed the arc of her limb, and I realized that while we'd been talking, people had poured into the square, and some of them were now encircling her table, inching closer to hear our conversation.

I lowered my voice. "Yes, but poisonous snakes, snakes that bite," I said. "Are they *not* part of voodoo?"

She shrugged, sat back in her seat, and pulled at an earlobe. "There are always those who follow another path."

A boisterous voice broke into our exchange. "Auntie, I see you're entertaining a celebrity."

I looked up into the laughing face of Napoleon DuBois.

He threw three balls into the air over our heads and began juggling. "Ladies and gentlemen, if you want to know what lies in store for you, here is the woman to see." He bowed to the priestess, and caught the balls behind his back, eliciting a laugh from three teenaged girls at the edge of the pack. He dropped the balls into his big pockets and came around the back of my chair. "Who'll be next to delve into the mysteries of the Tarot deck?" He grabbed my hand and pulled me from the seat with a flourish. A giggling teenager immediately took my place, her two friends squealing at her daring. "This is Ileana Montalvo," he told the teen in ringing tones, "a priestess, a voodoo priestess." He made his voice wobble on the "voodoo," extending the syllables into a long, eerie sound.

The priestess took up her role in the drama. In a strong voice I hadn't heard before, she exclaimed, "My ancestors drew pictures of the coming days. I am their descendant.

The blood of three continents runs in my veins." She pounded her chest with her fist. "I am African, Caribbean, French, and Spanish. I have Choctaw in me, too."

"In other words, you're a mutt," Napoleon teased.

"I'm Creole," she replied haughtily. "No one better in New Orleans. And you," she said, pointing at her nephew, "you're just a bad boy. Now you go and bother some other of these folks." She pointed at the teenager. "This child wants to know her future."

Napoleon doffed his top hat, swung his arm wide in an exaggerated bow to the fortune teller, and skated a short distance away. I was certain that the skit was one they'd enacted before, and she'd probably signaled him to interrupt when she'd tugged on one ear. Perhaps my questions were probing sore spots, or the public nature of our conference had made her edgy. Or I was taking up too much of her business time. She had yet to charge me for any of her services.

I checked my watch. It was time to pick up Wayne's garment bag back in my room at the Royal. The hotel staff had been fawning over me for two days since the milk snake had made its appearance in my bed. The concierge nearly begged to do something for me, so I'd asked him to arrange for a cab at ten forty-five. My transportation would probably be waiting when I got back. The funeral home was in the Garden District; it shouldn't take too long to get there.

Napoleon skated in front of me as I walked through Jackson Square. He turned around and threw three balls in the air, juggling as he glided backward.

"I hope you didn't mind my interrupting your tarot reading with my aunt, Mrs. Fletcher," he said, looking at me while the balls went round in a circle in front of him.

I stopped walking. "Was this her signal?" I yanked on my ear.

Napoleon laughed. "You caught us."

"I think we were finished anyway."

"Is your future looking bright, Mrs. Fletcher?"

"That remains to be seen."

He stopped juggling, his brows knit. "Auntie didn't give you bad news, did she?"

"I don't think so," I said, walking toward the gate.

"She's very good, you know. Lots of people go to her every week."

"I really don't believe in fortune-telling, Napoleon."

"That's okay. I like you anyway."

I laughed. We reached the end of the Square together and crossed the street.

"By the way, Mrs. Fletcher, thank you for the book," he said, juggling the balls again as he skated beside me. "I enjoyed it very much."

"You've finished it already? You're a fast reader."

"I am when I like what I'm reading."

"I'm delighted that you liked it."

"There was a lot about music in it, but not a lot about New Orleans," he said thoughtfully. "You missed some good places you could have written about."

"I'm sure I did," I said, "but a book can only cover so much."

"You're right, but I like to see my hometown in books. She looks different each time I read about her." He stopped juggling and pocketed the balls. "No one knows this city better than me." He knocked a thumb against his chest. "My Uncle Pascal had one of the buggies that takes the tourists around. When I was a kid, I used to go everywhere with him. He would let me drive the mule. Old Shakespeare, that was the mule's name. He knew the city, too. He always knew when we got near the stable and he'd pull like crazy in that direction, even if it wasn't the end of the day. Sometimes I'd have to get down and push against his side to get him to go the way my uncle wanted him to."

"Does your uncle still have the buggy?"

"Oh, yes. But my cousin Beatrice drives it now. Would you like a ride?"

"I think I would sometime."

While we'd been talking, an idea had occurred to me. I didn't know the city very well, and I could use the services of someone who did. Wayne had been my escort, and I'd been happy to put myself in his hands as he led me from one place to another. But I no longer had his expertise to rely upon. Here was someone who could be an informal tour guide, someone who was familiar with New Orleans, and also had an entrée into the voodoo community. Beaudin had offered the mayor's driver, who undoubtedly knew his way around the city, too. But I didn't think accepting such a favor was appropriate, and the more I thought about it, the less I liked the idea of Maurice Amadour, or his aide, keeping track of my movements.

"Napoleon?"

"Yes, ma'am."

"How would you like to show me around the city?"

He looked down at his clothes. "Dressed like this?"

"You look fine to me," I said. "I'll pay you for your time." I pulled a bill from my wallet and held it out to him.

He grinned at me. "My time is your time," he said, removing his top hat and tucking the money into a slot inside. "Where would you like to go?"

"I have to get back to my hotel," I said. "I'll explain while we're walking."

"Or while I'm gliding and you're walking," he said, lifting up one skate.

We reached St. Louis Street and turned toward the Royal. I told Napoleon about my upcoming errand, and other places I planned to visit.

"Do you know anything about Little Red LeCoeur the trumpet player?" I asked.

"Everyone knows his name here. He was a famous son of New Orleans."

"My friend died trying to find recordings Little Red may have made."

"Was your friend the one in the news, the one found in the cemetery?"

"Yes."

"I thought so," he said solemnly.

"Do you know who Elijah Williams is?"

He was silent a moment. "I know the name," he admitted.

"Do you know anyone in the city who could tell me about Elijah Williams?"

"Why would you ask *me*?"

I pointed to his skates. "You get around," I said playfully. "I think you probably know a lot of people."

"Let me think about it," he said. "Okay?"

"Okay."

We reached the front of the hotel. A black limousine sat at the curb; its uniformed chauffeur leaned against the driver's door. He straightened when he saw me, and tipped his cap.

"Uh-oh," I said. "This is not going to be as easy as I thought."

"What's the matter?" Napoleon asked.

"Nothing yet," I said. "Why don't you wait here for me?"

The concierge came out from behind his desk when I entered the lobby and clapped his hands in satisfaction. "Mrs. Fletcher," he said, "you wanted a cab, but I've got you something even better."

"That limousine is not for me, is it?"

"Yes, it is. Mr. Boudin sent it over this morning, and said to tell you the driver is prepared to take you anywhere you want to go."

The concierge was beaming at this fortunate turn of

events, and I was sorry to disappoint him. "Please tell the driver I won't be needing him today, but thank him for me. And I will be needing a cab."

"Of course, Mrs. Fletcher."

There was no limousine at the curb when I came outside again with Wayne's garment bag slung over my arm. There was no taxi either. The concierge was all apologies.

"I called the company, Mrs. Fletcher, but there are so many tourists in town, he couldn't tell me how long it would be."

"That's all right," I said. "I'll take public transportation." I looked at Napoleon, who'd been sitting on the curb listening. "Do you know how to get here?" I asked him, handing him the paper on which Archer had written the address and phone number of the funeral home.

"Just give me a few minutes, Mrs. Fletcher," he said, suddenly loping off down the street.

Fifteen minutes later, an open carriage with white leather seats and white wooden wheels drew up in front of the hotel. A young woman in a swallowtail coat hopped off the driver's seat, flipped down a set of steps, and held out her hand to me. "Hi, Mrs. Fletcher, I'm Beatrice. Napoleon sent me to pick you up."

"Where did he go?" I asked as I took her hand and climbed into the carriage.

"We'll get him in a minute. He went home to change." She handed me a yellow parasol that had been lying on the seat. "If it gets too hot in the sun, you can use this."

Beatrice scrambled back up to the driver's seat, clicked her tongue at the brown-and-black mule, and we slowly moved out into the traffic. Three blocks away, Napoleon waved to us from a corner. He still wore his checkered trousers, but had exchanged his skates for black-and-white high-top sneakers. The green suspenders and hoop around his waist were gone, replaced by a wide leather belt pulled tight to hold up the pants. A baseball cap covered his brown ringlets, and he'd scrubbed off his makeup. He leaped up into the seat beside me without waiting for Beatrice to stop the carriage. "Once she's got Keats moving, it's better not to let him stop."

"Keats?"

"All the mules in our family are named for poets. Shakespeare's retired now, but Keats and Shelley are still working. Beatrice is training a young one; we're going to name him Blake."

Beatrice guided the carriage out of the French Quarter and into the bustling traffic of the Central Business District. As we drove at a leisurely pace toward the Garden District, our one-buggy parade drew little attention, although I thought we must have been quite a sight. Napoleon had opened the yellow parasol to shield me from the heat of the sun, and Beatrice had donned a top hat similar to the one Napoleon wore for his Jackson Square act. The mule clopped along the busy streets, unfazed by the larger and faster vehicles passing him, or by the occasional honking horns. We reached St. Charles Avenue and drove on a roadway parallel to the green-and-red streetcars, which ran on rails down the grassy "neutral ground," what we'd call a median in Cabot Cove. Passing through the Lower Garden District, with its fast-food chains and rundown buildings, we crossed Jackson Avenue and entered a neighborhood of genteel houses with well-kept gardens. Some were lush, their tropical plants nearly obscuring the Italian Renaissance or Victorian Gothic buildings they surrounded; others were tailored with clipped, formal plantings in front of Greek Revival porticos.

The Montgomery Funeral Home was off St. Charles Avenue, a modest white wood clapboard house with black shutters and square columns, and little other embellishment, as if to reflect the seriousness of the business inside. I was relieved to see that the large blacktop parking lot on the side of the building was empty—no funeral service was in progress—except for a few black sedans and a glass-sided hearse parked in front of a large garage at the rear of the property.

I left Beatrice and Napoleon sitting in the carriage with Keats, who nibbled at a privet hedge that bordered the lot. I climbed the front steps, pushed a buzzer, and opened the unlocked door. The décor was suitably muted and dull. A plush brown carpet covered the vestibule floor, and stopped at the sills of the two rooms that flanked the entry, their varnished wooden doors thrown open. On the other side of the doorways, the carpet continued as a runner, leading down an aisle that separated two banks of pews in the left side room, and two sets of folding chairs in the room to my right. The windows in both rooms were concealed by dark-red velvet drapes with black trim. Ahead of me, a round mahogany table held an elaborate flower arrangement, the heavy scent of lilies overpowering whatever aroma more delicate flowers may have contributed to the stuffy air. I walked around the table, the floorboards creaking under the thick carpeting, and saw a door to an elevator. To its right was a stairwell leading to the lower level and a discreet sign that read OFFICE, with an arrow pointing down. I switched Wayne's garment bag to my left arm, gripped the railing with my right hand, and descended the stairs, treading carefully so as not to catch the heels of my shoes on the carpet's pile.

"May I help you?" a deep voice asked.

"Yes, I'm Jessica Fletcher. I called earlier and left a message." I was talking to a middle-aged man at the base of the stairs, who held out a hand for me to grasp. He wore a charcoal-gray suit, crisp white shirt, and navy-and-green tie. At least he's not wearing black, I thought.

"I got your message, Mrs. Fletcher. I'm Jordan Bunting, the manager. Let me take that from you, please." He lifted the garment bag from my arm and led me to a small office almost entirely taken up with a massive desk. He held the back of one of a pair of chairs in front of the desk and I sat. "I'll just hang this here for now," he said, hooking the garment bag over the top of the door. "Would you like some tea? I've just made a fresh pot."

"That would be lovely, thank you."

While Bunting went to get our tea, I looked around. The perimeter of the room on my side of the desk was lined with narrow chairs, which I assumed were there to accommodate members of large families when funeral arrangements were being made. The opposite side of the desk was framed by low black filing cabinets, with one high-backed office chair for its owner. There were no pictures on the cream-colored walls, only a black-and-white license, or diploma, hanging above one of the files; the type was too small for me to see from where I sat.

Bunting returned with a small tray, which he rested on a corner of the desk while pulling a slide-out shelf into position. He set cups and saucers on the shelf and seated himself in the chair next to mine. "Tell me again why you're here," he said, pouring tea from a porcelain pot with an English ivy design and a leather handle.

"I'm delivering funeral clothes for Wayne Copely," I said, "and I was hoping to speak with the undertaker who was on duty when his body came in."

"This is a family-run business, Mrs. Fletcher. We only have a small staff. That person would be Earl Montgomery."

"Is he here now?"

"Yes. We have a service this afternoon, and he's preparing the body. Perhaps I can answer any questions you have."

"Does that mean he won't have time to see me?"

"I'm afraid not," he said. "But I'm familiar with the Copely case. Did you want to review the arrangements Mr. Levinson made?"

"Oh, was Archer here already?"

"No. We've only spoken by phone. In fact, he left instructions for you to bring back Mr. Copely's personal effects when you dropped off the clothes. I can get them for you now, if you like."

"That's fine," I said. "I'd also like to take the things he wore the night he died."

"Most families don't want the old clothes back," he said. "They may be damaged or stained. Are you sure you want them?"

"If his clothes are in bad shape, I can look at them here," I said, "and decide what I should bring home."

"It's most irregular," he muttered to himself. "Let me check to see what we've done with them." He reached up to unhook Wayne's garment bag from the door. "I'll just take this with me."

He left the office, and I got up and leaned out the door to see him turn left at the end of the corridor. He returned two minutes later carrying a plastic bag, and wearing a mournful expression. "I'm terribly sorry, Mrs. Fletcher, but Mr. Copely's clothing has already been disposed of."

"Oh, dear," I said.

"We do have his shoes, however, but I haven't had time to clean them up for you," he said, indicating the plastic bag. "If you'd like to wait, I can do that now."

"No, no, please don't trouble yourself," I said. "The way they are is fine. I'm so pleased you have them." I took the bag from him.

"If there isn't anything else, Mrs, Fletcher, I'm afraid I'm needed upstairs."

"Thank you so much, Mr. Bunting," I said, picking up my teacup. "It was so kind of you to see me."

"May I escort you out?"

"Oh, I haven't finished my tea. You don't mind, do you,

if I linger here a moment longer? It's so peaceful in this room."

Bunting cleared his throat. "No, of course not. You take your time, Mrs. Fletcher. I'll be back in a little while."

"Thank you."

When I heard the creaking as he crossed the floor upstairs, I picked up the bag with Wayne's shoes and went down the hall in the direction Bunting had come from before. I turned left at the end of the corridor into a short hallway with two sets of double doors. I turned the knob on the first set of doors, pulled, and found myself looking out on an outdoor loading bay. An empty hearse was backed up to the platform. I closed that door as quietly as I could and went to the second set of doors. These were also unlocked, and when I opened them and slipped into the room, I knew I'd found the right place. Several coffins were stacked to my right, and four of what I assumed were refrigerated drawers were on my left. A hook on the wall held Wayne's garment bag. Straight ahead, a tiny man in black pants and a white business shirt, covered by a butcher's apron, was standing on a step stool, leaning over an open coffin on a draped stand and applying makeup to a corpse.

"That you again, Bunting?" he asked, not looking up from his work.

"Actually, no, Mr. Montgomery," I said. "I'm Jessica Fletcher. I left a message for you earlier today. Perhaps you remember?"

"Didn't Bunting take care of you?" he asked, still concentrating on his task.

"He did," I said, nodding, although he couldn't see me. "He was very efficient and kind. I just had some questions only you can answer."

"Pretty bold of you coming in here."

"Yes. I'm sorry for that."

"Well, I don't mind, if you don't. Take a seat. Gotta keep working. I have a deadline to meet."

"I understand about deadlines," I said, pulling a rolling stool away from the wall and perching on it.

"It's about Copely, isn't it?"

"Yes. Mr. Bunting was good enough to give me Mr. Copely's shoes."

"Usually, we burn the shoes along with the other clothes," he said, opening a box of face powder. "But these were so unusual, I kept 'em around. Planned to donate them to the thrift shop once I cleaned 'em up."

"Perhaps Wayne's sister will want to do that, too."

"Hmm."

"I wanted to ask you about Wayne's body, Mr. Montgomery. I know he was bitten by a snake, but did you notice any other marks or abrasions?"

"You mean, did anyone hit him on the head, or something?"

"Yes, that's what I mean."

"No. You'd know right away with that shaved head."

"I imagine you would."

"He was a mess though."

"Why?"

"You ever seen a bad snakebite?"

"I've never seen *any* snakebite."

"You can probably figure out where the fang marks are if you look real close, but as the venom spreads, it causes the whole limb to swell. The blood under the skin starts to boil up into these big black blisters that run down the arm. They put so much pressure on the skin, they burst, spraying blood everywhere. That's why the clothes were ruined. Too bloody to clean. Looks to me like he must've died pretty fast."

"I hope so," I said, sickened at the thought of Wayne suffering.

"Want to see his body?"

"No, I don't think so."

"His face looks okay," he said, picking up a comb. "Should be able to have an open coffin."

Holding the bag with Wayne's shoes, I thanked Mr. Montgomery and left, never having seen his face, nor he mine. Napoleon and Beatrice were very quiet when I climbed into the carriage and fell back against the white leather seat. I placed the bag on my lap and held it tightly as we lurched into the street and headed back to the French Quarter.

Chapter Seventeen

Napoleon and Beatrice dropped me off in front of Wayne's building with promises to collect me at my hotel the next morning. I turned the key in the lock of the third-floor apartment and walked in. The French doors had been secured; with no window open, the place was humid and stuffy. I dropped the bag containing Wayne's shoes on the sofa and opened the doors wide, letting a breeze into the room. The spicy scent of cooking came with it, but the freshness of the draft washed away the leaden air of death, lightening my mood.

I sat on the sofa, pulled out Wayne's black-and-white spectator shoes, and set them on top of the bag on the coffee table. Someone at the funeral home had stuffed them with newspaper to retain their shape. I inspected the heels and was surprised to see very few scuff marks. I had suspected that Wayne had been killed elsewhere and later placed at the crypt in the cemetery. But if his body had been moved, his shoes probably would bear the evidence. Wayne was no lightweight. Unless someone was able to pick him up without dragging his feet on the ground—an unconvincing scenario—there would have been heavy scuffing of the heels or other parts of the shoes as the body was pulled into position. It was likely that he died where he was found.

I noticed that one shoe was heavier than the other, and pulled out the newspaper to see why. Wedged into the toe was a plastic bag containing Wayne's wallet, and a few other items that must have been in his pockets the night he was found. I remembered Bunting telling me that Archer had requested I bring back Wayne's personal effects. I'd been so intent on getting his shoes, I'd forgotten to ask Bunting where he'd put them.

I emptied the bag onto the table. There was the infamous gris-gris on a leather thong, forty-seven cents in change, a chronographic watch, a yellow matchbook from a place called The Blazer Pub, a folded white handkerchief, and the wallet. His keys were missing, I realized. Steppe must still have them. Inside the leather billfold, I found eighty dollars and three credit cards, which ruled out robbery as a motive for the killing. Wayne also had a press pass, a telephone card, several business cards, and an old photograph showing him with Philippe Beaudin, standing on a dock, each holding up a fish. Folded in among the bills was a piece of paper, obviously torn from a calendar. At the top of page, the word "Friday" appeared with the first three letters of April; the rest of the date was torn away. Scribbled sideways across the page, not indicating any specific time, was BROADBENT.

Could Wayne have been meeting Julian Broadbent the night he died? Julian had been conspicuous by his absence the next day at Jazz Fest. He's an investigative reporter. Might he have found the cylinder recordings of Little Red LeCoeur? Did he inadvertently send Wayne to meet his killer? Or was he a witness to Wayne's death? A participant? Questions simmered in my mind, and I had no answers.

Sighing, I returned the note to the wallet and dropped it back in the plastic bag along with the watch, handkerchief, gris-gris, and coins. I opened the yellow matchbook, noting the address of the pub, and threw it in with the cache of Wayne's things. I stuffed the bag back in one shoe, and stood up. Where was the box Clarice wanted?

In what passed for a kitchen, I checked the few cabinets

against the wall, as well as the shelves above them, and the ones under the freestanding bar. I scanned the bookcases in the living room, walked to the bedroom and looked there, gave the bathroom and hall closet a good search, but found nothing that resembled a hand-painted Chinese box. Perplexed, I went back into the living room, sat on the sofa, and let my eyes wander the room. I picked up Wayne's shoes and the bag on which they sat, took the whole package to the little bar that served the kitchen, and left it on the counter for Archer. When I turned to find the phone, my gaze fell on the coffee table I'd just been using. It was nothing more than a glass top sitting on a large red-and-gold painted box, much bigger than I'd anticipated. The Chinese box!

Laughing at how I could miss something in plain sight, I pulled off the glass top and balanced it against the sofa. I picked up the box. It was made of very light wood. I looked for a drawer, but even though the box had gold rings affixed to it in several places, when I pulled on them, nothing happened. I shook the box and heard something shuffling around inside. Wayne, you devil, I thought. You've left me another puzzle to solve. A wave of bittersweet memories swamped me: Wayne trotting me all over New Orleans, chatting about jazz and filling my brain with more facts than I could ever possibly remember; leading me through his favorite restaurants, introducing me to waiters and maître d's, and watching gleefully as I swooned over his favorite dishes; and talking late into the night about writing, our very different lives, and how nice it was to have become friends. I was sad to lose him, but grateful to have known him.

Gritting my teeth, I attacked the box, looking for clues to reveal its secret. I pressed the corners, tapped along the top, bottom, and sides, twisted the rings, pushed them, pulled them one at a time in varying order, then finally, when I twisted one ring and pulled on another, I heard a click and a narrow drawer popped open. Once the first drawer was found, the others quickly yielded to my persistence, and I sat back to examine their contents.

In the smallest drawer was a mini–tape cassette of the kind used in dictating equipment or, perhaps, his answering machine. In the two larger drawers were numerous sheets covered in Wayne's neat handwriting. I read a few paragraphs. These were manuscript pages for Wayne's book on Little Red LeCoeur. A third drawer contained Wayne's notes to himself, ideas for chapters, quotes from authorities, and other scraps of information. I gathered up all the papers and the tape, and shoved them in my shoulderbag. I'd return the papers to Clarice after I'd had a chance to review them to see if they held any clues to what I now considered Wayne's murder.

I pushed the drawers on the box closed, restoring it to its original shape, and took the tape I'd found in the first drawer into Wayne's bedroom. The telephone next to his bed had a built-in answering machine. I flipped open the lid, removed the tape that was there, replaced it with the one I'd just found, and pressed PLAY.

"You have two messages," an automated voice droned. The first was from his editor's secretary, asking Wayne to resend an article that had gotten lost in the office shuffle. The second message was not so benign. A whiny, high-pitched voice that raised goosebumps on my arms complained, "You never learn, do you, Copely? I've warned you before. I know where you are, where you go. You can't escape me now. I've been sharpening my blade for you. Do you remember what I plan to do with it?" I shivered as the speaker—I couldn't tell if it was a man or a woman—recited a terrible litany of the acts of torture he or she planned. I pressed REWIND, intending to listen again, when I heard the front door open. Quickly, I pulled out the tape and reinserted the original one.

"What are you doing?"

"Hello, Archer," I said calmly, slipping the tape into my pocket as I turned to face him. "I came in to check if there were any messages on Wayne's machine. I didn't know you'd be coming by."

"And are there any?"

"I don't see any flashing light. Would you like to check for yourself?"

"No." He had a briefcase under one arm, and a harried look to his face. I followed him into the living room, where he paused next to the round table. "What's that?" he said, pointing to the box I'd left on the sofa.

"Clarice asked me to pick it up for her. She said it belonged to their father."

Archer laid his briefcase on the round table, went to the sofa, picked up the box and gave it a good shake. "She can have it," he said, handing it back to me. "It's worthless."

"It made a nice coffee table," I said. "What should we do with the glass top?"

Archer shrugged. "Don't worry about it. I'll figure something out." His face was impassive, and his manner cool. He wasn't in a mood to be social. He sat at the table, drew several manila folders from his case, and began sorting papers.

"Mr. Bunting at Montgomery's said you'd made the funeral arrangements," I said. "When will it be?"

"Thursday at ten in the Cathedral. I had to wait till the brass band that I wanted was available." He looked up. "You brought in Wayne's clothes?"

"I delivered them this morning."

"Did they give you my message?"

"As a matter of fact, they did. Wayne's wallet and other items are on the bar over there along with his shoes."

"You carried back his shoes?" He jumped up, went to the bar, and dumped the items from the plastic bag on the counter to pick through them.

"Yes. They were all they had. They'd already disposed of his other clothing."

Archer turned around. "I didn't mean for you to fetch his clothes, just his wallet and watch, and these things. I should have been specific."

I thought to myself, I'm glad you weren't or I wouldn't have been able to lay to rest one concern I had about whether the body had been moved.

"I'm sorry you had to cart these back," he said, picking up the shoes and crossing the room. "I'll only have to get rid of them again."

"You and Clarice will probably want to give away most of Wayne's clothes," I said, trailing him into the bedroom and watching him line up the spectator shoes with Wayne's other footwear on the floor of the closet. I hoped he would get the hint that Clarice had a stake in these decisions, too.

"I'll have to take care of it," he said, wiping his hands down the side of his trousers. "Clarice still has Steve's suits hanging in her closet, and it's been months since he died."

In the living room, Archer went back to his task of sorting Wayne's papers, and I tried to figure out how I was going to get the Chinese box to Clarice.

"Do you think Wayne had any cord?" I asked.

"Try the drawer to the left of the sink."

I found some cord, wrapped it around the box, and started to devise a makeshift handle for myself. "Are those Wayne's papers?" I asked.

"Yes. I think he had a will, and I'm pretty sure he had insurance. If they're anywhere, they'd be in these files."

"I went to see Clarice yesterday," I said. "She told me you'd taken a lot of papers with you."

"She'd make a mess of the files if I left it to her," he said irritably. "And I didn't want her hovering over my shoulder." He glanced up at me. "You know she's not the sweet, delicate lady she appears to be."

"No?"

"No. She can be hard as nails when she takes something into her head. And she's greedy and selfish, whether she has money or not."

"I didn't know that," I said softly.

"Right now, she's desperate for money." Archer said. There was almost a hint of satisfaction in his tone. "Steve left her without a penny and a ton of debt."

"What will she do?" I asked.

"She's counting on Wayne to rescue her again. He always did, although I talked him out of it the last time. She was furious." He frowned, remembering.

"Why did you talk him out of it?"

"Because she's got to learn to take care of herself instead of just taking."

"Shouldn't that have been strictly between them?" I asked.

"Why? I was always the one to run her errands, take her to appointments, do her shopping, escort her in society while her drug addict husband nodded over his needle. And did she ever thank me? Was she ever grateful?" He cursed under his breath.

As I finished tying up the box for Clarice, I thought about how you never truly knew what went on in families, the unhappy relationships, the shifting alliances, the resentments. Archer considered himself part of the Copely family, not simply an employee. He'd been with Wayne for sixteen years. Yet Clarice was ready to drop him now that she had Alberta. And what about Wayne? Had he really been thinking about letting Archer go?

"Here it is," Archer called out. "I knew he had a will." He unfolded a long legal document, and smoothed it on the table. "He left me the apartment," he said excitedly.

"How nice for you," I said.

"There are a couple of other bequests. We have to divide

up his accounts, his royalties, and his belongings," he muttered, reading to himself. He put the will down. "There should be a life insurance policy here somewhere." He eagerly hunted through the papers until finding what he sought. He slipped the policy from its brown envelope. His eyes moved rapidly back and forth across the page, and then stopped, widening in surprise. "I can't believe it," he whispered. Reading again, his expression turned to thunder. He slapped the paper down on the table, grabbed his briefcase, and stormed out of the apartment.

I went to the table, picked up the insurance policy, and read it. The beneficiary was named on page two. It was Clarice Copely Cruz. And the policy was for a million dollars. A million dollars! Two million if double indemnity could be proved.

Chapter Eighteen

"Doris, does your tape recorder use minicassettes?"

"No, but my dictating machine does. Do you want to borrow it?"

"Yes, if you don't mind."

"I don't mind at all. I'll drop it off in ten minutes."

"You don't have to do that. I can come up."

"It's no bother. I'm going uptown to have tea with a colleague of mine at Tulane. I'll bring it by on my way out."

I'd walked back to the hotel from Wayne's apartment. It was another hot, busy day, the French Quarter filled with tourists, and all the taxis and carriages occupied. The red-and-gold box had been cumbersome to carry. Even with my cleverly tied cord handle, the box had bounced against my leg every third step, and holding it in front of me in my arms was no solution; it blocked my view. When I reached the hotel, I immediately gave my burden, along with Clarice's address, to the concierge, who promised the box would be delivered the next day.

I called Clarice when I got to my room, explained when the box would arrive, and told her about bringing Wayne's things back to his apartment. I did not mention Archer's presence or what he'd found among the papers. That responsibility was his.

"I found a photograph in Wayne's wallet I wanted to ask you about," I said. If she was taken aback by my going through his personal papers, she didn't let on. "It's a picture of Wayne and Philippe Beaudin holding up their fishing catch," I said. "They both look young; it must have been taken some time ago."

"Yes. They used to be fishing buddies."

"I hadn't realized they were ever that friendly."

"They were for a time, but then they took a dislike to each other."

"What happened?"

"About ten or fifteen years ago, they had a falling out over something—probably political, but I can't remember now—and they didn't speak for years."

"Years? That's a long time."

"Outsiders always think that way," she said, "but it's not at all unusual down here. We look like a big city, but we really have a small-town mentality. People are always squabbling and holding grudges."

"Had Wayne and Phil ever made up their differences?"

"They started talking again recently, probably because the mayor and his wife are my friends. They kept bumping into each other at our social functions and decided to let bygones be."

"I see."

"Phil is going to give the eulogy at the funeral, Thursday. Will you be there?"

"Of course."

"I'm going to pick out a little something of Wayne's for you to have as a keepsake. Would you like that?"

"I would like that very much."

My next call was to Detective Steppe. He wasn't in, but I left a message as to where I was going, and asked him to join me later at the Blazer Pub, if he could.

I sat on the edge of the bed with all of Wayne's papers spread around me. He'd already written fifty pages of his manuscript for his next book, but nothing I could see in them held any clues to his death. I sifted through his notes, read snippets of research, and paused at lists of names and phone numbers, including Blind Jack's. I'd already tried to call him several times to no avail. I spotted a small corner of blue peeking out from under the pile of papers, and pushed them aside to extract what appeared to be a hand-drawn map. 1 couldn't tell whether it depicted a local area; most of the places on it were abbreviations or initials. On the right side, Wayne had written EW in black ink and had circled the initials. *EW.* Could the letters stand for Elijah Williams? I folded the map and put it in my purse, thinking I'd show it to Napoleon in the morning in the hopes that he could decipher it.

I gathered up all the papers and looked for someplace to keep them secure, finally stashing them in the same flight bag where I'd stowed the mystery story by David Stewart, the student who'd interviewed me. I unzipped a side compartment and put in Wayne's papers, along with the cassette tape from his answering machine, the one containing the threatening message. The irony wasn't lost on me that here, enclosed in one section of my bag, were symbols of Wayne's life and death.

Bobby Pinto's cottage housed both home and business. It was painted white, with long green shutters covering the windows. The proprietor himself answered my knock. A muscular man of medium height with a gray ponytail, he wore faded blue jeans and a long-sleeved denim shirt unbuttoned over a T-shirt of indeterminate color. It might have been blue at one time. Heavy steel-toed boots were laced over the bottom of his jeans. He looked vaguely familiar; I didn't know why.

"This ain't a tourist attraction, you know."

"I'm Jessica Fletcher, Mr. Pinto," I said, "a friend of Doris Burns. I have some questions about snakes. Doris said you were the expert."

He grunted and held the door open for me to enter. I stepped directly into an office area with a battered desk and three tall file cabinets. A glass-front refrigerator contained rows of plastic-covered beakers holding cloudy fluids, which I assumed were venom.

He sat down at his desk and pointed to a visitor chair.

"I have the feeling I've seen you before," I said.

He straightened in his chair. "The TV people did a story on me," he said, obviously pleased. "Did you see it?"

"I'm afraid not," I said, smiling.

Behind him was a large aquarium tank in which the curved length of a snake seemed to be folded back on itself three times, the brown markings of its thick body pressed against the glass. Pinto followed my gaze. "That's Oscar," he said, cocking his head toward the tank. "He's a pet."

"What kind of snake is he?"

"Boa constrictor. Gettin' a bit big for his home now."

"What will you do?"

"Sell him to another collector, maybe."

"How long have you had him?" I asked.

"Ten years." He swiveled in his chair and lifted the rock that held down a screen covering the top of the tank. "Wanna see him?" He didn't wait for my answer. He dipped his arms in the tank and pulled Oscar out, cradling the snake's body like a baby. The snake's tail immediately wrapped around his arm, and Pinto lifted Oscar's body over his head and wore him like scarf, gently holding the boa's head in his palm.

I was grateful for the desk between us, but resisted moving my chair farther back. I sat quietly and watched the snake. It was beautiful in a way, its tan, brown, and black colors arranged in a pleasing pattern. It moved smoothly, gliding along Pinto's neck while he directed its head with his hand. Pinto visibly relaxed as he handled the snake, crooning to it, and sliding his hand along the reptile's belly.

"Would you like to touch him?" he asked, raising an eyebrow.

This is a test, I thought. I hesitated, not wanting to offend him, but not really eager to pet a snake.

"He's not slimy at all. That's what people think, but it's not true," he said, leaning forward and extending Oscar's body toward me, holding the snake's head away. "Go ahead."

Tentatively, I reached out and rubbed along the brown scales. The snake's body was dry, and smoother than I had expected.

"See?" Pinto said as I withdrew my hand. He seemed pleased that I hadn't rejected his offer. He returned Oscar to his tank, and went to wash his hands at a small sink next to the refrigerator. I followed his example.

"Come on, I'll show you around."

Pinto led me through the office to the next room, where racks of tanks were strung along the walls, from floor to shoulder height, each with a single bulb illuminating its reptilian residents. In the center of the room were three more tanks, one filled with rats, another with mice, half of them moving frantically back and forth. The third held crickets.

"Dinner," he said, nodding at the tanks in the center. He flipped a switch to illuminate the overhead lights. "This is my native species room," he said. "I caught all of these snakes right here in Louisiana." He rested his hand on the top of one rack. "These over here are nonvenomous. You've got your speckled kingsnake, your black-masked racer, your yellow-bellied water snake." He tapped each tank as he named the snakes. "Those over there are the venomous ones: copperhead, cottonmouth, coral snake. Got the constrictors upstairs, and the rattlesnakes out back."

"This one looks familiar," I said, looking at a red-and-black-banded specimen.

"That's a Louisiana milksnake."

My midnight visitor.

"Want me to take it out for you?"

"No, thank you," I said. "Touching one snake a day is sufficient."

He smiled at me for the first time, revealing a gold-rimmed tooth in front.

"I'd rather you tell me about your business, Mr. Pinto."

"If you wanna talk business," he said, "you gotta see my invention."

"Your invention?"

"Got a patent pending on it and everything."

We walked through to the next room, which was crammed with piles of packing boxes, shelves of basking lights, and sacks labeled REPTILE BARK and ASPEN BEDDING.

"See this?" he said, grabbing a tall box off the top of a stack of cartons. "I designed it."

It looked like an ordinary box to me. "What is it?" I asked.

"It's the Pinto Snake Transportation System," he said proudly. "Guy out in Metairie makes 'em for me. See my mark over here?" He pointed to a red circle surrounding the letters "PSTS" that were stamped in the corner of the box and on its top, and looked at me expectantly.

"What makes it special?" I asked.

A big grin spread over his face. "Keeps the snakes nice and comfy between here and their new home."

I smiled back. "How does it do that?" I asked, tossing him the question he obviously wanted to hear.

"It's divided, see?" he said enthusiastically, opening one end of the box. "This pulls out so you can wedge the snake's head in here, kind of like a cardboard collar, isolating it in this end of the box. And then the rest of the body can curl up in the bottom of the box. When you get the snake home, you open the bottom of the box and you can reach in and grab the snake behind the head, and it still has this protective cardboard collar on. Keeps you from getting bit."

"What happens if you open the wrong end of the box?"

"Nothing, as long as you don't stick your hand in," he said. "The collar prevents the snake from striking."

"Very impressive," I said.

"Gonna make a fortune on this one day."

"I hope you do," I said. "If you need all these boxes, you must sell a lot of snakes. Who buys them?"

"All kinds of people. Individual collectors, pet shops, voodoo temples, zoos. I got a website. Starting to get some business from there, too. Plus, I sell the venom to hospitals and drug companies."

"What kind of snake do you sell to the voodoo temples?"

"Constrictors," he said. "The hand-raised ones are easy to handle, as you saw."

I was quiet for a minute, thinking. "You mentioned venom. What kind of venom do you sell?"

"Mostly rattlesnake," he said. "They're in the back."

We walked into the last room. It must have been a kitchen at one time; an old sink stood alone on one wall. An oilcloth-covered table and two chairs were set up nearby. One shelf on the wall next to the sink held a few dishes and glasses. Above it, another shelf displayed a dusty collection of rattles, snakeskins, and reptile skulls. A narrow staircase led to the second floor. Straight ahead was a large picture window that overlooked an L-shaped enclosure that ran the width of the back room, and extended halfway down one side of the house. Ten-foot-tall chain-link fencing was covered with a fine metal mesh that reached across the top forming a roof for the area. Twined about large branches set on the ground, curled up in each corner, and slithering in and out of old automobile tires scattered about the area were dozens and dozens of rattlesnakes.

"Got close to a hundred of 'em by now," Pinto said, stripping off his denim shirt and hanging it on a peg. The sleeves and half the sides of his T-shirt were torn off, revealing the myriad tattoos Doris had mentioned, covering his biceps, shoulders, and torso. They were all pictures of snakes. "Don't like to wear sleeves when I'm playing with them," he said. "Got one caught up a sleeve once, and damn near killed me. Got plenty of scars to show for it."

"You're going to play with them?" I asked, incredulous.

"They like it. Gives 'em a little exercise."

Pinto picked up a long stick with a forked end, and opened a storm door leading to the pen. Most of the snakes shrank back out of his way. He used the stick to toss several others aside, and to pick one off a branch and set it down in front of him. Resting the stick against the side of the house, he pulled a white handkerchief from his pocket and dangled it in front of the snake like a matador with a red cape. The snake reared back, struck at the handkerchief—the white cloth fluttering up and out of the way—and flopped down on the ground, recoiling again and readying for another strike. Pinto danced around the snake, forcing it to turn and follow the handkerchief to strike, each time coming closer to the steel toe of Pinto's boot. The snake tired before the man did, and while a series of rattles sounded around the pen, the other snakes stayed away from their keeper.

"Are they all the same kind?" I asked, relieved, when he'd come back inside and locked the door behind him.

"They're all rattlers, but there're many different kinds," he said, pulling on his denim shirt again. "That little guy over there, hanging from the fence, that's a western pygmy rattlesnake. The one I played with and those three in the corner are eastern diamondbacks."

"Do you have any canebrake rattlesnakes?"

"Most of these are canebrakes," he said. "They have a tendency not to move too quickly, so they're easy for me to hook. Trapped one in a cemetery for the city last weekend."

"I heard about that," I said. "Is that usual? Have you caught many in the city?"

"Lots of snakes in the city these days because of the

drought," he replied. "Don't usually see a canebrake out of the country, but there's always a first time."

"Would you recognize a snake you'd caught before?"

"You mean can I tell them apart?" he said, waving his arm toward the collection of snakes in his enclosure.

"Can you?"

"Not really. Even though their markings are different from snake to snake, it'd be like recognizing one sparrow over his brother."

"Have you sold any canebrakes recently?"

"Sure," he said. "Sold one last week."

I pulled out the picture of Wayne that I'd cut from the newspaper and showed it to him. "Did you ever sell a snake to this man?"

"I was gonna say he doesn't look familiar," he said, hesitating.

"But he does?"

"I don't know him, but I've seen this picture before."

"Oh," I said, disappointed. "It was in Monday's paper. You must have seen it there."

"No," he said, shaking his head. "I don't read the paper. But there was a guy in here on Saturday asking the same questions you are. He showed me this picture."

"What did he look like?"

"Normal-looking white guy. I didn't notice anything unusual about him."

"Can you describe him at all?"

"Average height, average build, brown hair. That's all I remember."

I wondered if Detective Steppe had been here before me. I would have described him as heavyset, but who knew what Pinto considered "average." "Was he a policeman?" I asked.

"Didn't say. Didn't look like a cop, though," he said. "Dressed too nice for that."

*   *   *

It was another late evening when I finally closed the door to my hotel room. The bed had been turned down, and the French doors were secured; I checked, a habit I'd gotten into even though I rarely opened them. Detective Steppe had met me at The Blazer Pub, a neighborhood bar across the street from St. Louis Cemetery Number One. He'd been annoyed that I'd planned to go by myself, and had gotten there early to greet me with a scowl and a lecture.

"This is not a neighborhood for you to be wandering around after dark," he'd scolded.

"I'm sure I'm safe here with you," I countered.

"What if I hadn't been able to get here?"

"I would have asked the bartender to call a cab for me when I was ready to leave."

He shook his head. "I can't get used to these modern independent women," he said, giving me a wan smile. "I was raised to look after females, open doors for them, worry about their safety."

"I still like to have doors opened for me," I said. "But you don't have to worry about me any more than you would your male friends."

"I'll try to remember that." He took a sip of his beer, studied me over the rim of the glass, and said, "The word came down from the top."

"What word?" I asked.

"To close the case. It came straight from the superintendent, who got it from the mayor."

"Amadour himself?"

"Sounds that way."

"Well, that's a surprise, isn't it?"

"I knew it had to be something like that," he said. "Everyone hopped to it so quickly. It couldn't have been a decision made in the district. It had to come from higher up. And it came from as high up as you can go."

I wondered what the mayor's rationale might have been.

He had close ties with Wayne's sister. Was he protecting Clarice again, as he had when he cautioned me not to tell her about my suspicions? And why? Did he not want her to know that Wayne might have been murdered? Or did he suspect she might have a motive for killing him herself?

"Listen," Steppe said, "I'm exhausted. They've got me running around like a headless chicken. What are we doing here? You're not planning a trip to the cemetery tonight, are you?"

"No, but Wayne may have been here before his trip," I said, explaining about finding the matchbook among Wayne's personal items. "Didn't you see it?"

"I knew there was a matchbook," he said. "I saw it when one of the other guys emptied Copely's pockets into the evidence bag." He shrugged. "I figured I had time to examine all his stuff later on. After the ruling, I went to find the evidence bag, but it had already been sent to the mortuary with the body."

I looked around the pub. It was definitely not one of New Orleans's more elegant establishments. The smell of spilled beer and stale cigarettes pervaded the air, and the room was dimly lit, except for the area behind the bar. It would have been easy to miss a customer, especially if there had been a crowd on Friday night. We approached the bartender. Was he on duty last Friday night? Yes. Did he recognize this man? I showed him the picture of Wayne that had been in the *Times-Picayune*.

The bartender studied the photograph and rubbed his chin. "I might have seen him."

"Are you sure?" I asked.

"We don't get a lot of Anglos in here," he said drolly. "I was on the late shift. Seems I remember two white guys. They left shortly after I came on."

"What time would that be?" Steppe asked.

"Around midnight."

"What did the other man look like?" I asked.

"Medium height, jeans, T-shirt, baseball hat."

"Did you notice anything unusual about them?" I asked. "Were they arguing? Did they seem angry with each other?"

"Just the opposite, I'd say. Your friend here was pretty drunk," he said, tapping Wayne's picture. "He could barely stand up. His buddy had his arm around him and helped him out."

"You're sure it was this man?" I asked.

"Short guy, shaved head. Yeah, it was him."

"Just great," Steppe muttered on the way back to my hotel. "He was drunk. Maybe he did stumble on a rattler and get himself killed."

"I don't think so," I said. "Wayne didn't drink."

"Well, he did Friday night," he said, yawning, as we pulled up in front of the Royal.

"The bartender didn't come on duty till midnight," I said. "He never actually saw Wayne drinking, just saw the effects of what he thought was alcohol. Maybe Wayne was drugged. When do you get the toxicology reports back?"

"That's a real long shot," he said, rubbing his eyes. "I'm bushed. Can we talk about this in the morning? Why don't I come by about seven. I'll buy you coffee and we can go over everything we've got."

The red light was flashing on my telephone when I entered my room. It was Doris reminding me she would need the dictating machine back in the morning. Hers was the only call. So far, I hadn't received any communication in response to my announcement in Charlie Gable's column that I was pursuing the recordings of Little Red LeCoeur. It was disappointing.

I took my flight bag from the closet, put it on my bed, unzipped the side compartment, and pulled out the minicassette. I plugged in the dictating machine and slipped in the tape. The high, eerie voice filled the silence, whining about Wayne never learning.

"I've warned you before. I know where you are, where

you go. You can't escape me now. I've been sharpening my blade for you."

I took the little pad beside my phone and wrote down the full message. Something was bothering me, and it was more than the description of the torture the caller was threatening.

I listened again, cocking my head for any nuance I might have missed the first few times. My eyes fell on my flight bag. That's it, I thought. In David Stewart's story, the ventriloquist changed his real voice when he was working with the dummy. Had Wayne's tormenter changed his voice? It would have been easy to record the message in advance, altering the voice, and play it into Wayne's answering machine when he wasn't there. I rewound the tape and pushed PLAY. This time I rotated the speed knob, slowing down the tape while the caller was speaking. With each fraction of a turn, the voice got lower and lower, until the caller drew out the words in a slow, measured beat. It was a man's voice. It was a voice I knew.

Chapter Nineteen

Steppe called early Wednesday morning to cancel our appointment. He was exasperated. The department was sending him to a conference in Baton Rouge, and he wouldn't be back till Friday.

"Never went to one of these things before," he complained. "Seems to me they're trying to get me out of town."

We agreed he would call and leave his telephone number while I was at the mayor's party, and we would confer after the funeral Thursday when he had a break in his schedule. We hung up, and I thought about Steppe's suspicions. If the mayor and the police department didn't want Wayne's death investigated, he might be right; they could be moving him out of the picture. What will they do about me? I wondered.

The sky was overcast when I exited the lobby of the Royal Hotel. The lowering clouds and the still air increased the impact of the humidity, making it feel even hotter than the ninety-degree temperature registered on the thermometer. True to their word, Beatrice and Napoleon occupied the driver's bench of the white carriage parked in front of my hotel. They sat, heads together, speaking quietly. Spying me, Beatrice put on her top hat and straightened her white sundress. Napoleon had forsaken any part of his clown costume, and wore baggy khaki pants and a Little Red LeCoeur T-shirt. How appropriate, I thought. He'd fitted a baseball cap over his black curls, and turned the brim to the back.

"Where are we off to today, Mrs. Fletcher?" he asked as he handed me into the carriage.

"That depends on how good your map-reading skills are," I said, unfolding the crude chart I'd found among Wayne's papers.

Napoleon glanced at the map and started to laugh.

"What's so funny?" I asked.

"We're vibrating together, you and me. You asked if I knew about Little Red LeCoeur, and his recordings."

"That's right."

"Well, I know someone who does."

"In the French Quarter?"

"No, ma'am, but not too far."

"And who would that be?"

He grinned. "Can't tell you just yet."

"Is this a map to where this person lives?"

He nodded.

"Do you know how to get there?"

He looked down at the map and nodded again.

"Do you think this person would talk to me?"

"Just leave it to me, Mrs. Fletcher," he said, climbing into the driver's seat next to Beatrice. He whispered something to her, and she slapped the reins on Keats's rump and we moved out into the line of taxis and other traffic attempting to negotiate the French Quarter. Napoleon pulled a cellular phone from his front pocket and punched in a number. His voice was too low for me to hear, but he seemed satisfied with the conversation.

I smoothed out the folds of the blue paper on my lap and studied the abbreviations and initials along the network of lines that filled the page, trying to decipher what Napoleon had seen so easily. But my knowledge of places in New Orleans, much less outside the city, was limited, and the map kept its secrets from me.

Sometime later, Beatrice pulled on the reins and Keats

came to a stop on the levee along Lake Pontchartrain. Napoleon hopped off the driver's bench and held out his hand for me.

"What are we doing here?" I asked.

"There are no roads where you want to go," he replied. "We have to take a boat." He pointed to a flat-bottomed touring craft with rows of four seats across the beam, tied up at a terraced concrete seawall. "I need some money," he said apologetically. "We have to pay the captain."

While Napoleon negotiated with the "captain," a boy of about sixteen, I experience a twinge of trepidation that I had put myself into the hands of all these youngsters. But the boat looked sturdy enough, bobbing up and down as the wake made by larger vessels on the water reached the wall.

"Okay, we're set to go," Napoleon told me. "Beatrice will meet us when we get back."

The young captain, whose sea legs were better than mine, stood in the center of the boat and rode out the swells. He grasped my left hand and Napoleon took my right, and they guided me to the closest seat.

"I forgot to tell you when you called, if I don't get this back by two, my father will kill me," the captain told Napoleon. "He's got a tour group this afternoon."

"No sweat. We've got lots of time."

Napoleon dropped into the seat next to mine, and the young helmsman untied the lines and pushed off from the wall. He walked to the front of the boat, picked up two orange life vests, and dropped them at our feet. I struggled into mine, but Napoleon left his on the floor. We moved away from the concrete mooring slowly, but once clear of it, the captain opened the throttle. The wind whipped my hair and stung my eyes as the boat flew across the choppy water of the silver lake, and I put on my sunglasses to protect my eyes from the airstream. We cut across the wake of a yacht, and our boat tipped up in the air and slammed down in the water, spray rising on both sides of the bow and raining down on us. My arms were covered with water droplets, and tiny dark spots appeared on the parts of my blue blouse not covered by the life jacket.

"Can you get him to slow down?" I shouted to Napoleon, who was leaning back in his seat with both arms stretched along the tops of the adjacent chairs.

"What?" he yelled back.

I shouted my request again, and he reluctantly turned around and motioned to the captain.

At a slightly reduced speed, I began to enjoy being on the lake, although our competition for the right of way was daunting. Speedboats, sailboats, slower-moving tugboats, and fishing boats moved at various angles across the water, with no stoplights or yield signs to control the traffic. Fortunately, our young captain seemed to know the lay of the lake, and we zipped along, slowing down only when its breadth began to narrow. Ahead of us was a marina. We bypassed the piers and, instead, turned into a wide bayou.

Immediately, the air was still, thick with humidity and the sounds of insects and birds in the trees lining the waterway. Our captain chose a smaller branch and we glided up the stream, disturbing a great blue heron, which lifted into the air at our approach, its six-foot wing span creating a fleeting shadow over the boat. The water was dark, covered with patches of green algae, and the tupelo, gum, and cypress trees pressed in on us until there was no longer a distinct shoreline; we were surrounded by water and woods. There wasn't a sign of civilization until the captain rounded a curve to bring us to a rickety dock balanced on long poles sunk into the murky water. Tied up beneath the wooden platform was a small red pirogue, a Louisiana canoe.

"I'll wait two hours," the captain told Napoleon. "After that, I'm gone, so you better be here."

"No problem," Napoleon replied. As our boat knocked

against one of the pilings, he leaned over, grabbed the rope that tied the smaller vessel, and pulled it toward him. "You can leave the life jacket here, Mrs. Fletcher," he said. "You can stand up in this water, although I wouldn't recommend it."

"Why not?"

"Leeches," he replied. "Snakes, frogs, alligators. Lots of wildlife lives in this soup."

"I'll keep it in mind," I said.

"You might want this," he added, tossing me an aerosol can of insect repellent. I took his advice and sprayed my exposed skin.

The captain took the rope from Napoleon and held the canoe steady while we stepped into it. There was not a lot of room for both of us. Napoleon sat in the stern. I sat in the bow, facing him. Our knees were barely two feet apart. He pulled a paddle out from under the seats, pushed it against the bigger boat until he had room to maneuver, and aimed the bow into the woods. In minutes, I could no longer see the tourist boat and the dock it was tied to.

We paddled for what seemed a long spell, passing live oaks, black gums, and swamp maples. Several times I heard gurgles, and saw the surface of the water move, ripples growing out from where some creature had submerged itself, or a faint wake where another glided out of sight behind a tree. A low grunt echoed in the woods.

"That's a bull alligator," Napoleon told me, pointing out the log-like back of one of its kin drifting away from our boat.

We brushed away strands of Spanish moss that hung down from the trees, and swatted at flies buzzing around our heads in the steamy heat. We pushed through weeds and bumped against Cypress knees, the tree's roots that grow into the air about the base of the trunk and are believed to help the Cypress breathe. The boat was small and easy for

Napoleon to handle in the tangled growth of the swamp. I tried to see what markers were guiding him, but he was reading a language I'd never learned.

The clouds above darkened, and thunder rumbled in the distance. Perhaps a break in the drought was near. I hoped we wouldn't get caught in a storm in the swamp. Napoleon aimed at a place where the woods deepened, and we found ourselves in a daytime twilight, the water black, with gray mist hovering above its surface.

"We're here," he said softly.

I turned and could barely make out through the mist a cabin perched on stilts. A tin roof covered the small house that had siding cut from logs, a thin layer of bark still clinging to the boards like crust on a piece of bread. There was one window, and a lantern was placed on the sill. Napoleon tied the pirogue at the bottom of steps leading up to a small porch, and we climbed out.

"Missus," he called out. "We're here."

I looked at Napoleon. "Is someone expecting us?"

"I asked him to bring you here," said a tall woman, who stood silhouetted in the cabin door.

I looked at Napoleon. "She asked you to bring me here?"

He had the grace to look abashed. "I'll wait out here," he said, shrugging.

"Napoleon told me what you said in the newspaper," the woman said, beckoning me inside. "I'm Sarah Williams. Elijah was my husband."

Mrs. Williams closed the screen door and invited me to sit on the only chair in the room. A handsome woman with strong features and dark brown skin, she was dressed all in black, and wore a white turban that covered her hair except for a few stray gray curls that showed at her temples. She sat down on a thin mattress that had been set on a platform to serve as both bed and couch. It was covered with colorful fabrics and half a dozen pillows.

"I'm sorry about your husband, Mrs. Williams."

"He was a good man." She looked at me with sad eyes.

"I'm a widow myself," I volunteered.

"Then you know."

"Yes, I think I do."

We sat silently for a moment before she asked if I'd like some tea.

"Only if you're having some yourself," I replied.

She rose and filled a kettle from a gallon jug. One corner of the room had been made into an efficiency kitchen with a tiny sink, hotplate, and shelves holding boxes of foodstuff, canned goods, and dishes. Jugs of water sat on the floor. While she busied herself with the preparations, I took in the rest of her surroundings.

The room was cramped but furnished with more than just the simple basics someone would need to live. Beautifully patterned fabrics were draped from the walls and reached to the floor, probably concealing storage. Two polished maple dressers sat side by side. One held a stack of books, along with an elaborate metal triptych serving as an altar, in front of which were arranged multicolored candles, two crosses, and bowls of bones, herbs, and powdered substances I couldn't identify. A small oriental rug hung on the wall above the altar. Fastened to it were Mardi Gras masks made of feathers and ebony African masks. On top of the other dresser, glass canisters were filled with a jumble of everyday items—packets of tissues, a hairbrush and comb, pads of paper, lipsticks, individually wrapped mints, pens, coins, soaps, candles, matches—each in its separate container. A mirror hung on the wall above the canisters with more than a dozen photographs stuck in its frame. They were of Elijah and fishermen he'd guided.

"Thank you for coming," she said, her back to me.

"I must admit, I didn't know it was you I was meeting," I said. "Napoleon didn't tell me."

"He's a scoundrel, that Napoleon," she said loud enough for him to hear on the porch.

"He did say you knew about the cylinder recordings of Little Red LeCoeur."

"Two people have already died because of those recordings, Mrs. Fletcher. Don't you fear for your life, too?"

"One of those men was Wayne Copely, a dear friend of mine," I replied. "He was passionate about the music of Little Red. If he lost his life because of those recordings, I'd like to know why. And I'd like to find who killed him."

"Can't help you with that."

"What can you help me with? Why did you want to see me?"

She turned from the kettle and sat again.

"Do the recordings exist?" I asked.

"Yes."

I heaved a sigh of relief. Little Red's playing had been recorded. There was still a chance to fulfill Wayne's dream of bringing the art of this talented musician to a new generation. "Do you know where they are?" I asked.

"Yes."

"Will you tell me?"

"I don't know yet." She fingered the pleats in her black skirt.

The water in the kettle began to boil. She made the tea and handed me a cup. "I'm here many years," she said finally. "I'm tired of hiding."

"Why *are* you hiding?"

"Elijah come home one afternoon, pack up everything we have, and move us into the swamp. He wouldn't say why. One day, he earns money taking rich men fishing. He plays his music for me at night. The next day he is fishing so we can eat, and the music is gone. He don't have the heart to play no more."

"Did you ever find out what happened?"

"Some of it." She hesitated. "He wouldn't tell me all. Said I would be in danger if I knew."

"Please tell me what he told you."

"There was an argument and a man was killed. An important man. Elijah saw it happen, and we been running ever since."

"Did the killer see Elijah?"

"'Yes, and he knew him," she said, hugging herself and rocking back and forth. "Fifteen years, Mrs. Fletcher, fifteen years of living poor, hiding in the dark."

"Why didn't he go to the police?"

"You think the police is going to believe a poor black man's story about a rich white man's murder? He was afraid, Mrs. Fletcher, and he spent the rest of his life afraid."

"Why did he go to the cemetery?"

"He sees an ad in the paper looking for Little Red's recordings. Elijah thinks he can sell the cylinders and give our life a little ease. I tell him, maybe it's a trap, but he says he knows it's Copely. Copely wouldn't trick him. But when he goes to meet your friend, Elijah ends up dead. Would your friend do that?"

"He wouldn't, Mrs. Williams. I'm sure of it."

"You know what I think? I think the man Elijah saw do the killing finally found him. Must've been looking for him for fifteen years, and finally found him. That's what I think." A few tears slipped down her cheeks, and she wiped them away with her hand. She shook her head and sighed. "The music. That's what I missed the most when we was in hiding. The music. Before we ran away, he would play for me every night."

"What instrument did he play?"

"Trumpet, of course," she said. "He was the son of Little Red's nephew. But he never had the 'chops' of Little Red. Do you know what that is?"

"Chops? That means his technical command of the instrument, doesn't it?"

"Close enough. Little Red could make the trumpet sing like a bird and growl like a gator. He was some player, all right."

"And he was Elijah's great-uncle," I said. "Is that how Elijah got the cylinders?"

"Yes. Give him the boxes to keep safe, but he don't want them played. Against his beliefs."

Napoleon rapped his knuckles on the door. "We have to go, Mrs. Fletcher."

"All right," I called back. I stood up, and Elijah's widow opened the door for me. "Will you tell me where the cylinders are, Mrs. Williams?"

"After Elijah was killed, I sent them to his cousin," she said. "That's what I wanted to tell you. I don't want them no more. They're cursed for me. He should've had them anyway. He's a player, too. Good one."

"Who's Elijah's cousin?"

"I thought you might have known," she said. "He's famous around here."

"What's his name?"

"Blind Jack."

Chapter Twenty

"For more than two hundred years, we New Orleanians have been interring our dearly departed above ground in what we call 'Cities of the Dead.' Early settlers tried burying bodies, but the ground was so waterlogged, the graves they dug would fill with water. If they were able to bury the coffins—say, during a dry spell—as soon as the weather turned, the coffins would float to the surface again."

The tour leader held her lace-trimmed, hot-pink parasol aloft and gathered her small group of tourists around her like a mother hen with her chicks. We were about to enter St. Louis Number One, the cemetery where the infamous Marie Laveau was laid to rest, and where Elijah Williams and Wayne Copely had been murdered, their bodies abandoned at her tomb.

Napoleon and I had left Sarah Williams's cabin in time to link up with our young captain, who'd transported us back to New Orleans before he'd headed off to return his borrowed command. Beatrice awaited us on the levee. We'd taken a different route back on the way to the French Quarter, one that led past the cemetery, where a tour bus had been unloading its passengers.

"I've been meaning to see this cemetery," I said, looking at my watch.

"I wouldn't go there by myself, Mrs. Fletcher," Napoleon said. "It's too dangerous."

"That's true, but I may have a solution for that. Would you mind waiting here a moment?"

I'd convinced the guide to let me join her group and returned to the carriage to thank Napoleon and Beatrice. Thursday would be my last day in New Orleans. We arranged that they would drive me to the funeral, and I waved good-bye.

"You'll notice that the crypts here are not as elaborate as the ones you'll see in some of the other cemeteries," said the guide. "That's because it's the oldest; it was established in 1789, during the Spanish colonial period. There was an earlier one, but it's gone now, closed in 1788 when a yellow fever epidemic took more lives than it had space to accommodate."

Compared to the bracing ride across Lake Pontchartrain, the heat in the city was oppressive, the moisture in the air an added burden, like a heavy weight on my head. Our little party trooped in a ragged line behind the parasol, stopping to admire the classical proportions of tombs erected by some of the city's many benevolent societies, and the cast iron angels and other embellishments that adorned fences in front of family tombs. The ash-gray clouds had deepened into charcoal, and thunder was rolling toward us.

"The writer Walker Percy wrote about St. Louis Number One, describing its 'tiny lanes as crooked as old Jerusalem, meandering aimlessly between the cottages of the dead.' As you may have guessed from that quote, it's easy to get lost here, so please stay with the group. We're going to move pretty quickly so we don't get caught in the rain."

Crashes of thunder grew louder the deeper we walked into the cemetery. Despite the sultry air, a sudden chill crept up my spine, and I had the oddest feeling someone was watching. I looked behind me, but no one was there. When I turned back, my fellow tourists had moved rapidly ahead, and I had to jog to catch up with them.

They were standing in front of a plain, narrow tomb topped by a simple pediment. Graffiti covered its sides, except in a few places where the stucco had been recently patched. Scattered around it was the debris of visitors' offerings. Several half-spent candles had fallen over in front of the door, and the wind was rolling them like a child playing with a toy. Carnival beads were draped around a squat vase, its flowers long since dried and blown away.

"This is called the 'wishing tomb.' It's the burial place of the most famous voodoo queen, Marie Laveau. Those X's you see represent the wishes of those who have asked for her assistance; the red ones were made with pieces of crumbled brick. The inscription is in French. It says, 'Here lies Marie Philome Glapion, deceased June eleventh, eighteen ninety-seven, aged sixty-two years. She was a good mother, a good friend, and is regretted by all who knew her. Passersby, please pray for her.' "

The rumble of thunder was gathering strength, and flashes of lightning lit up the underbelly of the black clouds, giving them a sickly yellow hue. The wind blew sand from the concrete and stone platforms on which the tombs rested, and it swirled around our ankles and up into our faces. I raised my hand to shield my eyes from the sandstorm. The description by the mortician fueled my imagination. In my mind, I saw Wayne meeting a shadowy figure at the tomb. I envisioned his shock when the snake sank its fangs into his hand, collapsing as the poison coursed through his system, blisters boiling up on his arms, splitting, spilling his blood till his clothes were soaked with it. Did it happen here beside this wall? Was the last thing he saw the ragged artificial flowers taped to the corner? I detected a faint rust stain on the stone paving to the side of Laveau's crypt. Was that Wayne's blood?

I also thought about Elijah. With the hopes of giving his wife a little comfort, he'd been willing to part with a family legacy, only to have his life stolen in this same place, his body set down like another offering against the cold wall of the tomb. Had he been surprised to see his killer? Was it the man who'd pursued him for fifteen years?

I shivered. The eerie feeling of being observed returned, intensified.

A bolt of lightning split the sky to my left, its jagged claw scorching the spire of a tall tomb. It was followed by an ear-splitting crack of thunder right over my head. I heard the jangle of metal rattling around me. Something banged against my leg. It was part of a box with a familiar mark on it. I bent to retrieve it, but the wind lifted it out of my grasp and sent it cartwheeling down a grassy path. I ran after it, trying to grab it out of the clutches of the coming storm. It fell between two massive tombs, sheltered from the wind for the moment. I reached into the passage to get it. It was the top of a box. I held up my reading glasses to see better. Part of it had been torn away, and the mark was smudged, but there was no question that stamped on it was a red circle, the letters PSTS in the center. The Pinto Snake Transportation System.

I felt the first splat of rain on my head and hurried back to Marie Laveau's tomb. Squinting against the wind, I looked around to realize I was alone. No pink parasol to guide me. No trailing tourist to follow. My heart started racing. Which way did they go? The wind was furious now, pulling at my skirt and tearing at my hair, keening as it flailed the burial vaults all around. Rain pelted my face. I pushed against the current, leaning in the direction I thought the group had taken. Was Marie Laveau taunting me as I struggled to stand against the force of her power?

The wind stepped aside to come at me from another angle. I stumbled, regained my balance, and started forward again. The rain became a torrent, harder now, beating down on the stone, turning the dust into mud. I skidded and slipped, tumbling forward, my hands out to break my fall. I landed on a patch of grass. Inches from my head, a marble urn thudded to the ground, wrenched from its moorings by the storm. Breathing heavily, I knelt to get up, pausing to take an inventory of my joints and limbs for injury. I was bruised, but nothing was sprained or broken.

"Mrs. Fletcher, are you all right? You could have been killed." Strong hands helped me to my feet.

The wind had died down and the rain was gentler now. I put a hand up to straighten my hair, and Archer looked down at me.

"What luck! That urn just missed your head. If you hadn't fallen, it would have gotten you."

He handed me a dry bandanna that I used to wipe my face and hands. "Ordinarily, I wouldn't have considered falling down to be lucky, but in this case . . ." I said, shaking out the cloth and dabbing at my arms. "Thanks for the use of your handkerchief. I'll wash it before I return it."

"Don't worry about that. Are you okay?"

"Battered but unbowed," I replied, picking up my bag. "What are you doing here?"

He looked embarrassed. "This is the first time I've come here," he said. "I thought I needed a pilgrimage to the place where Wayne died."

"You picked a bad day for it."

"The weather suited my mood actually," he said. "What are you doing here—and alone? I thought Wayne warned you against wandering in this neighborhood without an escort."

"I was part of a tour group," I explained, "but when the storm blew up, they left, and I didn't see which way they turned."

He bent to examine the toppled urn. It was one of a pair that had been resting on matched pillars. It didn't look easy to dislodge.

"Let's get you back to your hotel," he said. "If we can find a cab."

As we made our way to the exit, I saw the tour guide hurrying toward us, her arm holding the parasol high. "Oh thank goodness, you're not lost. I did a head count when we got back to the bus and realized we'd left you behind. You're soaked. Come with me. I've got a sweater on the bus. We'll drop you off first. Did you hurt yourself?" She fussed over me all the way to the bus, and offered to drop Archer at my hotel, a proposition he declined.

"I'll see you later at the party," he called out as I mounted the stairs into the bus.

A hot shower and a nap did wonders for my bruises and my mood. I sat in my armchair, wrapped in the terrycloth robe the hotel had provided, and thought about my stay in New Orleans. The Big Easy, they called it. It hadn't been easy this time. Snakes, death, and danger had accompanied me. What a strange city it was with its sultry weather, spicy foods, high spirits, and voodoo traditions. It was like attending a full-time party with Gothic overtones. The only time my hometown of Cabot Cove approached as colorful an atmosphere was at Halloween. For the people I'd met in New Orleans, it was Halloween all the time. And I wanted to peek behind their masks, analyze what they'd been thinking.

Archer was upset that Wayne had left so much money to Clarice. His appearance at my side in the cemetery so soon after the falling urn missed me was alarming. Was he making a pilgrimage, or visiting the scene of the crime?

Clarice desperately needed money, and it must have rankled her when Wayne turned down her request for more. She was about to receive an influx of funds. Her brother's office and files had been available to her every day. She could have examined them at leisure. Would a million dollars have been enough for her to sacrifice her brother? It seemed to me that Archer and Clarice had battled for Wayne's attention. They were both spiteful and manipulative. Was one of them also a killer?

Mayor Amadour. How far would he go to protect Clarice? He'd stopped the investigation into Wayne's death. Was it to protect her—or himself? What did he really know about Wayne's death?

Beaudin was ambitious and charming, but I kept feeling he was holding something back. He'd held a grudge against Wayne for a long time. Was their recent reconciliation genuine? He and Broadbent had been cronies in the early days of the mayor's administration. Broadbent was an investigative reporter, but he'd been under the mayor's influence before. He'd disappeared the night Wayne died and was missing the day after. His animosity toward Wayne had been obvious at the Book Club Breakfast.

And how did all this tie in with the recordings of Little Red? Did someone want them enough to kill?

So many questions to answer. And for the first time since arriving in New Orleans, I thought I might have some of the answers. Hopefully, there would be more at tonight's party.

Chapter Twenty-one

"Mrs. Fletcher, I'm so delighted you could come."

Marguerite Amadour stood next to her husband in the large oval foyer of their home, welcoming guests to their party. The tinkle of a ragtime piano in another room could be heard over the buzz of voices as people crowded in. The mayor pumped my hand and directed me to a tuxedo-clad waiter holding a silver tray with glasses of champagne. "The bar is in the library if you'd like something a bit more potent; food is out back in the garden. Make yourself at home. We'll find you later for some conversation."

Doris and I had been driven to the party in a car sent by Charlie Gable of the *Times-Picayune*. He came forward to greet us as well. "Ladies, how wonderful you're here," he said, taking our arms and guiding us from the reception area into the living room. "You must come see what the Amadours have done."

The house was large, elegant, and old—an antique, like much of its furnishings. The walls were freshly painted and the floors highly polished, but elsewhere there were indications of the patina of age so prized by New Orleanians. An ancient mirror hung over the marble mantel, its silvered back worn away in many places. The wood surrounding the doorway to a small room off the living room was nicked and distressed, a sign, perhaps, of the many times over the years large pieces of furniture had been moved in or out, battling to make it through the constricted opening. In the center of the room, the Amadours had set a round Biedermeier table with a display of books of all the authors from Charlie's Book Club Breakfast. Copies of *Murder in a Minor Key* were piled high with one standing open on top. The works of Doris, Julian, and Wayne were similarly featured, alongside a framed photograph that had been taken at the program.

"Everyone has to pass this table on their way to the courtyard," Gable said, clearly delighted with the publicity we were getting. "Maurice plans to give away the books as gifts later on."

We followed the stream of visitors outside to a generously proportioned stone courtyard between two wings of the house, hemmed in by an array of banana trees spaced to allow a view of the gardens beyond. The evening air was refreshingly cool, the afternoon storm having blasted away the heat, and a beautiful sunset provided a delicate scrim against which the party was played. Food was one of the stars. Long tables had been set up with platters heaped high with Louisiana specialties. I recognized the crawfish boil with red potatoes and corn, and the Oysters Rockefeller that Wayne had introduced me to. There were also baskets of fried chicken, bowls of beans and rice, gumbo, barbecued shrimp, blackened fish, crawfish étouffée, fried green tomatoes, jambalaya, and even more dishes that I'd not seen before.

"There goes the diet," Doris moaned. "I guess I'll have to sacrifice myself."

"On you, it'll look good," said a voice behind us.

I saw her stiffen. "Julian, we haven't seen you for some time," she said coolly, picking up a plate and turning back to the buffet.

"I'm sorry," he said. "I was working and didn't have time to call." He grabbed a plate and followed her down the table, but she ignored him and concentrated on her choices. "You should understand," he said. "You told me you were going to be busy, too."

"Trouble in paradise?" Charlie murmured to me.

"Let them work it out," I said. "Would you like to show me around?"

"With pleasure."

As we crossed the flagstone paving, Charlie pointed out the doyennes of New Orleans society, and other influentials in the city. I saw Philippe Beaudin talking to a group of people. He was standing near a zydeco band that was setting up at the far end of the terrace, opposite the food. Charlie led me through open doors into the library where a group of men, including the mayor, were standing around the bar, puffing on cigars and drinking from silver mugs of mint julep. We walked down a black-and-white-tiled hallway to peek into the kitchen; the bustle of activity convinced us to get out of the way quickly. We ended up back outside in the garden, Marguerite Amadour's showpiece, admiring the beds of colorful flowers and plantings she had lovingly cultivated.

"You know, Jessica, the Amadours don't come from society stock," Charlie confided. "Maurice has had to fight for every success he's achieved. But Marguerite's talents in the garden, and elsewhere, helped introduce him to the right people politically and socially."

"She must be a great asset to him."

"She is, and I hope he appreciates her," he said. "He's been known to have a bit of a wandering eye."

The woman we were just discussing stood in a corner talking to guests whose backs were to me when we rejoined the party in the courtyard. She broke away when she saw me, excused herself to Charlie, and pulled me over to meet them.

"Isn't this wonderful?" she said. "Archer has brought Clarice. Come say hello."

Clarice gave me a wan smile when I greeted her. "Archer insisted," she said.

"It didn't take a lot," he said, his expression one of annoyance.

"Wayne isn't even buried yet," she said, looking around at the festivities. "Maybe I should go."

"You stay right here," Marguerite told her, hugging her shoulder. "You have to get back into circulation sometime, and these people are all your friends. Besides, look at the mountain of food I've got. I need you to eat your share." She looked at me. "Have you sampled any of our goodies yet, Jessica?"

"I will in a little while," I replied.

"Well, *you* are not so easily excused," she said to Clarice, and drew her over to the buffet, leaving me standing with Archer.

"Have you told her about the insurance yet?" I asked him.

"No," he said. "Let her wonder a little longer."

"Isn't that cruel?"

"I'll tell her soon," he said, backpedaling. "But not here. I'll tell her tomorrow. It'll take the edge off the funeral."

"I don't think anything can do that," I whispered to myself when he left to follow Clarice.

The band started to play a Cajun favorite, and several couples began to dance. I remembered my lessons at the fais-do-do and Wayne's enjoyment in teaching me. "Tonight," I promised him silently, "there might be some justice for you. Tonight, I hope to expose your killer."

"Knew I'd find you here," a male voice said from behind me.

I turned to see Detective Steppe.

"I thought you were in Baton Rouge till Friday," I said.

"Change in plans," he said, his voice low to avoid being overheard. "Is there somewhere we can talk?"

I led him out into the garden and stopped under one of the banana trees. "What's happened?" I asked.

"Teddy called me at the conference. The tox report came back," he said. "Along with the snake venom, the lab found a hefty dose of GHB in Copely's veins." He squinted at a piece of paper. "It stands for gamma hydroxy butyrate."

"That's what's called the date-rape drug, isn't it?"

"Right. About the only good thing is that Copely probably didn't know what hit him."

"But it confirms that he was murdered, doesn't it?"

"You can sure make a good argument for it," he said, "which I've done."

"How?"

"Called the ME. He said he'll talk to the superintendent about reopening the case."

"I'm relieved," I said.

"Now all we need is a perp," Steppe said. "What've you got?"

I gave him an outline of my visit to Bobby Pinto, Sarah Williams, and the cemetery. I had a theory and so did he. We discussed how to proceed.

"I need to make a call," he said. "Give me a minute." He walked farther into the garden, dug his cell phone out of his pocket, and dialed. I watched him talk, but his words didn't reach me.

"There you are," Marguerite Amadour called to me as she crossed the terrace. "I've been looking all over for you. Maurice wants to see all the authors in the library before he makes any announcements about the books."

Steppe walked back to my side and Marguerite smiled up at him. "I don't believe we've met."

"Let me introduce you," I said quickly. I didn't want him to reveal his identity yet. "This is Christopher Steppe. He's a friend of mine. I hope you don't mind that I asked him to join me."

"Not at all. You're more than welcome. Please follow me."

"Thank you, Mrs. Amadour," Steppe said, slipping his cell phone back in his pocket and grinning at me.

The mayor was holding forth with an unlit cigar in one hand and a mint julep in the other when Steppe and I entered the library and took empty chairs opposite a brown leather Chesterfield sofa. Clarice and Archer sat on either side of the sofa, Doris between them. Broadbent was perched on one of the barstools behind the mayor. Archer gave Steppe a quizzical look.

"Got a lot of important people here tonight," Amadour said, pacing in front of the bar. "Talk 'em up. Might be able to give your careers a boost."

Charlie Gable winked at me from across the room where he was leaning against a pool table.

Philippe Beaudin poked his head in the door and looked around. "Okay, Maurice. You've got everybody?"

"Yup. C'mon in here, Phil. Take a seat."

Beaudin did as he was instructed but looked as though he'd rather be out at the party. He checked his watch, and craned his neck to see through the doors to the terrace.

"So, Mrs. Fletcher," the mayor said, "I've talked to the others about their books already. I'm interested in yours. You're a mystery writer, I know."

"That's right."

"In fact, I've heard tell you've even solved some mysteries in real life. Pretty impressive. Got any mysteries you can solve here?"

"As a matter of fact, Mr. Mayor, I believe I have."

The smile faded from the mayor's face, and there was a stunned silence in the room.

Recovering, the mayor broke it. "Well," he boomed,

"that's great! Always after a little entertainment. Give us a sample of your talent then. We'd all be interested in seeing that, wouldn't we, folks?"

"Maurice, you're embarrassing Mrs. Fletcher," his wife said. "That's no way to treat a guest."

"That's all right, Mrs. Amadour," I said, standing. "I'll be happy to comply. I have a few questions I'd like to ask first." I looked at her husband.

"Shoot!" said the mayor. "I'll tell you whatever I can."

I went to the bar. "I'd like to know, Mr. Mayor, why you directed the police department to stop investigating Wayne Copely's death."

There was a soft gasp from Clarice. Amadour frowned, put his drink on the bar, and faced me. "I did no such thing," he said. "The medical examiner told me it was an accident. It was his decision." His patented smile returned as quickly as it had vanished a moment before.

"But he was pressured to come to that conclusion," I said, "and the word around the police department was that the order came from City Hall."

"Never happened," he said. "I don't throw my weight around like that."

"Is that true, Mr. Beaudin?" I asked, turning to him.

"Maurice is right, Mrs. Fletcher. He'd never do that."

"But *you* might," I said to him. "As the mayor's right-hand man, you could give an order that the police department would assume came from the mayor. Isn't that right?"

Beaudin shifted position. "Why would I do that?"

"That's what I'd like to know," I said.

"I thought you wanted to know *if* I did it."

"Phil, just tell her you didn't do it," Amadour said.

"Well, actually, Maurice, I did."

Amadour was annoyed. "Whatever for?"

"There's a simple reason really, and it's absolutely justified."

"Go on," Amadour said.

"Superintendent Johnson had issued those warnings to tourists not to open their hotel doors if they don't know who's knocking, to travel in pairs, et cetera," Beaudin said. "He got a lot of press. It went all over the country."

"So?" Amadour interrupted.

"So, the hotel operators and the merchants were livid. They've been screaming at me that they're getting cancellations and losing business because we don't know how to keep Johnson's mouth shut."

"He's doing a good job," Amadour said. "I'm not about to muzzle him."

"Well, between his list of warnings, and the recent murder of that Williams guy in the cemetery, the Businessmen's Association and the Chamber of Commerce were upset. If we had a second investigation, they might have thrown their support to your opponent. I couldn't take the chance. Besides, Copely was bitten by a snake. What else could it have been but an accident?"

Amadour fumed and looked at me. "I didn't know anything about it."

Clarice cleared her throat. "Jessica," she said, "do you think Wayne's death was accidental?"

"I know Wayne's death was *not* accidental," I said.

Everyone started talking at once.

"How can you say such an irresponsible thing?" Amadour demanded.

"I hope you know what you're doing," Beaudin said, glaring at me.

"I'd be interested in what Mrs. Fletcher knows," Julian put in.

"So would I," said Archer.

Clarice started to cry. "I knew it," she said. "And they'll think I did it."

"They probably will, Clarice," I said, flashing a look at Steppe, who sat quietly, taking it all in.

"Why?" Doris asked. "Why will people think Clarice killed her brother?"

"Because his life was insured for a million dollars," I said, "and Clarice is his beneficiary."

Archer glared at me. "I told you I would tell her."

"She already knew," I said. "I just wanted to see how responsible *you* were."

"I told Wayne not to do it," she said, sniffling. "I said I didn't want the money if he had to die for me to have it. I told him it was no substitute for going to the police."

"Why would he want to go to the police?" Amadour asked.

Clarice was weeping steadily. Doris got up to give Marguerite her seat, and the mayor's wife put her arms around her friend. "I was praying his death was really an accident." Clarice sobbed into her shoulder.

"Why should Wayne have gone to the police?" the mayor asked again.

"Because he was getting death threats," Clarice wailed.

Amadour looked at his aide. "Did you know this?"

"How the hell would I know that?" asked Beaudin. "If I had any idea, I never would have stopped the investigation. You know that, Maurice."

"That better be true," the mayor said.

"Thanks a lot," Beaudin said, affronted. "We've worked together long enough. Don't you trust me? Of course I didn't know about any death threats."

"But Archer knew, didn't you, Archer?" I asked.

Clarice stopped crying. "He did?" She looked at Archer. "Wayne said he didn't tell you about them."

"Wayne didn't pay any attention to them," Archer said resentfully. "Why should *I*?"

"Maybe you didn't pay attention to them," I said, "because it was you who made the recent series of calls."

"The hell I did."

"Would you like to listen to what's on this?" I asked, holding up the cassette tape I'd brought with me. "I found this in Wayne's apartment. It has a really nasty message on it, but the voice was peculiar, and I wondered about it. When I slowed down the tape on a different machine, I found out why."

Archer turned pale.

"It was your voice," I said, watching him closely. "You recorded that death threat, speeded up the tape, and played it into Wayne's machine. Not very nice for someone who was supposed to be his friend."

He stammered. "He, he, he was growing away from me."

"You snake!" Clarice growled.

"No, you don't understand," he said to her. I would never have hurt Wayne. I loved him. He was my life."

"Then why did you leave death threats on his answering machine?" I asked.

"Because he was getting tired of me, pushing me out."

"He wanted you to grow up," Clarice snapped.

"I just wanted him to turn to me for help," Archer said miserably. "All he had to do was ask. I would have made sure he never got another threat. That's all he had to do."

"Phil, get one of the cops outside and have this guy arrested," the mayor ordered.

"I didn't kill him. I swear I didn't," Archer said, tears flowing freely down his cheeks. "I made the calls, it's true, but I would never hurt him."

"Go on, Phil." Amadour waved his cigar at him. "Get the cop."

"Not just yet, Mr. Beaudin," I said.

"I think we've had enough of your parlor games, Mrs. Fletcher," Beaudin replied.

"Sit down, please," I said, and he complied. I turned to Broadbent and spoke his name.

Julian's head snapped up. "What?"

"Why did you go to see Bobby Pinto?"

"What makes you think I did?" he asked.

"I went to see him myself, thanks to Doris," I said, "and showed him the picture of Wayne that had been in Monday's paper. He said a man answering your description had shown him the same picture."

"So what?" Broadbent said, amused. "There are lots of guys answering my description. Look around."

"That's true," I acknowledged. "But you showed him the picture on Saturday. It wasn't published in the paper till Monday. Only someone who had access to the newspaper's photo morgue would have had a copy of that photograph."

Broadbent laughed. "Didn't think of that, Mrs. Fletcher. You got me there."

"Was it you who met Wayne Thursday night?"

"Yes," Broadbent said. "I'd seen an ad about the cylinders, and had arranged through a friend to meet him. I didn't think he knew it was me, but he did. I was going to give him a hard time. We weren't the best of friends. But he talked me into helping him instead."

"And then?"

"And then he was killed the next night. Frankly, I was worried I'd be considered a suspect."

"Is that why you've been out of touch?" I asked Broadbent.

"That's right."

"But his death was declared an accident."

"I didn't believe it," he said. "You aren't the only one who thinks Copely was murdered, Mrs. Fletcher."

I tried to avoid looking at Steppe. No one had asked who he was, and I wasn't ready to introduce him yet.

"And what have you found out about Wayne's death?" I asked Broadbent.

"That a man answering my description bought a rattlesnake from Bobby Pinto," he said.

"Did you do that, Archer?"

"No." He shivered. "I wouldn't go near those things."

"What about you, Mr. Beaudin?" I asked. "Did you buy the snake from Bobby Pinto?"

"I never heard of him."

"How can you say you never heard of him?" I asked. "Didn't you hire him to trap snakes in the cemetery following Wayne's death?"

"No," he said. "The cops did that."

"But at your suggestion," I said. "Isn't that true?"

"What are you getting at, Mrs. Fletcher?"

"You suggested that the police hire Bobby Pinto to catch the snakes, and he did catch them," I said. "In fact, he caught the very snake he'd sold to you only a few days before."

"You're crazy."

"Am I? We can ask Bobby Pinto if he knows you."

"I may have met the guy once. I forget."

"In fact, you met him last Thursday," I said. "I saw you talking to him, right across the street from Antoine's where Wayne and I had just had lunch."

Steppe rose from his seat and went to stand near the door, and Broadbent moved in front of the French doors, which led to the courtyard.

Beaudin jumped up. "You're being ridiculous," he shouted. "Why would I want to kill Copely? He was an old friend."

"You hadn't talked in years, but you made up recently. Isn't that right? You wanted to get closer to Wayne to find out what he might learn about the cylinders."

"What are you talking about?"

"The cylinder recordings of Little Red LeCoeur," I said.

"You knew who had them. You wanted Wayne to help you find him."

"He told *me* that finding the cylinders would make Wayne rich and famous," Archer put in, "and I convinced Wayne to search for them."

The room was silent. All eyes were on Beaudin.

"What's the big deal if I told Archer about the cylinders?" Beaudin asked.

"The big deal is that the man who had the cylinders was Elijah Williams," I said. "You used Wayne's interest in the cylinders to track Elijah down. Wayne took out ads, and so did you. And then you used Wayne's name to lure Williams to the cemetery, where you killed him."

"That's crazy. I never even met Williams."

"You're lying, Mr. Beaudin," I said. "You knew him well. You fished together for years. In fact, you used to recommend him as a fishing guide to all your influential friends—until, of course, he became a danger to you."

"What do you mean?" Beaudin was sweating.

"He was the man who saw you kill Virgil Franklin," I said. I turned to Mayor Amadour. "You remember that name, don't you, Mr. Mayor, the man who was leading you in the polls in your first try for office?"

"Virgil died in a fishing accident, Mrs. Fletcher," the mayor said, tapping his fingers nervously on the bar.

"It was no accident," I said. "Elijah Williams saw the man who killed Franklin. And he," I said, pointing to Beaudin, "saw Williams, too. You'd been chasing your fishing buddy for fifteen years, hadn't you, Mr. Beaudin? And you finally caught up with him last month. And then you killed Wayne because you were afraid he knew the truth. You slipped a note in his pocket at Jazz Fest. I saw you do it. Was that when you told Wayne to meet you at The Blazer Pub?"

"You can't prove anything," Beaudin said, his voice rising. "You haven't got any proof."

"I disagree," I said calmly. "Bobby Pinto will identify you as the man who bought the canebrake rattlesnake from him. The bartender at The Blazer will identify you as the man who was with Wayne an hour before he died."

Steppe spoke up from the door. "The police are at your apartment right now, Mr. Beaudin, looking for the drug you used at the pub to make Copley light in the head."

"Who the hell is he?" Beaudin demanded.

"Detective Christopher Steppe, NOPD." He held up his badge for everyone to see.

Beaudin sank back into his chair.

"Wayne got so dizzy from that drug, he asked for your help," I said. "You helped him—right into the cemetery—and gave him the box with the snake. You told him it was the wax cylinder recordings of Little Red LeCoeur, the ones he'd been passionately searching for. When he reached into the box, the snake bit him, and ten minutes later he was dead. You looped a gris-gris around his neck and propped him up at Marie Laveau's tomb so that the police would look to the voodoo community first if they suspected murder. And then luck smiled on you. A local snake expert announced that the drought was causing reptiles to move into the city in search of food and water. You must have been very pleased with that."

"This is all speculation," Beaudin snarled.

"I'm curious about one thing," I said. "Did you arrange to have a snake put in my hotel room?"

"I don't know what you're talking about," he said, "and you'd better have more than you've shown, if you think you can pin anything on me.'"

"You want more proof, Mr. Beaudin? What do you think of this?" I unzipped my bag and pulled out the top of the Pinto Snake Transportation System, holding it by its edge with a handkerchief. "Your fingerprints are on this, Mr. Beaudin. It's part of the box you used to carry the snake. And I also have a copy of the note you sent Elijah, pretending to be Wayne, and arranging for him to meet you at the cemetery. His wife, Sarah Williams, gave it to me. I'm sure a handwriting analysis will prove it was written by you."

Beaudin looked around frantically. "She's making it all up. Maurice, you don't believe her, do you?"

"I always worried about the timeliness of Virgil's death," Amadour said, shaking his head. "Didn't you have any confidence in me, Phil? We could have won. It just would have taken a little longer."

"A little longer?" Beaudin spat, eyes flaming. "More like never. You never would have made it without me. You were a loser. I made you into a winner."

"You bastard!" Archer launched himself at Beaudin, but Broadbent grabbed him and pulled him away.

Steppe pulled out his handcuffs. I think it's time you came with me, Mr. Beaudin."

Archer collapsed, sobbing hysterically. "Wayne, oh Wayne," he cried. Clarice bent down and put her arms around him.

Chapter Twenty-two

Blind Jack stood at the pulpit and concluded his eulogy for Wayne. "He was a cat who loved music, and shared his love with the world," he said. His voice was low and gravelly, as if the years had exposed it to the elements and it had become rusty. "My man Wayne was straight-up smart. He understood that not everyone can be a player, but everyone *can* be a lover of jazz. He helped them learn, taught them how to listen to the soul of a musician singin' through his instrument. Or her instrument—be lots of female players, too, these days. In jazz, we talk about a band that swings. It's the highest praise you can give. Means we're all tuned in to each other's vibes; we hear that soul singin' and we add our own voice. Together we make a sound that takes us to a higher plane, lifts the spirit, fills the heart—both ours and whoever listens and understands. Wayne, he listened and understood. In his own way, he could really swing."

Archer walked to a small table that had been placed in front of the chancel rail, and adjusted the microphone so its head was in the center of the funnel-shaped horn of the cylinder player. He fitted the wax cylinder onto the phonograph and turned the crank. Everyone in the cathedral leaned forward tensely. There was a slight crackling sound, and then a voice announced, "This is Mr. Alphonse LeCoeur playing 'Amazing Grace.'" The strains of the traditional hymn filled the cathedral with a surprisingly clear sound.

The cylinder had survived. There was a collective sigh. This was the music Wayne had sought, the music he had died for, trying to bring to a new generation. And here at last it was—but never to be heard by him.

Little Red played the hymn through once, slowly, and then took the familiar notes and began improvising on them, increasing the tempo and adding frills and embellishments, offering a whole new interpretation of the beloved piece, exciting, uplifting, and modern, a musical precursor of all that was to come in the future, just as Wayne had suspected it would be.

On the steps of the cathedral, I smiled at Detective Steppe, who stood next to me. "The music was wonderful," I said. "Wayne would have been so pleased to know he contributed to the first public playing of Little Red's recordings."

"Maybe," he said, "but they've got bad mojo." He shook his head. "How did you figure out that it was Beaudin who used the cylinders to lure Williams and Copely to their deaths?"

"I was pretty sure he was the one," I replied, "but I became convinced when he kept lying about whom he knew."

"Okay, you saw him with Pinto, but how did you know he knew Williams?"

"Beaudin was an avid fisherman, born and raised in the swamps. Elijah Williams was a popular guide in the same place. Sarah Williams had photographs of the people Elijah had taken fishing. One of them was of Wayne and Beaudin, the same photo I'd found in Wayne's wallet."

"Did Copely know it was Williams who had the cylinders?"

"It's possible. Wayne was always a jazz aficionado, and the three of them could have talked about music while they fished together. When he started looking for the cylinders, he might have known who had them, but not where to reach him."

"Probably not," Steppe said. "After all, Williams had been missing for fifteen years."

"True," I said, "and I think Wayne might have suspected why. What he didn't know was that Sarah Williams had given the cylinders to Blind Jack after Elijah's death."

"So that's why Blind Jack took off after Copely was killed."

"He told me this morning that he had been planning to tell Wayne that he was Elijah's cousin, and that he had the cylinders."

"But then he heard about Copely and figured the killer would find out he had the recordings, and come after him. Right?"

"Right."

"I remember you telling me Copely was supposed to meet Blind Jack the night he was killed."

"Yes, but he never showed up," I said. "Beaudin got to him first. And you know what happened after that."

"Who gets the cylinders now?"

"I imagine they'll be sold to a recording company that's able to record them digitally and market the results."

"There should be some money in that."

"I hope so," I said, "The only heirs of Little Red are Blind Jack and Elijah Williams's widow, Sarah. I hope there'll be enough to let her move out of the swamp and back into society."

"Speaking of Sarah Williams," Steppe said, "you didn't tell me yesterday that you have a copy of the note Beaudin sent Elijah."

"That's because I don't," I replied. "I was bluffing. Before I left, I asked her if there was a note, and she said Elijah took it with him. I figured Beaudin would certainly have searched the body, found it and destroyed it. But it wasn't too much of a stretch to think Elijah might have copied the note and left it with his wife."

"Kind of like an insurance policy to help find the guy, if anything happened to Elijah."

"Exactly."

He thought for a minute. "Not that it makes a difference, but I don't know if we'll be able to lift Beaudin's prints from the Pinto box," he said.

"I wasn't sure you could either," I said, "but he was so cool, I wanted to rattle him and see what he'd do."

"Very clever," he said. "Our guys found the GHB in his house, like we thought. And actually, we don't really need the prints, now that he's confessed. It's nice to have three murders solved all at the same time."

"Three? Oh, you mean Virgil Franklin's," I said. "Yes, his was the one that started it all, wasn't it?"

"Once Beaudin killed him, he had to ensure that crime never came to light," Steppe said. "Killing Elijah, even fifteen years later, got rid of the witness, but then he had to keep going, in case Williams had talked. Beaudin was the one who searched the apartment, looking for any notes that might implicate him."

"He tried to control everything and everyone," I added. "He wanted me to use the mayor's car and driver so he could keep track of where I went. I even thought he put a snake in my room to try to scare me, but apparently that was really a result of the drought."

"The voodoo community is relieved," he said. "They're talking again. It seems there were a lot of people who worried about Beaudin. They knew he was dangerous, even if they weren't sure why."

"Fifteen years is a long time to keep a secret," I said. "If Elijah told even one person, the word would have gotten out. That kind of story would spread quickly, and make people fearful of the kind of retribution a man in his position could carry out. I think Elijah's widow knew it, too, but was too scared to say Beaudin's name."

"Amadour's really rattled," Steppe said. "In his story in today's paper, Broadbent says the mayor is considering not running for reelection."

"He may change his mind when he's had some time to think about it," I said.

While we'd been talking, Wayne's coffin had been loaded into the glass-sided hearse drawn by two white horses, and the mourners had gathered behind it. Leading the hearse in a slow procession was the brass band Archer had hired, with Blind Jack in front, his manager holding his elbow to guide him. Blind Jack lifted his trumpet, and the first clear notes of "Amazing Grace" filled the warm morning air. He played it slowly and reverently, the classical way the hymn is heard at a funeral service. The band, the hearse, and the mourners started the short walk to Lafayette Cemetery, where the Copely family crypt was located.

Spectators lined the street to watch the funeral procession, a spectacle unique to New Orleans. Some people saluted the hearse with their beer cans. Others joined the convoy, stepping along with the music as the band segued into "A Closer Walk with Thee," giving the hymn a faster tempo than is usually heard. Clarice and Archer walked behind the hearse, holding on to each other, their differences forgotten in their mutual grief. The mayor and his wife accompanied them. Steppe and I were farther back in the crowd along with Napoleon and Beatrice, who were enjoying participating in the pageantry. Doris and Julian were behind us.

"This is pretty different from what you have at home, isn't it, Mrs. Fletcher?" Napoleon asked.

"We have nothing like it," I agreed.

"A jazz funeral is really a celebration," he said. "We celebrate what a good life he had."

"He did have a good life," I said.

"We celebrate the better place he's going to," Beatrice added.

At Lafayette Cemetery, the door to the family crypt was open and Wayne Copely's coffin was lovingly deposited inside, his friends and relatives looking on. A short prayer was said. As the service ended, the band struck up "Oh, Didn't He Ramble," the long-established tune that accompanies mourners leaving the cemetery. The lively music pulled people along, observers now joining the parade, dancing in the street behind the band, and the family. When the song ended, Blind Jack lifted his trumpet to begin a new song. The sun glinted off the polished brass of his horn as he played the opening notes. They hung, shimmering in the air, and everyone stopped to listen intently. Jack paused and started playing again. It was "Amazing Grace," but this time, the hymn was an echo of Little Red's interpretation. This time, it was cheerful, full of fire and promise, a paean to life and the joy that is music.

Here's a preview of the
Provence—To Die For
available now.

He was dead. There was no doubt. His body was slumped against the arched door in the wall to the right, the papers he'd been consulting earlier scattered about him on the floor. A red stain above his heart was spreading down the front of his white shirt. His eyes were open, the vivid blue fading, and his mouth gaped, forming an "o," the expression of surprise that must have greeted his murderer. Apart from the papers on the floor there was no sign of a struggle. No over turned chair. No defense wounds on his hands. No clothing askew.

I knelt down and placed two fingers on his neck where a pulse should have been, and felt only cool skin.

The dead man was Emil Bertrand, renowned chef and owner of the restaurant *L'Homme Qui Court*, which had achieved a coveted one-star rating from the famed Michelin guide. He'd been the guest instructor this morning at the cooking class offered by the Hotel Melissande. I'd been one of his students.

It was my first trip to Provence, the region of southern France known for its quaint villages, summer festivals, fields of purple lavender, wild thyme, wonderful wine, and a fungus prized by chefs the world 'round—the black truffle.

I was coming off a particularly hectic summer in which friends, some invited and some not, had decided Cabot Cove was a great place to visit in July and August. I didn't know where September and October had gone. I only knew that various projects, some work-related and some community based, seemed to vacuum up all the hours in the days, until I began to feel I would never have time to sit down.

But that was all behind me now. Ahead were two months in the French countryside, in a borrowed house, with lots of time for reading and relaxing and learning the secrets of cooking in the Provençal style. At least, that had been my plan.

A slight breeze ruffled the papers on the floor a I stood. The door in the archway on the opposite wall was partly open. A sliver of light could be seen along the jamb, and the undulating sound of the Klaxon horns of emergency vehicles leaked into the room. Reluctant to leave my fingerprints, I pulled a handkerchief form my bag and used it to draw open the heavy wooden door. It led to a small paved area outside. I scanned the ground for evidence, something the killer might have dropped if he or she had departed this way. A short flight of stairs connected to the street level. I climbed it and found myself halfway up a steep hill. The street was deserted. I couldn't see over the top of the hill; not even a car crossed the intersection at its base. If someone had escaped through this door, they were gone now. Then something sparkled up at me from the curb. I leaned over and picked it up. It was an earring, which I put in my pocket. The sirens were deafening now. I retraced my steps and, using the handkerchief again, drew the door almost closed behind me. After the bright glare of daylight, my eyes had difficulty adjusting to the gloom, but I knew one thing. I was no longer alone.

"Bonjour Madame," said a voice filled with irony. "May I ask what you are doing here?"

"Oh, my," I said. "You certainly gave me a start."

"I could say the same of you," he said in near perfect English.

The speaker was a debonair man in a gray suit. A black trench coat was slung over one arm. His auburn hair was streaked with gray and he wore it slicked back from his fore-head, which emphasized the high-bridged prominent nose and the piercing look in his hard brown eyes. A colleague in a tweed jacket was leaning over Bertrand, his fingers probing the same area of the chef's neck where mine had been earlier.

I put out my hand. "I'm Jessica Fletcher," I said. "I was one of Chef Bertrand's students this morning."

"You are American?" he asked, ignoring my hand.

"Yes. I'm staying at the home of a friend who lives in St. Marc. I came to Avignon this morning to take Monsieur Bertrand's cooking class." I cocked my head toward the kitchen classroom.

"You have your passport with you, yes?"

"As a matter of fact, I do." I opened my bag, pulled out my passport and handed it to him.

He flipped it open to the photograph, checked it against my face, paged forward to the date-of-entry stamp and gave it back. "Why is it that you are down here?" he asked sternly.

"I was having tea with some of the other students when Madame Poutine—she was also in our class—accosted us. She was distraught, and crying that the chef had been killed. I thought she might be mistaken in what she'd seen. I rushed down here hoping he might be alive, in need of medical help. But, as you see, she was right."

"You are a doctor?"

"Heavens, no!"

"A nurse perhaps?"

"No. I have no medical degree."

"Yet you came down here to offer the chef medical help."

"I know that sounds odd," I said, "but if he'd had a heart attack or choked on something, I thought I could lend assistance until an ambulance arrived."

"And, of course, you are trained to lend assistance. No?"

"In a way, yes," I said, relieved I could answer in the affirmative. "I've taken several first-aid courses, and CPR; that's cardiopulmonary resuscitation."

"I know what CPR is."

"Well, I wasn't sure if it was the same in French."

"And what were you doing outside, if I may ask?"

"Certainly," I said, "I noticed that the door was ajar, and wanted to see where it led. I thought perhaps the killer was making his escape."

"And was this killer 'making his escape'?"

"No. No one was outside."

"You don't seem at all disturbed to be confronted by a dead man. Women are usually—how do you say?—delicate. They scream or faint at the sight of a corpse."

"That's not—"

He interrupted me. "They don't look so calmly around, notice the door is a bit open, and go investigate. *Vous gardez votre sang froid.* You are very cool." He raised an eyebrow and glared at me. "But what if the killer *had* been around, Madame Fletcher? Would you know what to do if he pointed a gun at you?"

"Oh, he wasn't . . ." I stopped mid-sentence.

"You were about to say?"

I sighed. "I was about to say that I don't think Monsieur Bertrand was shot. And I also don't think that the killer would hang around outside, waiting to be discovered."

"And why is it, Madame, that you don't believe the victim was shot? Did you see another murder weapon?"

"No, but I also don't see any shell casing," I replied. "And there wasn't a shell casing outside the door, or anything that could be a murder weapon. I checked. From the hole in his shirt, it looks to me like Chef Bertrand was stabbed, although since I didn't examine him, I can't say what the instrument might have been."

"You intrigue me, Madame," he said. "You are not, by any chance, a homicide detective?"

"No, but I have made a study of the subject for some time."

"And why is that?"

"I study murders because I write murder mysteries.

That's how I make my living, Detective . . . I'm sorry, I don't believe you gave me your name."

"The rank is Inspector, Madame. I am Inspector LeClerq."

"Inspector LeClerq, while you and I are conversing, the killer could be getting away. Chef Bertrand was alive an hour ago. The person responsible for his death may still be in the hotel. We should be looking for the murder weapon. We're giving the killer too much time to dispose of the evidence."

"We?" His eyebrows rose. "You seem to think, Madame, that Sergeant Thierry and I are inadequate to the task. That we require your assistance."

"I didn't mean to imply. . . ."

"Please allow us to do our job," he said. "The Avignon *Gendarmerie* is well equipped to investigate all crimes. We can do more than arrest the pickpockets and petty thieves who arrive each summer along with the tourists."

"I'm sure that's true," I said, trying to think how I'd gotten into this argument. I heard my name called.

Mallory raced through the archway from the hall, and drew to a halt at the sight of the two policemen. "Mrs. Fletcher, are you all right?" The American teenager I'd met on the train to Avignon last week had surprised me this morning when she'd shown up in my cooking class. She was a lonely child, drifting around France, perhaps running away from school or home. I meant to find out. Another mystery to solve, but first, this one."

"Yes, dear. I'm fine."

"I heard upstairs . . ." She was trying to catch her breath. "That there had been a murder." She shook her head. "You weren't around." A deep breath. "I got worried. And they wouldn't let me downstairs to look for you."

"Then how did you get here?" LeClerq asked.

Mallory flushed. "There's a set of stairs from the hotel's dining room." She pointed behind her. "It goes to the other end of the hotel kitchen."

Just then the elevator doors opened and two men entered

the room. One was carrying a small case, and the other held a camera with a flash unit.

"It's getting a bit crowded in this place," Inspector LeClerq grumbled. "Perhaps you would be good enough to wait upstairs with the others so we may finish our work down here.

Thierry had positioned his body to block Mallory's view of the chef, but now he moved aside to allow the newcomers to conduct their part of the investigation. Mallory gasped when she glimpsed the lifeless body of Emil Bertrand. "Oh my gosh. Is it him?"

'I think Inspector LeClerq is right," I said, taking Mallory's arm and turning her around. "We should wait for him upstairs. Why don't you show me where this other staircase is."

We walked down the hall to the hotel kitchen, Mallory excitedly burbling about how she had searched for me upstairs and begged the officer guarding the stairwell to let her try the lower floor. I recognized the signs of an adrenaline release. I twould take awhile for her to come down from its intensity. I took her arm as we walked and patted her hand. "You can see, I'm just fine," I said. "Thank you for worrying about me."

As we passed the door to the office used by the hotel chefs, I heard a sound, as if something had fallen off a desk or shelf. I put my ear to the wooden panel and my hand on the knob. Someone was inside. I twisted the knob and the door opened. Guy, the *sous-chef* who'd assisted Bertrand this morning, was on his knees, frantically gathering a sheaf of papers and folders that had slid off the overloaded desk.

"Hello," he said, pressing the folders to his chest. "I've got to clean up this mess one of these days. I can't find anything anymore."

"Where have you been, Guy?" I asked, wondering if he was trying to shield the front of his uniform from view.

He looked confused. "I went up to my apartment to get the materials for tomorrow's class, and then I . . . and then I came back. There's a lot of work to do to prepare for these classes. Why do you ask?" He was tripping over his words, not at all the self-assured *sous-chef* from the morning.

"How did you manage to get in here without running into the police upstairs?"

"There are police upstairs?" A few papers slipped out of his grasp and fell to the floor. He made a grab for them.

"Oh, Guy, the most terrible thing," Mallory began. I squeezed her arm, and she stopped abruptly.

"How long have you been here?" I asked, watching his face closely. I sensed someone behind me and whirled around.

"You're doing my job again, Madame Fletcher." The fierce eyes of Inspector LeClerq bored into mine.

My idyllic vacation in Provence was getting off to a rocky start.

MARTINIS & MAYHEM   185129

Jessica can't wait for drinks and dinner on Fisherman's Wharf, a ride on the cable cars, and a romantic rendezvous with Scottish policeman George Sutherland in San Francisco. But what she doesn't know is that solving a murder may be penciled into her agenda.

BRANDY & BULLETS   184912

A posh retreat in cozy Cabot Cove, Maine, offers struggling artists a European spa, psychiatry, and even hypnotism. No one, however, expects a creative killer. And when an old friend mysteriously disappears, Jessica fears a twisted genius is at work writing a scenario for murder—putting her own life in danger.

RUM & RAZORS   183835

From the moment Jessica arrives at a four-star inn nestled by a beautiful lagoon, she senses trouble in paradise. She finds hotel owner Walter Marschalk's throat-slit corpse at the edge of the lagoon. It's time for Jessica to unpack her talent for sleuthing and discover if the murderer is a slick business partner, a young travel writer, a rival hotelier, or even the lovely widow Laurie Marschalk.

MANHATTANS & MURDER   181425

Promoting her latest book brings bestselling mystery writer Jessica Fletcher to New York for Christmas. Her schedule includes book signings, "Larry King Live," restaurants, department stores... and murder?

Available wherever books are sold or at penguin.com

SIGNET   (0451)

FROM THE MYSTERY SERIES
MURDER,
SHE WROTE
by Jessica Fletcher & Donald Bain

Based on the Universal television series
Created by Peter S. Fischer, Richard Levinson & William Link